"This book has a lot of twists and turns and ups and downs. There is never a dull moment until you are finished with the ride and think, What the heck, let's go again."   —*Rendezvous*

"Fans of offbeat romantic romps will enjoy *Maybe Baby*."
—*Midwest Book Review*

"A lighthearted romp . . . [with] laugh-out-loud moments [and] warmly affectionate ones."
—*Romantic Times BOOKclub Magazine*

"Light and fun . . . This zany story is a blast . . . you've got a couple of hours of great reading."   —*FreshFiction.com*

"Perfect . . . Hilarious . . . a delightfully spirited read."
—*WritersUnlimited.com*

"Well written with likable characters and realistic dialogue . . . For a wonderful and fun read, I highly recommend *Maybe Baby*."   —*RomRevToday.com*

more . . .

"Funny and slapsticky, with a plot so crazy it must be read to believe it. And keep the tissues handy for the flowing of tears caused by hysterical laughter. A great read."

—NovelTalk.com

EX AND THE SINGLE GIRL

"I swallowed *Ex and the Single Girl* in a single sitting, so caught up was I in the lively misadventures of Rich's latest heroine. With wit to match Jennifer Crusie's, Lani Diane Rich charmed me with her story."

—Joshilyn Jackson, author of *Gods in Alabama*

"Rich again proves herself [to be] a chick-lit heavy-hitter. Funny, moving, and with great characters and a clever story, this book hits all the right notes."

—*Romantic Times BOOKclub Magazine*

"A sweet . . . book about following your dreams (and your dream man)." —*Publishers Weekly*

"Funny . . . sweet . . . full of quirky, likable characters and the charms of small-town life . . . Will appeal to fans of Rebecca Wells's Ya-Yas." —*Booklist*

"What raises this novel above many other chick-lit titles is its depth . . . You'll read it quickly for its sweet sass, but you'll reread it to savor its bittersweet truths."

—*Ventura County Star* (CA)

"Sweetly engaging. B+."   —*Entertainment Weekly*

"A fast, fun read, especially for those who enjoy the quirky characters of authors like Jennifer Crusie and Eileen Rendahl. Strongly recommended."   —*Library Journal*

TIME OFF FOR GOOD BEHAVIOR

"I love Lani Diane Rich's thirty-something heroine, Wanda. The world hands her lemons, and she snarls and throws them back at the world. Fast, funny, and always true to herself, Wanda is one of those heroines you want to have lunch with."
—Jennifer Crusie, best-selling author of *Bet Me* and *Faking It*

"A sparkling debut, full of punch, pace, and wonderfully tender moments. I devoured it in one sitting. Lani Diane Rich's gutsy, wisecracking heroine, Wanda Lane, speaks to any woman who has ever doubted her right to be loved."
—Sue Margolis, author of *Apocalipstick*

"A warm and funny story. A perfect read for a rainy afternoon. Or *any* afternoon."
—Karen Brichoux, author of *Coffee and Kung Fu*

"This effervescent debut novel will strike a chord with every woman who has ever been tempted to give her life an extreme makeover."
—Wendy Markham, author of *Bride Needs Groom*

Also by Lani Diane Rich

Ex and the Single Girl
Maybe Baby
Time Off for Good Behavior

The Comeback Kiss

Lani Diane Rich

NEW YORK   BOSTON

Copyright © 2006 by Diane Schwalbe
Excerpt from *Hard to Get* copyright © 2006 by Diane Schwalbe
All rights reserved. No part of this book may be reproduced in any form or by any electronic or mechanical means, including information storage and retrieval systems, without permission in writing from the publisher, except by a reviewer who may quote brief passages in a review.

Warner Forever and the Warner Forever logo are registered trademarks.

Illustration by Hiro Kimura
Cover design by Diane Luger
Book design by Stratford Publishing Services

Warner Books
1271 Avenue of the Americas
New York, NY 10020

Printed in the United States of America

First Printing: May 2006

10 9 8 7 6 5 4 3 2 1

For Fish, who taught me that comeback kisses
are the best ones of all.
I love you.

Acknowledgments

So many people saw me through this book that I'm pretty sure half my word count will come from the thanks alone. But I'll try to make it as short and sweet as I can, because I know you people reading this (thank you, by the way) have stuff to do. Here goes:

To CJ Barry, who held my hand through the writing of this novel and tried not to be terrified on my behalf when I told her I'd written two-thirds of the book and still didn't know who my villain was. Well, babe, I know now. So there. Nyah.

To Robin La Fevers, whose infinite wisdom, patience, and faith kept me from just throwing in the towel and getting a real job.

To the Cherries, for answering my endless research questions, giving me the straight poop on Girl Scout cookies, and putting up with my wailing and gnashing of teeth.

To my agent, the incredible Stephanie Kip Rostan, for her limitless enthusiasm and willingness to let me call her Punkin.

To Beth de Guzman, whose fabulous editorial guidance

and endless well of patience made writing this book a much less terrifying experience than it would have been otherwise.

To my fellow Literary Chicks, Alesia Holliday, Michelle Cunnah, Beth Kendrick, Whitney Gaskell, and Eileen Rendahl, who make me look good through the company I keep.

To my wonderful husband and baby girls, for still loving and supporting me even when I'm tight on deadline, haven't cooked a hot meal in weeks, and am cranky as all get out.

And last, but not least, to everyone who read *Maybe Baby* and wrote me saying Finn was hot. I thought so, too. This *Kiss* is for you—mwah!

Chapter One

I knew I should have sent her to boarding school, Tessa Scuderi thought as she sat at her kitchen table listening to her sixteen-year-old sister explain how Robby Parker had knocked her up in a round of passion under the bleachers during the Lucy's Lake High Christmas Dance six weeks ago.

"I'm so sorry to have disappointed you." Izzy sniffled, the moisture in her eyes shimmering in the soft glow from the light fixture hanging over their heads. "It was just a big, stupid mistake, and now I'll have to pay for it for the rest of my life."

"Oh, cruel fate," Tessa said flatly, lifting her coffee mug to her lips. "You're not getting a car."

Izzy's eyes widened with pretend shock, then narrowed with genuine frustration. She smacked her hand down on the old linoleum table. "Oh, come on!"

Tessa pulled her elbows back and stared at the table. "God, this thing is ugly. Why am I only just noticing it now?"

"That could have *totally* been true! What if I was really pregnant?"

"Impossible." Tessa shrugged and put her elbows back on the table. "No one who has ever actually had sex would use a phrase like 'round of passion.'"

"Hey!" Izzy's voice was sharp and offended. "I got that from a romance novel."

"I rest my case." Tessa sipped her coffee and thought about the table. Maybe she should replace it. But it was such a hassle. The downside of living in small-town Vermont was how long it took to get to a damn Wal-Mart.

"I could be *pregnant*," Izzy went on. "That is *so* much worse than having my own car."

Tessa couldn't help but smile. "And what? You thought that if I believed you were pregnant for a few minutes, then I'd let you have a car out of sheer relief?"

Izzy shrugged, lifted her coffee mug, and sulked. "It was a theory."

"It was a bad one." Tessa glanced at the clock: 6:45 in the morning. She had to give Izzy credit for strategy; getting to Tessa early in the morning was a good move.

Not good enough, but the kid was only sixteen.

"Look, Iz, I've got enough stress in my life without worrying about you getting speeding tickets—"

"I would drive like George Washington's grandmother, I swear."

"—or a flat tire on the side of a dark highway littered with sexual predators."

"I'll get AAA and a can of Mace."

"And if I'm concerned about you getting pregnant—which, just between us girls, is the dark fear that keeps me awake nights praying to every variation of God known to man—then giving you a car is the very last thing I would do." She looked Izzy in the eye and spoke firmly. "This discussion is over."

Izzy's eyes rolled up in a dramatic arc. "Just because you lost your virginity in the back of a car—"

"Little tip," Tessa said. "Using my past against me does not help your case."

"If I'm going to lose my virginity, I don't need a car to do it."

"But you do need a convenient location, and I'm sure as hell not going to be the one who gives it to you."

"God! You are such a tool. I'm not even dating anyone."

Tessa suddenly felt bone-tired. She shouldn't feel that tired at twenty-eight, should she? "The tool is closing this discussion. You want some more coffee?"

Izzy slumped back in her chair. "Mom would have let me get a car."

A heavy silence fell over the room, accentuating the absence they both felt so strongly. Tessa drained the last of her coffee, listening to the ticking of the wall clock as she breathed in deep, not sure what to say. What do you say to a kid who was orphaned at the age of six? Ten years she'd been trying to think of something, and always, she came up blank.

"Sorry," Izzy mumbled finally.

Tessa smiled. There was very little Izzy could do that Tessa wouldn't instantly forgive, and Izzy knew it. "It's okay."

Izzy leaned one elbow on the table as the fingers of her other hand picked lazily at her Pop-Tart. "You know what's weird?"

"That parents keep letting their children play at Michael Jackson's house?"

"That you still have a picture of that old car on the refrigerator."

Izzy nodded toward the worn and faded photo, drawing Tessa's focus to it as well. Tessa couldn't help but smile. That car had been so cool. It was a vintage 1974 VW Thing, a boxy, funky-looking model that didn't sell well and didn't last long; theorists were split on whether the blame fell on the name or the design. But Tessa had loved it with all her heart. She'd gotten it for a song from Oliver's on the edge of town, had spent a summer painting colorful daisies all over it, stems intertwining like lovers . . .

"Man," she breathed to herself, staring at the picture, transfixed in the memory of her last carefree summer. "You just can't replace something like that, you know?"

"If you loved it so much, why'd you give it to Finn?"

Tessa's shoulders tensed at the name. *Correction: I gave him my virginity. Bastard took the car.*

But that wasn't the official story, so Tessa kept quiet, suddenly feeling the weight of all the lies she'd piled on the memory of that night ten years ago settling heavily on her existence. At the moment, though, it was more than she cared to think about, and it was definitely way more than she intended to explain to her little sister. She pushed herself up from the kitchen table, smoothing her hands over the skirt of her waitress uniform.

"You got all your homework, right?"

Izzy sighed a martyr's sigh. "Yes, Warden."

"I'd have gone with 'Der Führer' over 'Warden.' It's got more punch." Tessa led the way out of the kitchen, through the living room, and to the front door, the same as she did every day. "And you're not getting a car."

Izzy trailed behind her, like a sad, sole duckling. "Tammy Myers's mom gave her a truck for her sixteenth birthday."

"Tammy Myers's mom is an idiot." Tessa grabbed her coat off the rack by the front door, and handed off Izzy's to her.

Same as she did every day.

"God, you are wound tight. You know what you need? A man."

Tessa fought the urge to laugh as her sister puffed up, nodding her head furiously.

"That's right. I said it. You need to get laid."

Tessa grabbed her house keys from the basket that sat on the half-moon table, then turned to her sister with a beatific smile, cupping Izzy's sweet face gently in both hands.

"Darling Isabella, love of my pathetic and sexless life, you cannot manipulate, cajole, or otherwise engage me to the point where I will let you have a car," she said. "You forget that when I was a teenager, I was just like you, only about a thousand times worse. I know all your tricks, and I am immune."

"I hate walking to school every day," Izzy whined, shrugging Tessa's hands away.

"Builds character."

She stuffed her arms into her coat. "By the time I get there, my feet are frostbitten. How will you feel when I have to have a toe amputated?"

"It's two blocks, Bette Davis. That's the beauty of living

in the middle of town. Everything's within safe walking distance."

Izzy stared at Tessa for a minute, then finally huffed and pulled the door open. "Damnit. I really thought the pregnancy thing would work. You know, contrast and compare."

"I'll give you credit, it was a nice strategy, but you still have much to learn, Grasshoppah." Tessa stepped out onto the porch, locked the door behind her, same as she did every day. It wasn't until she turned and bumped into Izzy, who had frozen on the porch right behind Tessa, that the routine of Tessa's life finally broke.

"Oh, my God," Izzy breathed, the words stepping out into the frigid February air in white puffs.

"What?" Tessa said, but her eyes landed almost instantly on the *what,* and she froze as well. Time seemed to slow down as she stared at the street in front of her house.

"That's not . . . ," Izzy said, pointing. "That can't be . . ."

"No." Tessa finally willed her legs to move forward. "It's not. Go to school."

"No way," Izzy said. "I want to—"

"School," Tessa said, her voice hard. "Now."

Izzy muttered some complaints, hauled her backpack up over her shoulder, and marched off in the direction of the school. Tessa watched until her sister was out of sight, then slowly moved forward. Her feet felt strange beneath her, unconnected to either her legs or the ground, just numbly carrying her to the thing she was absolutely sure could not possibly be parked in front of her house.

And yet. There it was. Boxy. Yellow. Covered with flowers she'd painted herself. She rubbed at her eyes and took a step closer, focusing on the driver's-side door. Two daisies, pink in the centers with orange petals, the stems wound together with the initials D.F. and T.S. spelled out discreetly in their twirly waves. She moved closer, opened the door, and glanced around the empty interior, then froze when she saw the keys dangling from the ignition. She slumped down into the front seat and pulled them out, her heart pounding as she held the key chain up in the waxing morning light.

It was the same key chain she'd had in high school, a simple silver rectangle with "Tessa" engraved in the center. On the day she got the car, Finn had given her that key chain.

And then, eight months later, he'd taken it back.

Which led to the question—who had returned it?

Finn.

Her heart rate revved up, and she instantly tamped it down. She cared more about the car than Finn. It was the car she had missed all these years, the car she had wanted returned to her. And now that it was here . . .

She twirled the keys in her hand, her teenage years coming back to her in flashes. Laughing with Finn, kissing Finn, sneaking away with Finn, stealing the town bell with—

Oh. Crap. She gasped and gripped the steering wheel tightly in her hands as, for the second time that morning, the weight of a decade's worth of lies fell down on her. Finn couldn't be back. He wasn't supposed to come back. Ever. She'd been banking on it, counting on it, and if she'd miscalculated, it would ruin everything.

Tessa twisted around, glancing in the backseat for some evidence of what had happened, hoping against all hope that maybe the police had left a note explaining that they had confiscated and returned it, or that there was a fairy godmother sitting in the back with a wand at the ready. There was nothing except a snow brush and an empty Tic Tac container. Her heart pounded in erratic rhythms as her eyes darted about, finally catching on something lying on the headrest behind her. She reached up and plucked it off, and even in the faint morning light, she knew exactly what she was seeing.

One short red hair, slightly stiff with styling gel.

"Well," she said finally. "Shit."

"Hey, Babs." Dermot Finnegan huddled in an alley, leaning against the brick wall of Lucy's Lake's only movie theater as he held his cell phone to his ear, feeling like a criminal even though he hadn't done anything illegal yet that day. "Where's my car?"

"Finn?" A yawn stretched through the phone. "Is that you?"

"Yeah, Babs, it's me. Where's my car?"

"Goodness," she said. "What time is it?"

Finn glanced over his shoulder at the street behind him. It was still empty, for now. He tugged his brown knit hat down over his ears and forehead. "I have no idea, but the sky's kinda pink. I hear it's called sunrise. It's really not as great as they make it out in the movies. Now where's my car?"

"What car?"

Finn rubbed his fingers over his eyes and tried to keep his voice even. "The car you said would be here."

"Oh," she said, her voice gaining strength. "That's tomorrow."

Finn went still. "Gee. You don't say. Because the eight

thousand times we talked about it last week, I could have sworn you said it was today."

"Hmmm, really?" He heard the rustle of papers in the background. "See? I've got it right here. *Rental car. Max's Diner, Lucy's Lake, Vermont. Tuesday, February 10.* That's tomorrow."

Finn raised his eyes skyward. "Beg to differ, crumb cake. Today's Tuesday, but it's the ninth. Now, think. When you made the arrangements, did you say Tuesday or the tenth?"

Finn already knew the answer. For fifteen months now, he'd been working—for lack of a better word—for Babs Wiley McGregor, the slightly off-center widow of Manhattan real estate king Bryson McGregor. He should have known this wouldn't go smoothly. Things involving Babs, no matter how tangentially, rarely did. But getting paid to do odd little "favors" for Babs's nutty rich friends beat petty bird thieving, his previous occupation, by a country mile. As of yet, none of Babs's insane friends had bitten him, crapped on him, or woken him up in the middle of the night with incessant chirping.

"I said the ninth. And I'm almost certain . . . wait, my calendar's right here . . ." There was a pause. "Oh. Whoops."

Finn heard voices on the street behind him and slid deeper into the alley, pushing himself flat against the wall.

"I need that car, Babs. Now. There's no way I'm making it to Boston by tonight if I have to hitch."

"Oh, that's okay," Babs said. "Now that I'm looking at my calendar, I realize that the favor isn't until Saturday night anyway. Isn't that funny?"

Finn glanced out at the street. A woman huddled in a

white coat passed by, leaving a thick trail of perfume in her wake. Finn huddled flat against the brick wall; the woman passed without noticing him. A lucky break, but every moment he spent in Lucy's Lake made it that much more likely he'd be spotted, and that was not part of the plan.

"No," Finn said. "Not funny unless public hangings are your brand of comedy. People in this town don't like me much."

"Oh, tosh," Babs said. "What's not to like? I think you're absolutely charming."

"No argument," Finn said. "But these people haven't seen me since I was a teenager, and I was a little"—he paused, searching for the right adjective to describe himself in high school—"*unruly* back then."

"Everybody was unruly as a teenager. When Dana was in high school—"

"I blew up the nativity scene in front of the church using half a pound of black powder and a homemade mortar," Finn said. Although that was among the least of his youthful infractions, he figured it trumped anything Babs's daughter had ever even thought about doing.

Babs paused. "Well, lots of kids—"

"During the outdoor Christmas Eve vigil."

"Ooh," Babs gushed, drawing from her endless supply of fierce loyalty. "Like fireworks. Must have been lovely."

"Reverend Diggs was a Vietnam vet," Finn said. "He dove to the ground, knocking over the school librarian, whose flaming candle flew out of her hand and landed on the mayor's toupee. Do I need to keep going?"

"I don't think so." Babs paused. "Dana set a priest on fire once, did I ever tell you about that?"

"No, but it sounds like a great story." Finn glanced over his shoulder again. "Look, people in small towns like this are long on memory and short on forgiveness, and if the term 'lynch mob' means anything to you, you'll get me a car. Now."

Babs sighed. "I'll try. But it's not like you're in the hub of civilization. Why can't you just wait it out until tomorrow? I'm sure it's not as bad as you think."

"Babs—"

"Okay, okay. I'll make some calls and see what I can do. But I do think you're overreacting, Dermot."

"Point of information: Calling me Dermot does nothing to endear you to me right now."

"You really should go see your family," Babs went on, ignoring him. "You've got five whole days and nothing to do. I'm sure they'd be happy to see you."

Finn opened his mouth to speak, then paused as realization sank in. "Hey. Babs. Just to soothe my curiosity— you didn't do this on purpose, did you?"

Her voice rose half an octave and dripped innocence. "Do what, dear?"

"Hey, and there's my answer," he said, running one gloved hand over his head. "Look. I told you. I don't wanna see them, and they don't want to see me. I came here to do one thing, and I did it, and now I need to get out of here."

"Oh! I've got a beep," Babs said suddenly, although Finn heard no interruption on the line. "It's Dana. I'll be in touch."

"Get me that car!" Finn said quickly before Babs disconnected the call. He flipped his cell shut and tucked it into his pocket, then let out a grating chuckle.

He was an idiot. He knew when he started on this whole

thing that it was a bad idea. It had been a bad idea to go back to Westchester and drive by the house of the old lady he'd sold the Thing to. It had been a bad idea to hit the doorbell, and pay twice the car's value to a woman who probably wouldn't have noticed if he had just hot-wired it and took it straight from her driveway.

A few years back, that's exactly what he would have done, without a second thought. Hell, a few years back, he wouldn't have gone looking for the damn thing in the first place.

He'd been much, much smarter then than he was now.

Finn looked down the length of the alley, the back of which jutted up against the parking lot of Max's, the two spaces separated only by a cheap metal guardrail and some trees thinned by the winter. He had to get out of there before Tessa saw the car and announced his presence in town.

Tessa. He could still see her face in his mind. Light freckles sprinkled over nose and cheeks. Blushed lips. Chocolate brown eyes that flashed murder when provoked. Oval-shaped face framed by thick dark curls she always complained about but never cut. Something coursed through him, and it took a moment for him to recognize it as a mixture of regret and excitement.

Over a girl he hadn't seen in ten years; a girl who would probably kill him with her bare hands given half a chance.

He pulled up the collar of his jacket around his face and hunched into it as he headed out to the sidewalk. If he could get to the edge of town, he could probably hole up in the shack next to the lake until he figured a way out of town that didn't involve relying on Babs friggin'

McGregor, which had been just one in a long string of mistakes he'd made in recent months.

Well, it was over. The stupidity, the guilt, and the lame attempt at making up for something that couldn't be made up for. From now on, he was the old Finn, the smart Finn, the Finn who moved through life free and easy, letting the past stay in the past.

Head down, he took a left out of the alley and kept his eyes on his feet. It wasn't until he smelled the smoke that he slowed down and looked up. At first, he couldn't tell where it was coming from, and he was about to dismiss it as someone's fireplace smoke when he heard panicked sounds coming from across the street. He grazed his eyes over the buildings there and saw smoke creeping out from under one of the doors, then lifted his focus to the sign over the awning.

FOR PET'S SAKE.

I should let it burn down just for the name alone, he thought. He looked down the street one way and then the other. No one. Nothing. He heard what sounded like a high-pitched bark, and saw that the smoke creeping out from under the door was thickening.

Something in FOR PET'S SAKE was definitely on fire.

Hopefully, it was the person who'd named it.

"Well," he muttered to himself as he felt the struggle between smart and stupid start to stir within him. "Shit."

Chapter Two

Finn clenched his fists in his pockets, decided that smart was gonna win this time, and started walking in the direction he'd been heading. It was early, but he was sure someone would be coming by soon. Someone who belonged here, someone who cared about what happened in Lucy's Lake.

Someone *not* him. He had bigger problems to think about right now, like how he was going to convince the car rental place in Brattleboro to deliver a car to him out in the middle of friggin' nowhere.

He'd made a few long, determined strides before the barking grew louder, more frenzied. Finn grunted and stopped again, looking impatiently up and down the deserted street.

"Christ," he muttered. "What the hell is wrong with you people?"

He stepped out into the street and glanced at the apartment windows above the offices for the *Lucy's Lake Weekly,* just three buildings down from the pet store. Back in the day, Stella Hodgkiss had owned the *Weekly;* probably still did. Seemed fitting that the same woman who knew when the mayor's wife farted in church showed no sign of waking up when the damn town was on fire.

Finn looked back to the pet shop. He hated pet shops. During his bird thieving days he'd worked in one to get leads on the good, rare birds, and it had sucked. Full of weird dogs that seemed to be bred for funky looks and nervous urination, big-eyed fish that died the moment people got them home, and hairless cats that were even uglier than regular cats. He'd be doing the town a favor if he just kept walking.

He took one more step, then stopped and closed his eyes.

"Shit," he grumbled, then turned on one heel and darted across the street. He pulled his cell phone out of his pocket and dialed 911. Two rings sounded, followed by a woman's voice.

"Nine-one-one, what's your—"

"FOR PET'S SAKE is on fire. Get someone down here now, or Max is gonna have to get some creative dog-meat specials on the menu."

There was a rustling as the woman put her hand over the receiver and yelled to someone that the pet store was on fire, then came back on the line. "They're on their way. Who's calling, please?"

Finn flipped the phone shut and picked up the pace as he stepped up on the sidewalk in front of the store. A sign in the window read, *Closed for Vacation until Feb. 16.* Through the window, he could see orange light flickering through the crack under the office door at the back, which meant the fire was probably mostly contained in there, for the moment. The smoke was another story; it filled the store, thicker toward the ceiling but still menacing even down low.

Finn looked around for something he could use to break the glass panes in the front door. There was nothing. He tightened his gloved hand into a fist and slammed it through the pane, then reached in and undid the lock. The smoke hit him hard in the face as he entered, and he ducked back outside to take a big breath of fresh air before putting the collar of his jacket over his mouth and running in.

From what he could tell, it should be quick work. There were two puppies and a few kittens in cages along one wall, and some birds squawking in the back. He headed to the birds first, as they were closest to the fire.

African grays, he thought, grabbing a cage in each hand and mentally calculating how much he'd get for the pair on the street in Manhattan as he carried them outside.

Not that he was going to steal them. It was just that old habits die hard. And the market was glutted with grays, anyway.

He darted back inside, searched under the register for the keys to the animal crates. He unlocked them, letting a springer spaniel and a shih tzu puppy loose. Another dog, some kind of border collie mutt mixture, was barking by the office door as the puppies ran around Finn's legs like frantic, furry bumper cars. Moments later he chased the dogs out, carrying two more birdcages with him. One of them was filled with common parakeets not worth stealing, but the other cage held a macaw that looked young and in relatively good health, smoke inhalation notwithstanding.

Macaws still got a decent price in New York. He'd bet they'd get about the same in a place like, say, Boston.

He set the macaw off to the side, slightly behind a wrought-iron bench in front of the drugstore next to the pet shop. He'd sworn he'd never do another bird job, but it wasn't every day that a macaw just dropped in his lap.

And Smart Finn? Would absolutely steal that bird.

When the fire truck finally arrived three minutes later, he was carrying out the last of the animals, two small kittens that had been frolicking in the front window display.

"The fire's in the back office," he said to Matt Tarpey, a big hulk of a guy who'd been the fire chief since Finn was a kid. "Door's closed, but a few more minutes, there won't be a door."

Tarpey shouted some orders to his guys, who went to work pulling out the hose as people started to gather in the street. Finn ducked back toward the bench to make his escape with the macaw, then remembered he was still holding the kittens. He turned back and was instantly blinded by a flashing camera. He blinked a few times to get his vision back, and when he did, he saw Stella from the *Lucy's Lake Weekly*.

So much for slipping out of town unnoticed, he thought.

"Dermot Finnegan," she said, her beady little eyes locking on him as she released the camera slung around her neck. "I could just kill you with my own two hands."

"Yeah," he said. "Get in line. Better yet, take these kittens off my hands, and I'll save you the trouble by kicking my own ass out of town. No mob required."

Stella's face suddenly flashed into a smile as she moved forward and put her hand on his shoulder. Startled, Finn instinctively flinched back, taking a moment to process that her expression held none of the hatred and vitriol he was expecting.

"I'm so glad you're here," she said. "I was supposed to be keeping an eye on the place while Vickie was away, and—" Stella put her hand to her mouth, eyes moist, then clutched it to her chest. "I didn't even wake up until I heard the fire truck. Thank you."

Finn shrugged. "No problem. Well. See ya."

Stella grabbed his hand and squeezed it, smiling up at him. "Why didn't you tell us you were coming home? I would have made you a dinner."

Finn tried to recall if he'd ever heard "made you a dinner" used as a euphemism for "beat you with a tire iron." Before he could respond, she threw her arm around his neck and hugged him.

"I haven't forgotten what you did for Frank and me," she said quietly into his ear. "And now this . . ." The kittens mewed and she pulled back, her eyes now full-on teary. "It's so good to have you home again."

Finn blinked, tossed a look at the macaw behind him, then looked back at Stella. "What I did for . . . what?"

She sniffed. "Oh, don't be so modest. Although I don't know how in the world you found out exactly the amount of our deductible for his foot surgery. We never would have been able to afford it without you, even with the insurance. Seven hundred and fifty dollars is a lot of money to people like us." She squeezed his hand again, and Finn felt a stab of panic that he was in the social clutches of a Stella gone mad, as he had no idea what the hell she was talking about.

She sniffed again. "Your uncle will be so happy to see you."

"You know what?" Finn said quickly. "Maybe don't tell Max."

"Oh, of course, you want to surprise him," Stella said, wiping at the edges of her eyes. "But don't wait too long. News travels fast around here, you know."

Finn stared down at her. Stella had to be in her sixties, but her eyes were still as bright and sharp as ever. When had she lost her mind? Not that it mattered. He'd been gone a long time, and what had happened in Lucy's Lake in the interim was not his deal. His deal was getting gone again, and if he could just distract Stella for one minute, he could probably get gone with that macaw . . .

"Hey, there's Matt Tarpey," Finn said, holding out the kittens to her and motioning toward the fire truck with his head. "Get him with the kittens. Talk about a money shot. The Pulitzer people'll be eating out of your hand."

"Oh, Tarpey gets plenty of press!" she said, taking a step back and aiming her camera at Finn. "You're the hero of this piece. Let me get a few more pictures. You looked a little startled when I took that first one."

"No kidding," he said flatly, holding the kittens and pulling on a tight smile. Behind Stella he could see a crowd starting to gather, distracted for the moment by the bright fire engine. He sighed. If he was going to get that macaw and get out of there, he had to move fast.

Stella flashed the camera at him a few more times, and he stepped forward and pushed the kittens at her.

"Great to see you, Stella. Give my love to Frank," he said, taking a step backward.

"Wait. Let me get these to a safe place and I'll come right back." Stella grinned at him. "Don't think you're getting out of that dinner."

Finn grinned back. "I can smell the pot roast already."

Stella turned toward the fire truck with the kittens. Finn scanned the crowd; no one was watching him. He dipped down and his fingers were just grazing the handle on the macaw cage when he felt a hand on his shoulder. He closed his eyes and cursed under his breath, then turned to face the person who'd come up behind him.

"Well," he said as he looked into deep brown eyes, flashing murder at him.

"Shit," Tessa said, withdrawing her hand from Finn's shoulder. She'd hoped it wouldn't be him, that somehow all the evidence that Finn had returned was wrong, but she couldn't really feign surprise. She paused for a moment, waiting for the heart attack and the panic and all that nonsense, but instead, she just felt kind of numb. This was not how she had imagined this moment. She thought she'd be panicked, babbling, unable to string one coherent thought together. But she was actually feeling pretty calm.

"Dermot Finnegan," she said slowly. He smiled down at her, cocking his head to the side as he did.

"Contessa Scuderi . . . ," he began, feeding on an old joke that was never funny in the first place.

"*Tessa,*" she said. "Don't start with that crap."

". . . mistress of all she surveys."

His eyes connected with hers, and she felt that hitch in her chest and where the hell did that come from and she had to get him out of here or someone would figure out Finn wasn't the person she'd told them he was and . . .

Ah, hello. Here's the panic. She placed her hand over her chest, felt her heart bouncing around in her rib cage like a straitjacketed mental patient in a rubber room. *Yep, that's about how I imagined this moment.*

Finn put down the birdcage he was holding and touched her arm. "You okay? You don't look good."

"I can't breathe," she said.

"I have that effect on women," Finn said, grinning down at her. "Don't worry. It'll pass."

"It's not you, you big idiot," she spat.

"You gotta let me flatter myself, Tess," he said. "If I don't do it, who will?"

He smiled down at her with total focus, making her feel like the only person in his world.

Just like old times.

She looked up into his crystal blue eyes, which were laughing, as usual, never taking anything seriously, not even her.

Just like old times.

She put her hand to her forehead. She had to think. She had to think fast.

"Tessa?" he said, his voice suddenly tentative and concerned. She felt something tweak inside, followed by a rush of something powerful and oddly not pissed off. Which wasn't possible. If it felt even remotely good to see him then that meant she'd missed him, and if she'd missed him then that meant she still felt something for him, and if she still felt something for him . . .

Well, she just didn't. And that was that.

"We have to talk," she said quickly. She took a few steps down a side street, away from the crowd. It would afford them a few minutes of privacy, and that was all she needed. Just enough time to somehow convince him to leave and never come back. When Finn caught up to her, she turned and looked up at him.

"What are you doing here?" she shot out in a harsh whisper.

"Being a hero, apparently," he said, tucking his hands into his pockets, and giving her his trademark lopsided smile. "Concrete proof that wonders never do cease. How'd you find me?"

"Saw the car. Smelled the smoke. Put two and two together."

"Hey." Finn's eyebrows locked together in what appeared to be sincere indignation, but with Finn you never could tell. "I didn't set the place on fire."

Tessa gave a dismissive wave. "Whatever. Look. I don't have much time—"

"I busted into a burning building and saved those animals." He held out his arm, showing off the singed area on the elbow of his jacket. "Life. Limb. Risked. Credit?"

"*Whatever,*" she said again, talking low and fast. "I can't tell you everything because there just isn't time, but the *Reader's Digest* version is that I've led everyone in this town to believe you're some kind of benevolent hero, and if you don't get out of here, you'll completely screw up my life. Again. So . . . bye."

"Benevolent hero?" Finn said. "Is that why Stella Hodgkiss invited me over for dinner?"

"She invited you to dinner?" Tessa put one hand over her stomach. "Oh, God. Pepto moment. You didn't say yes, did you?"

"Tessa . . ." He stared at her, looking both amused and confused. "What's going on?"

Tessa sighed, glanced over her shoulder, then leaned in and spoke without moving her lips. "The town bell."

Finn laughed. "The town what?"

"Agh!" she said, whacking him on the shoulder. "Keep your voice down."

Finn continued to chuckle, and she couldn't believe how difficult it was to fight the desire to clock him one across the chin. *This must be what it feels like to be a man . . .*

Finn regained himself. "Look, I know it was probably a big deal to these people when we stole the town bell—"

"Shhhh!"

"—but they were the idiots who left it out in the open on a trailer to wait for the repairman. They were begging us to steal it. And they got it back. No harm, no foul."

Tessa narrowed her eyes at him. "No harm? They got it back *three months later*. After you dumped it in Manhattan. Meanwhile, I'm back here fighting off the friggin' Spanish Inquisition. Big foul, Finn. Big. Damn. Foul."

"Well, no one expects the Spanish Inquisition," Finn deadpanned.

"Look," she said, ignoring his joke, "I don't know why you brought my Thing back, but if you're looking for forgiveness, you know what? You've got it. Now, make it up to me by leaving and never, ever coming back, okay?"

She glanced over his shoulder nervously, although she couldn't see the crowd from where she stood. Didn't matter. It wouldn't be long before the distraction wore off and people came looking for Finn. The Big Hero. Lucy's Lake's own personal Guardian Angel.

Finn cocked his head to the side and eyed her, a playful smile forming on his lips. "Can't."

Panic gripped her at her edges. "Can't? Why can't? What can't? You got here. Get gone."

"I don't have a car."

She pulled out the silver key chain, stuffing it in his hand. "It's at the house, right where you left it. I don't know why you brought it here in the first place, but I don't want it, so you take it. Shoo. Go away."

He recoiled. "*Shoo?* What am I, a dog now?"

"No. Dogs are loyal. Now go."

He put the keys back in her hand and closed her fingers over them, all traces of amusement gone from his face. "You don't want it, fine. Then sell it. But it's yours and I'm not taking it."

She huffed in frustration. "I don't need a car. I have a car."

He shrugged. "Give it to your sister, then. Izzy's gotta be coming up on sixteen about now, right?"

"She'll be seventeen in May," Tessa said. "And it doesn't matter, because there's no way in hell I'm giving my little sister that car."

"Why not?" he said. "It was good enough for you."

"It's got bad karma, and the last thing Izzy needs is . . ." She stopped, regrouped. "Hey, let's revisit that part where you were leaving."

"The karma can't be all bad," Finn said, a sly smile forming on his lips. "I remember having some pretty good times in the Thing."

"Shut up," Tessa said, but could feel her cheeks starting to warm at the memory. His eyes locked with hers in a playful game, and despite herself Tessa felt that same old spark, remnants of teenage lust gone horribly, horribly wrong.

This is definitely not *how I imagined this moment.*

"Look, there's no time to argue," she said, pushing the keys at him again. "Just take it and go."

His smile faded and he shook his head. "I'll walk to the edge of town and hitch from there."

"You can't," she said. "Someone will see you, pick you up, and bring you back to town. Probably throw you a damn parade."

"A parade?" He chuckled. "I think I might need more than the *Reader's Digest* version of this story."

She met his eyes and the panic subsided, replaced by . . . what *was* she feeling? Abject terror? Disgust? The strange and unnerving desire to do things with Finn that would make the backseat of any decent car blush? Was she really that special brand of girl-dumb that threw all remnants of pride and reason out the window when first loves had the tactless nerve to come back?

Oh, holy hell. He needed to leave, and he needed to leave now.

"Wait here," she said through clenched teeth. "I'll bring the car around and I'll drive you out to I-91 and drop you there, and whatever happens to you from there on out is your problem."

She stepped out to pass him, but he grabbed her wrist and she stopped dead in her tracks at his touch, which zoomed up her arm like an electric current.

Old wiring, she thought. *Means nothing.*

He stood there looking at her, an odd half smile on his face.

"You look good," he said finally.

He reached up and nudged a curl away from her forehead

and suddenly she was eighteen again, crackling with energy and drowning in stupid.

"Finn, I don't have time to play ga—"

"Don't sell it," he said softly, his eyes uncharacteristically earnest.

"What?" she said, a strong sense of déjà vu washing over her as the current moment vaguely reflected one she'd had with him ten years back, in which Finn had done a conversational dance-and-dodge rather than saying what he'd really meant.

Which, as it turned out, had been good-bye.

She gently pulled her arm out of his grip. "We can argue about that in a minute. I'll be right back."

He smiled, but his eyes didn't, and the déjà vu hit again, stronger this time. Everything in her calmed as realization fell over her like a heavy blanket.

"You're not going to be here when I come back for you, are you?"

He released her wrist but didn't say anything.

"Fine," she said. "You know what? Fine. I'll play this scene again. As long as you're gone, and no one else sees you or gets a chance to talk to you, I don't care what happens to you."

"As long as I'm gone," he said.

"Right."

She didn't move, though, just stood there staring up at him, their faces so close she could smell the scent of him, which was kinda making her a little dizzy.

Old wiring, she thought, but didn't get to finish the thought, because suddenly, they were kissing. She didn't know how, or why, or what had come over her, but she was kissing Dermot Finnegan on the street behind the drugstore.

And it felt *good*. Way too good to be good for her.

After the first moment of surprise passed, one of his arms tightened around her waist and pulled her closer to him, lifting her off her toes for a moment, sending her world rocking. There was something in his response that was oddly fervent, unusual for Finn, who'd always been so cool, and the shock of it all emptied her mind of everything except the feel of his kisses that, she had to admit, were still toe-curling good.

Which was bad. Bad, bad, bad.

Tessa pushed her hand against his chest, and after a small struggle with both Finn and herself, managed to separate them enough that they could look at each other.

"What's going on here?" she asked, her voice breathless as she stumbled back on her heels.

"Don't blame me," he said, swinging her around in one deft motion and leaning her against the wall of the drugstore. "You started it."

"I did not!" she said, but barely got the words out before his lips were on hers again, him leaning over her as he pressed her against the wall. A whirlwind of sparks crackled all through her abdomen, moving lower, and this was stupid and dangerous and yet only about forty percent of her cared, and that just wasn't enough to make her break the kiss. They gasped and pulled at each other, his hand inside her coat, her fingers knocking off his knit cap as they wound through his hair, all the time her own voice lecturing in her head, like a broken record.

Never make the same mistake twice. Never make the same mistake twice. Never—

She put her hands on his shoulders, pushing him away. He looked as surprised as she felt, probably not so much by the kissing itself—they'd had more than their share of strange and inappropriate kissing back in the day—but by the power of it, the way it had taken them both over, a force unto itself.

"That," she gasped, gesturing vaguely back and forth between them, "is not going to happen again."

He took in a breath, then nodded. "Yeah. Okay." He watched her for a moment, and she saw his Adam's apple bob up and down as he swallowed before he could speak again. "Better go get that car, then."

"Yeah," she said. She pushed herself away from the wall and took a few wobbly steps toward Main, stopping when she saw Joe Finnegan standing there in his firefighter uniform, hand gripping his ax.

Oh, God, she thought. *This is* definitely *not how I imagined this moment.*

"Well," he said, his eyes on Finn. "Looks like at least one person is happy to see you, little brother."

Chapter Three

Finn blinked. Between the strangeness of being in Lucy's Lake, the all-night drive, the missing rental car, the fire, and kissing Tessa—mostly kissing Tessa—his Surreal-O-Meter was peaking out, and it took him a moment to fully process the fact that the older brother he hadn't seen in more than a decade was standing not ten feet away. But it was definitely Joe. Same dark eyes, dark hair. Same total lack of humor. And by all appearances he was still toting around that Curse-of-the-Good-Brother chip on his shoulder. All responsibility. No fun.

The firefighter getup was new, though.

"Hey, Joe," Finn said, giving Tessa a little squeeze on the elbow as he stepped away from her. It was their code from a lifetime ago, the classic let-me-know-when-you-need-me-to-cover-for-you signal, but he knew she'd remember it. After all, she remembered what it did to him when she ran her fingertips over the hair at the back of his neck. He could only hope that his shirt and coat were hanging low enough to mask the rather obvious after-effects of that little trick.

"Finn," Joe said, his face hard and unreadable. As always. Joe, the strong, silent Finnegan. The Big Protector. God, the way he was looking at Tessa right now . . .

Finn stopped, glanced at Tessa, then back at Joe. A thought ran through the back of his mind, but he squelched it. Instead, he widened his stance a touch and locked his eyes on Joe. "Love the getup, bro. But last I heard, you were going to be an electrician."

"I am." Joe lowered his ax slowly. "I volunteer with the fire department."

"Did Tarpey tell you I was here? You don't seem surprised to see me."

Joe gave a quick shrug. "Got called in on the fire. Passed by Tessa's and saw the Thing there on my way in. Kinda put two and two together."

Finn broke eye contact to shoot a look at Tessa. "Why does everybody think I set the place on fire?"

"Can't imagine," she said flatly, her left eyebrow quirking at him.

Okay. Maybe appealing to Tessa wasn't the wisest move. Finn turned his attention back to his brother.

"I *saved* those animals," he said, playing up the indignation. Granted, he also planned on stealing one, but they didn't know that. Apparently, the big hero mold Tessa had poured him into only fooled strangers who didn't know better.

"Tessa," Joe said, turning his focus to where Tessa stood. "You can go to the diner."

"She can also make her own decisions," Finn said, taking a step forward. Who the hell did Joe think he was, anyway, telling Tessa what to do?

Joe's jaw muscles worked in that I'm-so-manly-I-can't-express-my-anger-in-words kind of way. Finn clenched his fist at his side. Man, he'd been back in his brother's presence for less than two minutes, and already he wanted to hit him.

Had to be some kind of record.

Joe looked Finn up and down. "So, I guess dressing like a bum is the big new thing in Las Vegas, huh?"

Before Finn could react, he heard Tessa clear her throat. *The signal.*

"This is my vacation gear," Finn said. "Some people, they go for the Hawaiian shirt/Bermuda shorts thing—"

"I see you haven't changed that much," Joe interrupted. "Still incapable of a straight answer."

Finn met his brother's eye. "Yeah, but my left hook's doing fine."

Tessa groaned and put her hand to her forehead, and Finn heard her mumble, "Oh, Christ, here we go."

Joe took a few steps forward. "So, what brings you to town, Finn? Is it business . . . or personal?"

Joe's eyes drifted over to indicate Tessa. Tessa's eyes went down to the ground.

"Business," Finn said. "I'm on my way to a job in Boston."

Joe nodded. "So, you're taking cases outside of Vegas now, huh? Business must be good."

Cases? Finn kept his face impassive, waiting for Tessa to feed him what he needed. Which she did, expertly couching "P.I." in a coughing fit.

So. He was a private investigator now.

Okay.

"Yeah," he said to Joe. "Business is good."

He turned slightly toward Tessa. She cleared her throat

gently and put her hand to her chest, as though she was surprised and slightly alarmed—but not too much—by her sudden coughing fit. Finn caught a slight flash of gratitude in her eyes, but he only caught it because he knew her so well.

She was a better liar than he remembered, and he remembered her being pretty good back in the day. A rush of something—excitement, longing, fear, who the hell knew?—ran through him, and he turned his attention back to Joe, whose dark stare did a lot to dampen the effects Tessa was having on Finn.

"Look, little brother," Joe said. "You may have the town fooled with all the money you've been throwing around here—"

Tessa cleared her throat again and Finn ground his teeth. So, he'd been throwing money around. Well, that explained Stella Hodgkiss. Of course the *why* was another matter altogether. Tessa was creative when it came to covering up, but even she wouldn't go to that much trouble over the town bell. Something else was going on.

Joe continued. "But I know you better than that. You're not exactly the charity type." Joe looked at Tessa again. "Not if there's nothing in it for you."

There was something in Joe's expression as he looked at Tessa that struck an odd chord of possessiveness in Finn.

"Hey, Tess," he said, turning his eyes to her, "something going on here you want to fill me in on?"

Tessa shot him an indignant look. "Nothing that's any of your damn business."

Well. It was clearly going to take a while to get back on

Tessa's good side. Which he would, if he was staying in town.

Which he wasn't, so it didn't matter.

Joe took a step forward. "So, how long you here for, Finn? Just passing through to wreak some minor havoc, or planning on hanging around to inflict permanent damage?"

Finn glanced at Tessa, then looked back at Joe. "*Wreak some havoc?* Who uses phrases like that in everyday conversation? You wanna ask me a question, ask it. See, like this. Question: How long are you staying? Answer: Long as I damn well feel like staying, that's how long."

Joe took another step forward. "Look, you little punk—"

Finn took a step closer. "I'm taller than you."

"By a half inch."

"And yet, still taller."

Tessa let out an annoyed sigh and stepped between them. "He was just leaving. He stopped by just long enough to return my car and burn down the pet shop—"

Finn pointed his finger at her. "This is the last time I rescue animals for you people."

"—and he's on his way out." She turned to Finn, her face firm, one eyebrow raised. "Now."

"Really?" Joe said.

"Maybe," Finn said.

"*Now,*" Tessa said. She turned her back to Joe and gave Finn the most pathetic pleading look he'd ever seen. It killed him not to smile, but he trusted that if Tessa was playing this game, it was important not to give her away.

It was the least he could do, really.

"I'm late for my shift," she said, pushing past them and out to the street. "You two try not to kill each other."

Once she was behind Joe, she held up her keys at Finn and mouthed, "Get rid of him."

"Be sure to pick yourself up a lozenge for that throat, Tessa," Joe said, keeping his eyes on Finn.

Not everyone in town is buying your story, Tess, Finn thought.

Tessa shot Finn one quick, pleading look, then darted out into the street.

Finn looked back at Joe, who stared him down. Somewhere in the back of his imagination, Finn heard the menacing whistle of the theme from *The Good, The Bad, and The Ugly.* He hesitated a moment, then decided someone had to make the first move. He pulled on what he hoped was a conciliatory smile.

"So," he said, "duel at twenty paces?"

Joe didn't smile. Big surprise. Humorless ass.

"Don't you have a fire to put out?" Finn asked. "Isn't there a damsel in distress tied to a train track out there somewhere?"

"As long as you're here," Joe said, and Finn could tell it was killing him to say it, "you should go see Max."

"Hey, now there's some bad advice," Finn said.

"He's not getting any younger, you know."

Finn felt a slight stab of alarm at Joe's tone. "Why? What's wrong? Is he okay?"

Joe shrugged. "He's fine. He's just getting older, and whatever happened between you guys, as long as you're here, you should make it up."

Finn stared at his brother. For once, the hostility in his face was gone. It was still stony, impassive, and kinda square, but definitely not hostile. Finn relaxed his stance a bit.

"All right," he said. "I'll think about it."

Joe nodded, hesitated for a moment, then turned and stalked off.

Finn leaned back against the wall of the drugstore. All he'd wanted was to come into town, right a wrong, and get the hell out. He supposed he could still do that. He could grab his backpack, grab the macaw, and skip town. He pushed himself away from the wall, walked to the corner, and poked his head around to see Joe handing a leashed spaniel to one of the onlookers, delegating responsibility to the rubberneckers like a big damn hero who thinks he's better than everybody else.

Asshole.

Finn glanced down at the bench. His backpack was still underneath and, wonder of wonders, the cage with the macaw was still next to it.

Out of his peripheral vision, he thought he saw Joe look in his direction, and he ducked behind the corner and counted to sixty as he formulated his plan.

He could grab his pack and the cage, and then cut across Lowery's field to get to the lake. His toes would likely freeze solid before he got there, but if the shack was still there, he could probably count on the old cot and the woodstove and half a cord of firewood waiting there, as it had been every winter since he was a kid. Dick Lowery made sure of it; his land bordered the lake after which the town was named, and by stocking the shack with the basics he kept the fishermen, drunks, and revelers from wandering onto his property and dying of exposure. It was pretty much a win/win.

Get moving, he thought, but he stayed where he was, staring off in the direction Tessa had gone. He could still feel her under his hands, taste her on his lips. How did she do that? How did she stay with him even when she wasn't there?

That wasn't normal. It was a bad sign that she could still twist him up like this. If those kisses had lasted any longer, he didn't know if he'd still be able to form a thought. It had occurred to him that he might see her, but he'd never expected that she'd still pull on him like that, like a force of nature. He still couldn't believe he'd been stupid enough to kiss her, and yet, when they'd gotten that close, all the wires in his brain crossed and kissing her seemed like the only reasonable thing to do.

Which wasn't good. If there was one thing Finn liked to count on, it was his ability to think clearly. Something about Tessa messed with his head, so the best thing to do was to get as far away as humanly possible.

His internal count hit sixty and Finn peeked his head around the corner. The onlookers had dispersed, probably afraid of being forced by Joe to foster a pet or give blood. Great. His brother was actually good for something.

He glanced down at the bench. His pack was still there, but the macaw was gone. He looked up and saw Joe putting the cage in the front seat of the fire truck.

"Shit," he grumbled. Well, there went that part of the plan, the part where he actually got something out of coming back to this crap hole. Unless . . .

He looked in the direction of the diner. Unless he stayed one more day, took the time to track down the macaw. Then, maybe he could get a bottle of wine and sneak off somewhere with Tessa. Catch up on old times. Maybe have some new times . . .

Bad idea. He knew that if he stayed, it would be in the

running for the stupidest thing he would ever do, and there was certainly a healthy amount of competition for that slot. Smart Finn would have left already, but Stupid Finn had been ruling the day so far. He could feel them both pulling on him, pretty much in a dead heat.

Finally, he ducked out onto the sidewalk, grabbed his backpack, and made a choice.

Isabella Scuderi picked up a crate of violets from the cart and put them on the long display table near the entrance to FLOWERS, ETCETERA. She inhaled the earthy scent of the soil mixing with the sweetness of the flowers and smiled. This job definitely beat the hell out of AP Chem, which was where she would be if she hadn't dropped all her advance classes and gotten the afternoons off from school. It had been a hell of a fight convincing Tessa to let her graduate with her class instead of finishing early. Izzy had actually had to pull out reference materials from noted psychologists on the benefits of not skipping grades in school. She was lucky Tessa didn't require official in-person depositions from the experts.

That's probably what she'd have to do to get her own car. The way it was now, whenever she wanted to use the Mazda, she had to deliver a full itinerary to Tessa, who would make phone calls to check with mothers and chaperones, just to be sure. It would be impossible for Izzy to fly under Tessa's radar if she had to ask permission anytime she wanted to go farther than walking distance from their house.

It's not that I don't trust you, she'd always say, *it's just that sometimes I wish Mom hadn't trusted me so much.*

Of course, that's all she'd say about it. Izzy had no idea

what Tessa had done that was so bad, so damaging, that Izzy had to pay the price. Her sister had all her limbs and seemed to be in full working condition, aside from being overprotective to the point of making the Amish look laid-back. But maybe now that Tessa'd gotten her precious Thing back . . .

Yeah, right, Izzy thought. *I'm never getting a car.*

Her back pocket buzzed, and she reached for her cell phone, checking the caller ID window briefly before flipping it open and whispering, "Not yet." She flipped it shut and stuffed it back into her pocket just as Margie Fletcher came up from behind and put her hand on Izzy's shoulder. Izzy smiled, hoping that Margie wouldn't see her heart pounding under her apron.

"Great job, Izzy," Margie said, beaming at the display. A monkey could have put the display together, but because it was Izzy, Margie beamed. Margie's sweetness almost made Izzy feel guilty about what she was planning, but she was only doing what she had to do.

"I'm almost done," Izzy said, then cleared her throat. She was so nervous. She shouldn't be so nervous, should she? "Is there anything else you need me to do?"

Say yes, say yes, say yes, Izzy chanted internally. She needed to have an excuse to stay just a little while longer, just long enough to get into Margie's office . . .

"Hmmm, no, I think you can—"

The bell on the front door chimed, and Mrs. Sunberg came in, waddling behind a tremendous ficus tree. Margie hurried to the front of the store, listening as Mrs. Sunberg complained that the left side kept drying up and dying. Izzy's eyes shot to Margie's office door, slightly ajar behind the counter.

This is it, Izzy thought, her heart rate kicking up. She pushed the cart back into the storage room, then poked her head out. Margie's back was to her.

Now or never.

She slipped sideways behind the counter and into Margie's office, carefully returning the door to its slightly ajar state. She took a moment to get her breath, then headed for the daisy still-life that sat on the wall behind Margie's desk.

Geez. A painting over the safe in the office. Izzy had bit her tongue over that trite safety measure—any thief worth his or her salt would have no trouble robbing this place blind—but Margie's naiveté worked toward Izzy's gain, so despite the fact that Margie had been one of her mother's best friends, and Izzy really liked her a lot, she'd kept her mouth shut.

She started on the combination. It had taken two months of sneaking peeks through the crack in the door while Margie worked the safe in order to figure out what the numbers were. She clicked carefully to 50, then pulled out the cell phone in her pocket, hit her speed dial. After two rings, Sosie answered, and Izzy said, "Now."

"Now?" Sosie sounded nervous. Then again, Sosie was always nervous. "Are you sure you really want to do this? Maybe you should just call the police or—"

"Sose," Izzy whispered harshly. She'd explained her position on this a thousand times; there was no time to go through it again now. "Help me, or I'm going to Juvie."

Sosie gave a short whine, then said, "Okay," and hung up. Izzy tucked the phone in her back pocket with one hand as she carefully dialed 23 into the combination lock with the other.

The bells on the door jingled. Either another customer had come in, which would be good, or Mrs. Sunberg had left, which would be bad. Izzy felt some sweat on the back of her neck.

Come on, Sosie. Come on . . .

Izzy maneuvered the lock to 46 and held her breath waiting for the phone to ring.

"Come on, come on," she muttered. She could hear footsteps and no talking, which meant no other customer. Margie was a chatterbox; she couldn't stand not to be social. Izzy had caught her talking to the garden gnomes once or twice. If there was no one in the store, Margie would probably be heading for the office; if she caught Izzy now, it would be all over. Izzy swallowed hard as she imagined how Tessa would react. Even if Margie didn't press charges—which she probably wouldn't—Tessa would be really upset.

Izzy'd probably never leave the house again.

She'd probably be homeschooled.

Oh, Jesus, Sosie, come on . . .

The counter phone rang.

That's my girl, Izzy thought. If anyone could keep Margie distracted with a thousand inane questions, it was Sosie. Izzy twirled the combination to the last number—18—and listened for Margie to start talking before she gently lifted the latch. A thrill ran through her as the safe opened, and she had to do a little jig to keep herself from giggling with glee.

This was it. The last thing she needed. All the planning, and the mulling, and the maneuvering had finally come to this.

She started rummaging through the safe. There was

some cash in a bank pouch, various deposit slips and random account information, and two credit cards. Izzy rummaged farther and found Margie's passport.

"Damn," she muttered. *Where was it?*

"Well," she heard Margie saying from the shop, "I suppose if you wanted to try and crossbreed a hydrangea with a hyacinth . . . I suppose you could . . . but that's really not what we do here . . ."

She felt along the safe for a false bottom, a false side. Something. Damnit. Izzy had looked almost everywhere else—Margie's car, every nook in FLOWERS, ETCETERA. The only place left was Margie's house, and Izzy'd need a car to get there. Then she'd have to figure out a way to break in. Then . . .

"I have to go now," she heard Margie say quickly into the phone. This followed by the sound of the phone hanging up and the clack of Margie's heels on the hardwood floors as she headed into the office.

"What are you doing?" Margie asked as she walked in, a mere nanosecond after Izzy set the painting straight on the wall, her heart pumping like a freight train. Izzy smiled and picked up an object from Margie's desk.

"Stapler," Izzy said. "I need a stapler."

Margie pulled a scrunchy out of her pocket, and drew her dishwater blonde hair back into a ponytail. "What for?"

Izzy went blank, then started to laugh. "Oh, man. Now I can't remember. Don't you hate it when that happens? You go into a room for something—"

Margie smiled. "Oh, I know. Happens to me all the time."

Izzy put the stapler down and looked at her watch. "I

have to run. I'm meeting Sosie at the mall, and then I've got to check in with Tessa at Max's. You know how she gets when I'm late." She rolled her eyes, playing up more annoyance than she actually felt because petulant teenagers don't arouse suspicion as easily as compliant ones.

"Don't give her a hard time. She just worries about you," Margie said. As Izzy passed, Margie reached out and touched her arm. "It's been really good having you here, Izzy. It's a little like having your mom back."

Izzy nodded, smiled back. "Yeah."

She grabbed her backpack from under the counter and hightailed it out, not letting the smile fade from her face until the door had shut firmly behind her.

Chapter Four

Tessa stared out the front window of the diner as she poured Astrid's coffee. Her eyes focused lazily on the backward image of the Max's Diner logo painted on the front window, but her mind definitely qualified as being somewhere else.

Or, more accurately, with someone else. It was about three o'clock, almost eight hours since she'd been caught kissing Dermot Finnegan behind the drugstore, and she could still feel him. His fingers in her hair, his breath on her lips, his everything all smooshed up against *her* everything . . .

God. Izzy'd been right. If kissing Finn, the man who had been the bane of her existence for ten years, had this effect on her, maybe she really did need to get laid.

"Watch it there, sweetie," Astrid said, putting her wiry hand on Tessa's pouring arm. Tessa pulled the carafe back just as the coffee was about to flow over the mug.

"Oh." Tessa stared down at the mug. Good thing Astrid took her coffee black; there was no room for sugar or cream. "Sorry."

"No problem," Astrid said, her smile overly bright, her eyes focusing tightly on Tessa, watching for anything worth reporting. It hadn't taken long for the news of Finn's return to fly through town. Stella Hodgkiss was the heart of the gossip mill in Lucy's Lake, and by seven-thirty that morning, Max's breakfast business had tripled with people wanting to be at the heart of the action should Finn want to visit his uncle or his old girlfriend. Nothing happening followed by a whole lot more nothing had driven out most of the voyeurs, and now it was pretty much just the die-hard gossips—Astrid the laundry lady and a passel of PTA moms.

"You look awfully distracted," Astrid said. "There something you want to talk about, honey?"

Tessa thought seriously about that. Did she want to talk about the most surreal morning of her young life, in which the car she'd been mourning for ten years had been mysteriously returned, and she'd practically gotten busy in public with a man she thought she hated? Did she want to talk about the aching and irritating disappointment she'd felt when she'd gone back to take him out of town, and he was nowhere to be found?

She met Astrid's grin with a distracted smile. "No. Thanks. No."

Astrid leaned forward over her coffee, the official Lucy's Lake body language for *There's gossip a-comin'*. "So . . . I hear they haven't gotten in touch with Vickie yet. She didn't tell Stella where she was going, just that she was going on vacation. And then her place catches fire. Don't you think that's strange?"

Tessa shrugged. "For this town? Not so much."

"I bet she'll want to give Finn a reward. You know, for

saving the place. Is he going to be in town for a while, do you know?"

Tessa forced a tight-lipped smile. "I really don't know." *And I'm not conflicted at all about it.* "Can I get you anything else?"

Astrid's disappointment registered on her face, and she sat back. "No, thanks, hon. I think I'll be working on this coffee for a while."

Tessa nodded and glanced back at the counter, where Max Finnegan stood punching buttons on the register. Max was her boss, Finn's uncle, and possibly the crankiest man in the state of Vermont. He'd reacted to the news of Finn's return the same way he reacted to everything— one shake of his white-haired head and a rude grumble under his breath. Tessa could tell that Finn's return was hitting Max hard; she'd known the man her entire life, and she knew when he was really upset and when he was just being Max.

She also knew that he'd never admit to being upset, so there was no point in directly addressing anything. She slid casually behind the counter and started to refill her carafe.

"Get outta here, Tess," Max grunted. "Your shift was over an hour ago."

"That's okay," she said. "I can hang out for a while."

"Did I sound like I was asking?"

She leaned one hip against the counter. "Don't know. Been a while since I've heard you ask politely for anything. What's it sound like?"

Max turned to her, his blue eyes narrowing at her. Apparently, despite her best efforts to be casually rude, he'd sensed her sympathy. "Go home."

"Fine." She jerked the strings on her apron loose. "Remind me not to try and help you next time."

"If I have to remind you, I'll fire you," he grumbled, then grabbed the carafe and brushed past her to go refill the PTA ladies' coffee.

Tessa hesitated for a moment as she watched Max with the PTA ladies. She didn't want to leave him in case Finn showed up, but she knew from experience that at times of emotional intensity, Max liked to be left alone.

She pushed against the swinging door and stepped into the kitchen just as a short girl with a shoulder-length black bob, severe bangs, and dark eye makeup skipped into the kitchen through the back door. It took a moment for Tessa to recognize her sister, and when she did, she practically dropped her apron.

"Iz?" she sputtered. "What—what—what . . . ?" Tessa put her hand to her forehead and tried not to imagine her sister's curly golden locks lying on the basement floor in the home of one of Izzy's crazy friends. "It's a wig, right? Tell me it's a wig. Even if you're lying. Please lie to me, Iz."

"It's a wig, you freak," Izzy said, cracking her gum and giving Tessa one of her trademark light-up-the-room smiles. "I'm trying out my flapper look for the Come As You Aren't Ball on Saturday night." She put her hands on her hips and gave Tessa a cutesy wink. "You like?"

"Oh, hell," Tessa whined. "You're going to that thing?"

"Um, yeah," Izzy said. "I told you last month. Sosie's aunt Grace is organizing it. It's to raise money to renovate the old covered bridge on Morning Road. Or maybe it's for the library? I don't know. It's for a good cause, though. Baby ducks?" Izzy thought for a moment, then shrugged. "Whatever. I'm sure I told you about it."

"No," Tessa said. "You didn't. Now I have to chaperone. You know they're gonna make me bring the punch. I always get stuck with the punch."

"Then don't chaperone," Izzy said. "I'm going with Sosie, her aunt and uncle will be there, and we're not even planning to start smoking the crack and fondling the boys until later on, so your time will be best spent staking out the alley behind the VFW afterward." Izzy grinned and cracked her gum again. "And, hey, with the alley? No punch. Although I believe it is BYO crack pipe."

Tessa quirked one eyebrow at her sister. "Don't be a wiseass."

"But speaking of needing a chaperone, dear sister," Izzy said, her eyes wide with glee, "what's this I hear about you making out with Dermot Finnegan behind the drugstore this morning?"

Oh, for Christ's sake. "We weren't making out. And how did you hear about that, anyway?"

Izzy pulled out a cherry red lipstick and ducked her head so she could see her reflection in the bottom of a hanging pot.

"Melissa Moss was in there this morning—buying a pregnancy test, like she needs one. She does that every month like everybody doesn't know she's a virgin and as if anybody cares. Anyway, she saw you guys through the window. It was all over the school by second period so I'm guessing when you get home, the answering machine will be a smoking, charred shell of what it once was." She pulled away from the pot and smacked her lips, then casually retracted the lipstick back into the tube. "Speaking of smoking and charred, what's the word on Vickie's shop?"

Tessa shrugged. "Office fire. That's all I know. I'm just glad you're not working there anymore."

Izzy shifted on her feet, a strange expression on her face. "They don't know how it started? Seems kinda weird."

"Yeah," Tessa said. Weird didn't begin to describe the events of that morning. "So, how was Margie's?"

Izzy shrugged. "Fine."

"And your grades?"

"Excellent."

"Good, because the moment your grades slip—"

"You're making me go back to full days at school and blah blah nag blah." Izzy gave Tessa a look that was both irritated and loving. "You do know why all the adults on Charlie Brown sound like that, don't you?"

Tessa crossed the kitchen and hung her apron up on the pegs by the door. "Because the rotten kids they're responsible for have made them clinically insane?"

Izzy gave a short laugh, then leaned casually over the butcher-block island in the middle of the kitchen. "So . . . is Finn really a private detective like everyone says? That's so cool."

Tessa watched her sister for a moment. She'd learned a long time ago to be wary whenever Izzy was casual.

"Yeah," she said. "He is."

Izzy nodded. "And when do I get to see the man who steamed off my sister's panties in broad daylight?"

"A: The state of my panties are none of your business; and B: Never."

"Big party poop." Izzy grinned at Tessa, then her smile dimmed a bit as she glanced toward the door to the dining area. "How's Max doing?"

Tessa shrugged. "He's Max."

Izzy nodded. "Well, I'm starving. I'm gonna go scam a burger and fries for me and Sosie."

"Sosie?"

"Yeah," Izzy said, rolling her eyes. "She's meeting me here so we can pretend to study for our history test but really talk about boys. I told you—"

Tessa held up her hand. "Yeah, yeah, I remember. Just don't be home too late, okay?"

Izzy grinned, jaunted across the kitchen, and launched the door to the dining area open with her hip. "And you and me? Are *so* gonna talk later."

She blew a kiss to Tessa and disappeared. Tessa stared as the door flapped back and forth in her sister's wake, wondering what the kid was up to. Typically, Izzy's brand of trouble was a lot like Tessa's had been. All about the fun, no thought for the consequences. But something in Izzy's face had set off a warning bell in Tessa's head, and she'd learned long ago that instinct was the only thing that counted for anything in parenting.

Or sistering. Whatever it was she'd been doing for the last ten years.

She grabbed her coat from a peg at the back of the kitchen and pushed out through the side door into the crisp day. The sun was bright enough to make her squint but did little to ward off the harsh chill of the Vermont winter. She stuffed her hand in her pocket and ran her fingers over the set of keys there. She heard a noise behind her and her heart skipped a beat as she twirled around, giving no time for her brain to shut down the fervent wish that she'd find Finn standing there.

But no one was there. A staccato breeze kicked a plastic bag down the alley between the diner and Astrid's

Laundry and Dry Cleaning. Tessa stuffed her hand back in her pocket.

Finn wasn't coming back. He was running away again.

Which was a good, good thing.

She was almost sure of it.

Finn's eyes flew open and for a disorienting moment he had no idea where he was. Then his focus gripped on the features of Lowery's old shack—the shelf with various canned goods, the hodgepodge series of pots and pans hanging from rusty nails in the wall, the old woodstove shooting out warmth from the corner of the room—and the surreality of the past day came rushing back. He sighed, laid back again, and rested his arm on his forehead.

Even with the midday nap, it had been a long fucking day.

After the run-ins with Tessa and Joe, Finn decided the only thing to do was hang low in the shack by the lake. He'd done what he came to town to do, and anything else would just be asking for trouble. So he'd hoisted his pack over his shoulder and headed for Lowery's field. He'd found the shack pretty much the way he'd expected to find it—fully stocked and vacant. He'd made a fire, cooked some beans, and pulled the sleeping bags out from under the bed. That was the last thing he remembered.

He swung his feet over the side of the old cot and glanced at the woodstove, which was still cranking out the heat. He looked through the window at the sky, drenched orange-pink by the sunset. It was about five-thirty, he estimated.

If he didn't think of something soon, he'd be stuck in that shack for the foreseeable future. He'd already called information and gotten three car rental places in Brattleboro; not a one was willing to drive forty-five minutes to drop a car off for him. He hadn't really expected they would, but it was worth a shot. Now Babs was his only hope, and both her home phone and her cell had gone straight to voice mail, pretty much cinching his suspicions that he'd been punk'd by his sixty-year-old boss.

Which, if he'd been thinking about anything other than getting that car back to Tessa, he should have seen coming a mile away. For Babs, meddling was a religious experience, and Finn had no one but his own stupid self to blame. He'd confided in her during a moment of weakness, and he'd pay for it for the rest of his life.

Not that it mattered much now. Damage was done. And he may be stranded, but he was also resourceful. He'd find a way to get a car tomorrow, if he had to hitch all the way to Brattleboro to do it. Then he'd go to Boston, do the favor for Babs's friends, and double his fee while he was at it. Babs took on these favors to stave off boredom, and always received her payment in the form of donations to charity, but Finn was a mercenary, and after all this hassle, damnit, he was going to get paid, and paid well.

Not that kissing Tessa had been exactly a hassle. Actually, that had been something of a religious experience in itself. Being stuck in Lucy's Lake, though? Big. Damn. Hassle.

He pushed himself up off the bed and grabbed the matches from the shelf to light the lantern, but stopped when he heard a noise outside the shack.

Christ, he thought, closing his eyes. *Can't a guy hole up in a shack in peace?*

He wasn't entirely irritated, though. Part of him suspected it might be Tessa; it wouldn't be unlike her to guess where he'd gone and come looking for him. Of course, that was the same part of him that had him pressing Tessa up against the wall of the drugstore that morning. While he liked that part, it wasn't the part he wanted doing his thinking at the moment; it had no appreciation for strategy. Still, as he walked over to the door and peeked out the small crack between the warped wood panes, Finn couldn't entirely squelch the stab of disappointment that no one was there.

And there was reason #597 to get the hell out of Dodge.

He turned and took a few steps toward the lantern, then heard it again. A soft scratching sound, followed by a whimper of some kind. Finn struck the match and lit the lantern, then walked over to the door and pulled it open.

Staring up at him was the border collie–looking mutt he'd chased out of the burning pet shop that morning. The dog looked up at Finn and wagged its tail.

"Hate to be the sugar in your gas tank," Finn said, "but cute doesn't work on me. The only thing I hate more than birds is dogs. Beat it."

The dog stopped wagging its tail but didn't move. Finn started to shut the door, but the dog stuffed one paw under the door and gave a loud, overly dramatic screech as the door barely slid over it.

"What the . . . ?" Finn pulled the door back open to see that the dog was just fine.

"Hey," he said. "Cheap trick." He raised his eyebrows. "Nice play, though."

Finn moved to shut the door once again, more gently this time, but the dog wouldn't budge. Finn put some weight behind it and the dog dug in its heels, pushing its side and shoulder against the door.

Finn glared down at the dog. There was no getting rid of it without hurting it, and it took less energy to let it in than to kick it.

"Fine," he said as he stepped to the side of the doorway, allowing the dog passage. "But keep your distance and if you pee on anything, I'm making me a big plate of mutt flambé. We clear?"

The dog assumed an expression of victory and took its sweet time moving into the room, so Finn deliberately closed the door on a wisp of tail hair to make his point. The dog shot Finn a *What the hell, man?* look and jumped up on the bed before Finn could stop it.

Finn grabbed another can of beans and cooked them up in silence, letting the dog finish them off when he'd had his fill. They both sighed, sitting on the bed, staring at the door.

"So," Finn said after a while, "is Riker's Island still the best place in town to hustle pool?"

The dog looked at him and shrugged. *It's better than sitting around here all night.*

Finn grabbed his boots, which had been getting dry and toasty by the fire for the past few hours, and stuck one foot in.

"Town full of dog people," he muttered, pulling the laces tight, "and you had to pick me."

Chapter Five

Babs Wiley McGregor turned up the heat under the large skillet, keeping a watchful eye on the blue flames licking up underneath. Her kitchen and cookware, like everything else in her Manhattan penthouse, was of the highest quality. Surely that counted for something.

"Okay," she said, breathing a sigh of relief as she reached for her glass of chilled chardonnay. "Step one: Success."

She grabbed the remote and pointed it at the small TV/VCR perched in the corner of the room. The tape began to play, and the energetic female chef jumped into action, talking a mile a minute about fresh herbs as she dumped an armful of ingredients on the counter.

"Goodness," Babs said, grabbing the remote again and pausing the tape. "No wonder she can make meals in thirty minutes. That woman could perform a triple bypass in thirty minutes." She glanced down at the recipe printout she'd gotten off the Internet, then poked her head into the bag of ingredients she'd had delivered from the market down the street. "Now, which of you little lovelies are the shallots?"

Since none of the various bits of whatnot jumped out of the bag at her yelling, "We are the shallots!" Babs grabbed the one ingredient she could immediately identify—the olive oil—and splashed some into the skillet, just like the woman on television. Filled with a sense of purpose, Babs smiled to herself as she took another sip of wine.

She was cooking.

Traditionally, the women in Babs's line didn't cook. There seemed to be some kind of genetic anomaly that made it not only challenging but dangerous. Her great-aunt Corrine had lost the tip of her pinkie finger in a cole-slaw incident and had become a cautionary tale passed down through generations of cook-hiring and takeout-ordering women. But Babs had turned sixty last year, and the world was running short on things she hadn't tried yet. If she had to risk a little bit of pinkie to maintain some variety, well, damnit, she'd do it.

She was just about to dip back into the shopping bag when the phone rang.

"Mom," Dana's voice came through the line, "I just got your message. What's up?"

"Nothing," Babs said. "Just wanted to call and say hello, see how you were doing."

"We're not pregnant, and we're not trying right now, Mom. Leave it alone."

Babs reached for the bag and poked her nose in. "I'm offended. You've only been married for six months. I wouldn't think about pressuring you for grandchildren yet. But are you sure you're not pregnant, darling? The women in our family are frighteningly fertile. You were a little piece of serendipity yourself, you know. Your father and I were vacationing in Lake George—"

"Agh, enough," Dana said. "And yes, I'm sure I'm not pregnant."

"Well, be sure to take that folic acid I sent you, just in case. Which reminds me—do you know of any car rental companies that might deliver a car for me?"

"How does folic acid remind you—?" There was a short pause, and Babs could practically hear the suspicious wheels in Dana's mind begin to grind. Not that they didn't have cause to grind; Babs was the first to admit she had a tendency to get into . . . scrapes. "Mom, where are you, and are you being held at gunpoint?"

Babs sighed. "You're just never going to let me live that down, are you? Anyway, it's not for me. It's for Finn. I seem to have inadvertently stranded him in Vermont."

Another short pause. Their conversations tended to have quite a few of those. "How do you inadvertently strand someone?"

"It's a long story," Babs said, "but I did, and now I'm in a bit of a pinch. Do you know what shallots look like, darling? They're not long and green, are they?"

"Blind leading the blind, Mom; I have no idea. So what are you going to do about Finn?"

Babs set the long green things aside on the counter. "Oh, I don't know. Can you believe I can't find a single car rental place that will deliver a car to Lucy's Lake?"

"You've been living in Manhattan too long," Dana said. "They'll deliver the Hope Diamond in Manhattan if you know who to call. It's not like that everywhere. Where is Lucy's Lake?"

"According to the last person I spoke to, it's—and I quote—'forty miles east of the Middle of Freaking Nowhere.' I tell you, if I had any idea how difficult it would be to get a car to him, I would have gone in a different direction."

Dana released a sigh. "Oh, God. Tell me you didn't strand him there on purpose."

"He hadn't spoken to his uncle, the man who raised him from the age of six, in ten years. Of course I stranded him there on purpose. But it was meant to be only for a day or so, and getting him out is proving to be a bit of a sticky wicket." Babs held a plastic bag up to the light. "Okay, now *those* I know are carrots."

"You're not cooking, are you? Remember Great-aunt Corrine."

Babs pulled out a bag of tiny, brown onion-looking things. "Who in the world yanked these things out of the earth and decided to eat them? I mean, what would possess a person to do such a thing?"

"Oh, I don't know," Dana said. "People get weird when they're about to starve. Back to Finn . . . what are you going to do?"

Babs sighed. "I can't identify the shallots."

"Focus, please," Dana said. "We're talking about Finn. You can't just leave him there."

"Oh, I'm not going to just leave him there," Babs said. "What kind of person do you think I am? I'll bring him a car myself if I have to." She gave a short laugh as a thought hit her. "Do you know I've never been to Vermont?"

At that moment, a petulant screech assaulted her eardrums. She wheeled around to discover that the skillet had burst into flames.

"Oh, dear. Big fire," she said, and dropped the phone.

As the alarm wailed on, she calmly yanked the cute little red fire extinguisher off the wall, pulled the pin, and covered her range top with white foam. When she was done, she flicked off the gas, turned the extinguisher upside down, and swung it at the fire alarm, dismantling the horrid thing with one careful blow. She put the fire extinguisher down, wiped her hands on her apron, and picked up the phone to hear both Dana and her husband, Nick, calling her name frantically.

"I'm fine," Babs said. "If there's one thing my people know how to do, it's put out a kitchen fire."

"Mom!" Dana sputtered. "You scared me half to death!"

"Babs," Nick's voice came through over Dana's; he must have gotten on their other extension. "Are you okay?"

"Don't ever say 'big fire' and just drop the phone like that ever, ever again!" Dana said.

"You would prefer I stayed on the phone and burned up in the big fire?"

Short pause. "Well, no, of course not, but . . ."

"Babs," Nick said again, his voice insistent, but calm. "Are you hurt?"

Babs puffed some air upward to get a wayward strand of hair out of her eyes. "I'm fine. I have to go; my alarm is wired to alert the NYFD and they'll be here any minute. If you need me anytime in the next few days, call me on my cell phone. I'll be leaving for Vermont first thing in the morning."

"Vermont?" Nick asked.

"Long story," Dana said.

"Love you both," Babs said in a singsong voice. "Now, go make me a grandchild."

She clicked the phone off and opened the drawer that held her yellow pages, flipping through them as she hit speed dial.

"Demetrios?" she said when the familiar voice answered. "This is Babs McGregor. Can you deliver the usual?"

"Absolutely, Mrs. McGregor," Demetrios said in his thick Greek accent. "Is there anything else I can help you with?"

"Yes, actually," she said as her fingers traced over the yellow pages to Automobile Rentals. "Can you recommend a good car rental place?"

"No dogs."

Finn glanced at the bartender, a big, hulking guy he didn't recognize, and decided to name him Surly.

"What?"

Surly jerked his chin at Finn's feet. Finn glanced down as the dog shuttled past him.

"Not my dog," he said, and ambled toward the bar, watching with mild amusement as Surly zipped out from behind the bar and approached the dog, first trying to nudge it back outside with his foot, then pushing with his hands. Finn had to give the dog its due; it managed to hold its ground without resorting to so much as a growl, living on sheer piss and vinegar and the ability to wriggle out of Surly's grip like a greased pig. After a while, someone in the back yelled, "Let him stay. This place is dirtier than that dog, anyway." Muttering some parting-shot curses at the dog, Surly returned to the bar, giving Finn a black look as he did.

"What'll it be?"

"Pepsi," Finn said. Surly watched him for a moment.

"Just a Pepsi?" he asked finally.

"What, you don't have Pepsi?" Finn asked, keeping his

expression flat as he felt the damn dog nestle down under his bar stool. The bartender muttered something under his breath and poured Finn's drink from the fountain. Finn spun around on his stool and checked out Riker's. It hadn't changed much, still didn't live up to the toughness of its name. While Riker's tried real hard to get the dive thing going with the wood-paneled walls and cheap lighting accented by neon beer signs, it was still a small-town bar in picturesque Vermont. Hell, back in the day, Riker's had been the Sunday afternoon meeting place for the Lucy's Lake Knit Wits. There was an array of hand-knitted coasters on the tables that indicated it probably still was.

Finn let his eyes wander over to the pool table, analyzing the possibilities for picking up some extra cash that night. The first pool game he'd ever hustled had been at Riker's Island, and the first rule of pool hustling was to never hit the same place twice, but since he hadn't been to Riker's in well over a decade he figured he might be able to bend that rule just a bit.

"No chance," a voice grumbled over his shoulder. He didn't need to turn his head to know who it was.

"Bottle of Guinness, Russell," Joe said as he settled on the stool next to Finn's. Finn glanced at the bartender.

Russell? Nope, guy was a Surly if ever he saw one. Finn turned his attention back to the pool table. Three guys. No waiting. The only problem was . . .

Joe turned on his seat as well, back to the bar, and tilted the neck of his beer bottle in the direction of the guy lining up a bank shot. "Don't even try it. That's Tony Dale."

Finn blinked and looked closer, realizing that Joe was right. Finn's old geometry teacher took the bank shot and missed, and Finn mourned an opportunity lost. The second rule of hustling was to never take anyone who could identify you to the police by name. He reached for his Pepsi and took a sip.

Still, hanging out at Riker's beat the hell out of hanging out in Lowery's shack. Not by a wide margin, granted, but it was either this place or the ancient Pac-Man console at the Gas 'n Sip.

"Nice dog," Joe said flatly.

Finn kept his eyes on the pool game. "Not my dog."

More silence. Finn could feel the cold air coming off Joe in waves. The two of them had never exactly gotten along, but now Joe was acting seriously pissed off. Which begged the question . . .

"What are you doing here, bro?" Finn said. "Trying to keep me out of trouble?"

"No," Joe said, his voice flat. "I gave up on that a while back." He took a sip of his beer. "But I do have something to say, and if you end up hanging around, I just want it said."

Joe paused. Finn sipped his drink. Neither one looked at the other.

"Left my crystal ball at home, man," Finn said finally.

"Leave her alone." The warning was so low, Finn almost wasn't sure he'd heard right, but when he turned to look at Joe, he knew he had.

"Something going on with you two?" he asked, disturbed by how much the thought disturbed him. What Tessa did was none of his business, although he knew in his gut that Tessa never would have kissed him if she was with anyone, and especially not if she was with Joe. It was a cold comfort, but it was something.

"Not at the moment, no," Joe said.

Finn caught that one square in the chest. "So, by not at the moment, you mean . . . ?"

"We dated. Briefly. A few years back."

Finn sipped his drink, trying to guess what kind of body-snatching alien attack would result in Tessa's dating Joe. Because it would have to have been a body-snatching alien attack.

"No kidding," he said finally. "Who knew we'd ever have something in common?"

Joe shot a look at Finn. "I don't want to see her get hurt."

"Something else we have in common," Finn said.

"Good." Joe took a sip of his beer. "Then you'll be leaving her alone."

"You may not have noticed during the few weeks you were dating—"

"Months."

"Whatever." *Months? Christ.* "Tessa can take care of herself."

"Yeah," Joe said. "She can. But she's stupid when it comes to you. Always has been."

"Do you use that kind of sweet talk on her? Because that might be your problem."

"I don't have a problem," Joe said.

Finn watched his brother for a moment, then turned his eyes back to the pool game. "Glad to hear it."

They each took a drink, then Joe was the next to speak. "You didn't happen to see anything unusual at Vickie's this morning?"

Finn scoffed. "Before or after I set the place on fire?"

Joe shot him a look. Finn decided to let it go.

"Nothing but smoke and screaming birds," he said. He

took a sip of his Pepsi and added casually, "Speaking of which, who'd you stick the macaw with?"

"Seems a little weird," Joe said. "In the last ten years, we've had exactly two suspicious fires. One on the night you left, and now one on the day you come back."

Finn's trouble radar went off. "The night I left?"

Joe paused, his beer halfway to his mouth, an expression of slight surprise on his face.

"Yeah," Joe said slowly. "Karen Scuderi's craft shop."

Finn took a moment to absorb the information. Karen Scuderi. Tessa's mom. Holy shit, he pitied the person who set that fire. If there was one person you didn't want to piss off, it was Karen Scuderi. Sweetest woman in the world until you did something to make her mad—like, for instance, getting caught backstage at the school play with her daughter—then, watch out. He still had a scar on his right shoulder where the two-by-four had landed.

"Wow," Finn said. "Karen must have been pissed. What happened?"

Joe eyed him for a moment, then looked back at the pool game.

"She died in a car accident that night. There was some evidence she'd been running from the fire. Soot on her clothes and whatnot. The theory is that she was disoriented from smoke inhalation. She wrapped her car around a tree."

"Oh." Tessa's mom. God. Finn blinked and stared blankly at the dartboard across the bar. "Wow."

So that's why Tessa was still there, still working at Max's. She'd been raising Izzy by herself. Doing everything.

By herself.

"So," Joe said after a minute, "you didn't know?"

"Huh?" Finn said, his mind still on Tessa. He looked at his brother, shook his head. "No."

"Seems weird. You knew about Father Gregory's hearing aid, but not about Tessa's mom."

Father Gregory's hearing aid? Finn shrugged and kept quiet. The best way to ruin a perfectly good lie was to talk about it. Letting people draw their own conclusions was pretty much the only way to fly.

"Kind of a strange coincidence, though, don't you think?"

"What?" Finn said, trying to connect the dots between Tessa's mom and the father's hearing.

Joe watched him for a moment. "The fires."

Finn tightened his grip on his glass. "You got something to say, Joe, come out and say it."

Joe said nothing, just stared at Finn. Finn felt angry heat crawling up the back of his neck.

"What the hell, man? You think *I* set those fires?"

Joe shrugged. "I'd like to think not."

"Then here's a tip: Think not." Finn took a moment to tamp his anger down. "You know you're not required to assume the worst about me all the time, right?"

Joe let out a sharp laugh. "Assuming the worst is how I found you here tonight."

"Really?" Finn said. "And here I thought it was our tight brotherly bond."

Joe raised one eyebrow at Finn. "You gonna tell me you didn't come in here to hustle pool?"

"So what? Is that a crime?" Finn let out an indignant huff, then regrouped as he realized that, yes, technically, it was a crime. This only heightened his desire to haul off and hit his brother. Instead, he leaned closer and met Joe's eyes dead-on.

"Look, I didn't start either of those fires. I'm into petty thievery, general lying, and bad spy movies. I don't set fires and I don't kill people, especially not the mother of the girl I—"

Finn let that sentence drop and leaned back. He and Tessa were a long time ago, and this wasn't about her anyway. It was about him, two suspicious fires, and one self-righteous brother.

"In that case," Joe said, "it might be in your best interests if you didn't leave town."

Finn watched his brother, incredulous. "So, what? You're telling me I'm an arson suspect now?"

Joe shrugged. "The fire at Karen's was ruled an accident, and as far as I know, they don't have any reason to suspect anything nefarious at Vickie's shop. Yet."

Finn relaxed. "Did you just actually use the word 'nefarious' in casual conversation?"

Joe ignored him. "If you leave as suddenly as you showed up, you're gonna look guilty."

"Did you remember it from the SATs or do you have one of those Word-of-the-Day calendars?"

"If you've got nothing to hide, you might as well stay a couple of days."

Finn could tell by the irritated look on Joe's face that his brother was clearly giving the advice to do the Right Thing, not because he particularly wanted Finn's company.

Joe eyed his brother. "If you had nothing to do with the fires, then it shouldn't be a problem for you."

They stared each other down for a moment. Finn smiled.

"It's the Word-of-the-Day calendar, isn't it?"

Joe took a sip of his beer, then said, "So, you came all the way back here after ten years just to return a thirty-year-old car?"

"Rumor has it."

"Okay." Joe seemed to relax a bit. "Glad we had this little talk."

Finn watched Joe for a minute. His brother's dark eyes never wavered from the pool table in the corner of the room. There wasn't a hint of a smile, or a hint that there was any enjoyment in his life at all.

With the possible exception of seeing his no-good brother end up in the clink for arson. But even as the thought occurred to him, Finn knew Joe was too good-hearted to truly enjoy something like that.

Which made Finn dislike him all the more.

"So," Finn said, turning his attention back to the pool game, "for a geometry teacher, Mr. Dale kinda sucks at pool, don't you think?"

Joe downed some more of his beer. "Car accident. Glass eye. Throws off the depth perception."

"No shit," Finn said.

Without so much as a flicker of a smile to acknowledge the lightening of the moment, Joe gave a small nod.

"No shit."

Chapter Six

Tessa sat in her living room, flipping through the channels on the television. There was a great documentary on about the Templars, but it couldn't hold her attention. She hit the button and got an episode of *Buffy the Vampire Slayer*. Took her a full minute to get restless again. She hit the clicker to see a romance author painting her furniture on a craft show. The woman had even painted her television in a blue checkerboard pattern.

Tessa smiled. Mom would have loved that.

She flicked the TV off and sat for a moment in the dark of her living room. Illumination drizzled in from the streetlights outside, giving her just enough light to meditate on the extreme blandness of the room. The sofa she sat on was beige. The walls white. The floors wood. The occasional throw rug cream-colored. It was like living in a large vat of vanilla ice cream.

It hadn't been like that when her mother was alive. Karen Scuderi had been all about the kitsch; the place had been littered with crafty items. Sweeping matron dolls on shelves in the kitchen, ceramic cats on top of the upright piano, school art projects displayed throughout the house. It had been her mother's paints that Tessa had borrowed to cover the Thing with flowers. They might not have had a lot of money, but one thing about the Scuderi women— they were colorful.

After the state had taken Izzy away, though, the kitsch and the color had been too much. Tessa had spent an entire weekend packing up everything of her mother's, even little art projects she and Izzy had done, and shut it all up in the attic. It had never occurred to Tessa that her home and her life were one big blah; she'd been too busy getting a job, proving herself a responsible adult, and covering up any evidence to the contrary. Then, once she got Izzy back, she had neither the time nor the inclination to brighten things up, to get back to the person she used to be. She hadn't even thought about the fact that she hadn't painted a single daisy in ten years.

Mom would have hated that.

Still, deep inside, Tessa knew it wasn't the lack of daisies in her life that was eating at her. At the diner she'd been able to distract herself with work, but since coming home, she'd been unable to outrun the tension she was feeling. She'd cooked dinner. Cleaned. Tried to read some magazines. Nothing had worked. Nothing could get Finn's face, the feel of his hands on her body, out of her mind. And it seemed the harder she tried to push him away, the more stubbornly he held on.

"One good kiss," she said out loud. "That's all it was. One good kiss. I've had plenty of good kisses in my life."

Of course, that wasn't exactly true. She'd dated a bit over the years, but none of the men had given her the zing that Finn did. Not even Joe, who had proved to Tessa once and for all that *looks good on paper* is not a reason to date someone. It certainly wasn't Joe's fault; he had been great. He'd paid attention to her. He'd brought her flowers. He wasn't too needy, nor was he too standoffish. He was good-looking, honorable, trustworthy. He was perfect, actually, the only problem being that there'd been no *zing*. Not like there was with Finn.

Of course, looking at it from another angle, Joe had never stolen her car. Big bonus points for Joe. And if it had been any other guy, she might have let it go on. But Joe was so *good*. He deserved two-sided *zing*.

The front door opened and closed, followed by the sound of Izzy's keys hitting the hall table. Tessa listened as her sister padded through the foyer and the large open French doorway that led into the living room. Izzy got three or four steps into the living room before seeing Tessa in the dark on the sofa, at which point she screamed and clutched at her chest.

"Jesus, Tessa!" Izzy said, catching her breath. "Lurk much?"

Tessa sighed and rested her head on the back of the sofa, staring up at the white ceiling. "Sorry. Just sittin' and thinkin'."

Izzy grinned, flew over, and bounced onto the sofa, folding her legs under her in midair before landing gracefully on the cushions.

"You wouldn't happen to be thinking about making out with your ex-boyfriend in a public street, would you?" Izzy batted her thickly mascaraed eyelashes at Tessa. "Come on, girl. Gimme some girl talk."

"I wasn't thinking about Finn," Tessa lied.

"Is he cute?" Izzy asked, taking off her black wig and

going to work on releasing her long blonde tresses from the elaborate web of bobby pins. "I'll bet he's cute. I remember cute. Of course, I was six when I saw him last."

Tessa pulled her head up from the back of the sofa and looked at her sister.

"Do you ever run out of energy?"

"I don't know," Izzy said, pulling out the last of the bobby pins and shaking her hair loose. "What's it feel like?"

"My life."

"Oh, my poor decrepit sister," Izzy said. There was a slight pause, then she said, "Is he still in town?"

"Who?"

Izzy rolled her eyes. "Finn. Doof."

"Why?" Tessa asked, suspicion deepening her voice.

"No reason. I just think it'd be fun to see him again, see if he's like I remember."

Tessa eyed her sister. "Hasn't changed a bit."

"Quit it with the hairy eyeball," Izzy said.

"The what?"

"I'm not up to anything," she said, with just the slightest hint of indignation. Not enough to cause a fight, just exactly the amount that seemed reasonable.

"You are up to something," Tessa said. "Just because I haven't figured it out yet doesn't make it not true."

"Geez," Izzy said, standing up. "Paranoid much?"

Tessa sighed. "Whatever it is, just make sure it doesn't involve Principal Hinkel's parking space."

"You know, you'd think he'd at least appreciate the artistry of it," Izzy said. "I mean, it was a total *Gaslight* reference. Classic. Most kids are spray-painting *Skool suks* on the gym walls, and the misspellings aren't even intentional, so they don't even have the irony going for them—"

"They'll take you away, Iz," Tessa interrupted.

Izzy was silent for a moment, then said stiffly, "No. They won't."

Tessa sighed. "They did it once."

"I was six."

"I remember what it was like and, Izzy, I can't go through that again."

Izzy looked up, and Tessa could see the guilt on her face. She hated doing that to Izzy, hated pulling the guilt trip card, but damnit, it was pretty much the only card she had left. She sighed, sat up, and put her hand on Izzy's.

"Iz, I know you don't believe me, but that social worker in Brattleboro is just waiting for either one of us to screw up, and she will, she'll take you away. I know it's only one more year of high school, but . . ." Tessa sat back. She didn't want to think about it. Her brain was mush as it was. "So whatever you're up to, I know I can't stop you. Just please. Don't get caught."

Izzy smiled. Not too much, not too little. Just the perfect amount. "Stop worrying. I'm not up to anything."

They exchanged looks—Izzy trying to convince, Tessa trying to believe.

"Stop looking at me like you expect me to screw things up," Izzy said. "It's gonna be okay. Really."

Tessa sighed. "Can't you just be the shy, demure, bookworm type that never gets in trouble? Just until you turn eighteen? Then, I promise, it's straight to Mexico with us. We'll drink questionable beer and get regrettable tattoos and we can both finally relax and have some fun."

Izzy laughed. "It's a deal. I'll be good. You start planning that trip."

Tessa smiled. "Deal." She watched her sister for a moment, wishing she could know what was going through her head. Izzy was a good kid, a great kid. She just didn't appreciate consequences, or the power of evil social workers.

"Well," Izzy said, "I need to shower off this Eau de French Fry. See you in the morning?"

"Sure," Tessa said, and watched as her sister disappeared up the stairs. She knew she should probably do more. Lock Izzy up in her room. Let her out only for school and the occasional church social. But she lacked the energy to monitor her sister day and night, and most of what Izzy did was relatively harmless, just mischievous enough to raise eyebrows in Brattleboro and get Izzy placed in foster care again. The thought alone made Tessa's heart seize up in panic. Izzy might not remember those three years too clearly, but Tessa did, and a repeat performance might just send her over the edge she'd been so carefully straddling all these years.

But for the moment, Izzy was safely upstairs, and there were bigger fish to fry. Like making sure Finn was out of town before someone started asking the right questions about the events of the night he left.

Stupid town bell.

Stupid Finn.

Finn.

Her chest filled with equal parts anger and longing at the thought of him. She smoothed the pillow on her lap, working from the center to the edges the way her mother used to when she needed to calm down.

It didn't work.

"Grr!" she growled, then punched the sofa pillow dead center. That felt good. She hit it again.

Even better.

She tossed the pillow on the sofa, turned to her side, and beat it with both fists until her hair was in her face and a small sheen of sweat formed on her forehead.

And yet, when she closed her eyes, there he was again, all laughing blue eyes and hands that seemed to know exactly where to go.

"Yagh!" she grunted, pushing herself up off the sofa. There was only one way she knew of to get it all out of her head. It was late and she was tired, but she was still going to have to do it, all because stupid Dermot Finnegan had chosen to come back into her stupid life and make everything stupid.

Big, stupid, redheaded jerk.

She grumbled all the way down the back hallway, grabbed her skates off the bench by the door, slamming the door behind her.

Finn's feet were almost completely numb by the time he reached the shack. He'd refused Joe's offer of a ride and didn't rethink that choice until he was halfway there and realized the stupid dog was still following him. It would have been much easier to shake it if he'd been riding in Joe's truck.

"You're gonna have to find some other mark, dog," Finn said, "because tomorrow I'm outta . . ."

He trailed off as some movement on the lake flashed in his peripheral vision. Thick clouds blocked most of the moonlight, and after watching for a few moments, he realized that even if there was something out there, he wouldn't be able to see it. Still, the black ice held his attention. Just about every major turning point of his young life had happened out there—first swim, first kiss, first Winter Festival where he picked his first pocket—and being back after being gone for so long made its pull feel stronger, somehow.

And suddenly, with a clarity so sharp it cut, he realized something.

It wasn't any better. The thing, the *whatever* inside him that had gone off-kilter . . . it wasn't any better. He wasn't going to be able to sleep tonight any more than he had been able to sleep in the past year. He'd been sure that returning Tessa's car would set him right, put him back to the guy he'd always been. He was happy being that guy. No strings. No commitments. No one depending on him, or expecting anything from him. The girls were good-looking and temporary, and the jobs were just jobs. No guilt, no complications.

Good times. Until he tried to steal a bird that ended up being more trouble than it was worth. Since then, everything had been wrong. The dreams began, and Tessa had starred in all of them. The locales varied, but the conversation never did.

You left, she'd say.

There are penguins in the park, he'd reply, despite the fact that he wanted to say, *It was for your own good.*

I had all my things packed, she'd say.

That's a spicy meatball, he'd say, really meaning, *You were gonna go to college.*

I waited all night for you, she'd say. *Just sat on my porch, waiting in the cold, until sunrise.*

Five tomatoes for a dollar, he'd say, aching to tell her he was sorry, but unable to get the words out.

She'd watch him and sigh, then turn away, trailing one last comment behind her.

I loved that car.

And then she'd disappear.

Returning the car was supposed to have put an end to that crap, but standing there, staring at the lake, he knew the restlessness hadn't gone anywhere. He could feel it like a stone in his gut.

"Five tomatoes for a dollar," he muttered to himself. He was about to turn back toward the shack when the clouds parted, allowing some moonlight to spill out, and he saw her. She was on the other edge of the lake, near the road. He had to rub his eyes and take a few steps closer to the lake to be sure it was really her.

It was, and the moment he saw her, he realized he should have expected her. Whenever Tessa was upset, she headed for the lake, swimming in the summers and skating in the winters. When she skated, it was always the same routine, over and over, until she felt better. *Forward, turn, backward, hop, twirl, forward, turn, backward . . .*

She was mesmerizing. The moonlight played off her dark curls, and it looked as though the tiniest stars Finn had ever seen were dancing around her like . . . like . . .

Like nothing he'd seen before. He took a few more steps toward the ice. The dog whimpered a bit and scratched at the door. Finn ignored it, his eyes following Tessa as she glided over the ice, and for the first time ever, he fully felt the weight of his regret, ten years in the making and tied to the very spot where he stood, which—give or take a few feet—was where he was standing when he first realized he loved her, while watching her dance on the ice.

Forward, turn, backward, hop, twirl, forward, turn, backward . . .

She was beautiful. Graceful.

And she should have had more.

He'd been so stupid. He'd left her, given her up because he thought she could do better. Better than him, better than Lucy's Lake. All he'd managed to do was double her loss. Boyfriend and mother gone on the same night. Tessa was supposed to go to college, get out of this town. She was supposed to backpack around Europe, write novels in San Francisco, paint in a Manhattan studio. Something cool. Something interesting. Something more than waiting tables in Max's Diner and making up stories about a guy she should have forgotten the moment he left the town limits.

The dog whimpered and scratched at the door again. Finn glanced behind him at the shack, and when he turned to look at Tessa again, the clouds had once again obscured the moon, and she was barely visible. With some effort, he turned his back on Tessa and trudged quietly to the shack.

Chapter Seven

"Can I get you some more coffee?" Tessa asked, holding up the carafe and blinking her eyes. Skating on the lake the night before had turned out to be a bad idea after all. Although it had worked to calm her for the moment, she'd spent the night tossing and turning, dreaming about tomatoes. Weird.

"No thanks, Tessa," Joe said, folding his newspaper in front of him. "You look like you could use some, though."

Tessa gave a weak smile. She'd already had three cups, and it was only ten o'clock. She peeled Joe's bill off her pad, scribbled "Fire Dept." on it—Max never charged law enforcement or firefighters—and headed for the front, her eyes bleary and her shoulders tight with whatever was bothering her. She couldn't quite put her finger on it. With any luck, Finn was already gone, on his way back to where-ever he'd come from. So that shouldn't be bothering her. And Izzy had promised to be on her best behavior, which meant no more crack pipe/biker boyfriend/unsavory tattoo jokes when Mary Ellen Neeley, the social worker assigned to their case, dropped in on one of her home visits.

And just last night while skating, Tessa had decided it was time to stop telling stories about Finn. She'd covered everything up well enough; it was time to let it all go and move on.

So all was well. All was fine. Life was good.

The front door opened, and a woman Tessa didn't recognize walked in, pushing all other thoughts out of Tessa's head. It wasn't that they never had new people there—occasionally, someone's uncle or cousin would visit from Wichita or Duluth. But this stranger looked as though she'd just stepped out of a Manhattan penthouse, and that was definitely unusual for Lucy's Lake.

The woman looked to be somewhere in her fifties, pretty with fair skin and large blue eyes accented with light smile lines, which seemed only to make her prettier. Crisp, short blonde hair poked out from under an eccentric Annie Hall-style hat. As her ivory cashmere coat fell open, Tessa saw that the Annie Hall thing was a theme.

The woman smiled brightly and beelined for Max, who instinctively straightened and took a half step back upon seeing her.

"Oh, my," she said, her face beaming as she held out her hand. "You must be Max. I'm so pleased to meet you."

Tessa looked from Max to the woman, then back to Max, who seemed a bit surprised himself, although with him it was sometimes hard to tell. He was rarely an easy read.

"Yeah," he said warily, reaching for the woman's hand and shaking it. "Can I help you?"

The woman released his hand and smiled even brighter. "I'm Babs Wiley McGregor. You can call me Babs."

Max shifted a sideways look to Tessa. Tessa shrugged.

The woman was acting as though they should know who she was, but the name wasn't ringing any bells for Tessa.

"Oh, Finn hasn't told you about me, has he?" You-Can-Call-Me-Babs said.

Tessa's mind raced. Who was this woman? Did Finn have a girlfriend? An *older* girlfriend? No, it couldn't be. She wasn't his type. Although, in ten years, his type could have changed.

But no—

Babs settled on one of the counter stools. "I'm his . . . well, employer. Of sorts. I guess. It's slightly overcomplicated, but none of that really matters. Is he here? I need to speak to him."

Employer. Of sorts. She guesses.

Tessa went from confused to panicked in 1.5 seconds flat.

"No, actually," she said, hurrying around the counter to stand next to Babs. "Um. He's not here. He left. He's gone." Tessa put her hand on Babs's arm and pushed lightly. "Nice to meet you, though. Bye."

"He left? Already?" Babs frowned, getting up from the stool but not moving any closer to the door. "That's disappointing."

"He left?"

Tessa spun around to find Joe standing right behind her, putting a few bucks on the counter and nudging them toward Max, who shook his head and nudged them back. "He's gone?"

"Um," Tessa said, looking from Joe to Max and back again. "Yeah. I think. Maybe. He said he was going to leave."

Joe huffed in irritation. "I told him not to leave town."

Tessa put her hand over her erratically pumping heart. "What the hell did you do that for?"

Joe sighed. "He might be a suspect in the fire at Vickie's."

"There was a fire?" Babs asked.

"Why?" Tessa said, her eyes on Joe. "He didn't start that fire."

Joe's face tightened a bit, but before he could say anything in response, Max picked up Joe's hand, slapped the bills into it, and closed Joe's fist around them.

"And I don't want to hear another goddamn word about it," he said, then turned and slammed into the kitchen, leaving the door swinging furiously behind him. Tessa and Joe exchanged a look, and then she turned to Babs.

"Um," she said, "sorry about that. He can be a little grumpy sometimes. But his heart is good."

Babs raised one eyebrow at the swinging door. "That's not all that's good." Babs used a napkin to fan herself, then turned a grin on Joe. "And you must be Finn's brother."

Surprise registered on Joe's face. "He told you about me?"

"Little bit," Babs said, "but I could tell because you've got the same mischievous sparkle in your eyes that Finn has."

"I do?" Joe asked.

"He does?" Tessa said, throwing a glance back at Joe.

"You said Finn works for you?" Joe said. "I thought he worked alone."

Babs scoffed. "Hardly. I get the clients, he just does the jobs. So, he really left, huh?"

"Um," Tessa said. "Are you hungry? We have a killer lemon Danish . . ."

"You said you drove here?" Joe said, settling on a stool next to Babs. "All the way here from Las Vegas? By yourself?"

Tessa's stomach flipped in panic. *Crappity crap crap shit.*

"You know, she's had a long drive; I'm sure she doesn't want to be pelted with questions, *Joe,*" Tessa said, shooting him a warning look, then turning a smile on Babs. "How about some coffee? Nothing beats Max's coffee. Cream? Sugar? Black?"

"Las Vegas?" Babs said, looking at Joe.

Tessa launched herself at Babs, grabbed her by the arm, and pulled her toward the door.

"You know," she rattled as she led Babs away, "I think I might know where Finn is why don't you let me bring you to him Joe tell Max I had to run out okay I'll be right back!"

She let the door shut behind them and took a breath of the chill air outside, hoping it would slow her panicked heart. When she regained her focus, Babs was smiling at her with glowing warmth.

"And you must be Tessa," she said, patting Tessa's hand. Tessa stopped moving and stared at Babs.

"Yes," Tessa said. "I am. How did you know?"

Babs smiled. "You're even prettier than I imagined. Although I knew you'd be pretty."

Tessa stared at her. "What . . . ? You mean . . . ?" She paused, fought not to say what she was thinking, and lost. "Finn said I was pretty?"

Babs laughed. "No, he didn't say a word about your looks. That's how I knew you were really something special." She moved down the cement steps into the parking lot. "There's something you should know about men: The less they say, the more there is to say."

"So . . . Finn ta-talked about me?" Tessa said, feeling a strange tightness in her throat.

"Of course," Babs said, slipping on a pair of sunglasses. "You're the whole reason for this little adventure, didn't you know? Now, where's that flower car? I've been just dying to see it. Is it really called a Thing? That's so cute I could just do a tap number right here in the parking lot."

"Um, it's at my house, just about a block away," Tessa said, pointing vaguely in the direction of her place. Babs smiled and hooked her arm in Tessa's.

"So, you say you know where Finn might be?"

Tessa swallowed and forced a smile. "I can only think of one place."

"I waited all night for you," Tessa said, standing in her skates on the black ice, staring at him with her arms crossed over her fuzzy white sweater. "Just sat on my porch, waiting in the cold, until sunrise."

Finn tried to move closer to her, but she skated lightly backward, nullifying any ground he gained.

I'm sorry, he thought.

"Five tomatoes for a dollar," he said.

knockknockknockknockknock

He blinked, glanced behind him. "Did you hear that?"

"Hear what?" she said.

knockknockknockknockknock

He looked at Tessa, who stared back at him, her arms laden with bags of produce.

"What the hell am I supposed to do with all these tomatoes?" she asked.

Then there was a sudden punch to his gut, and he bolted upright in the cot. Fur in his face, a yelp, sleeping bag to the floor, dog scrambling to its feet.

Finn sat there and stared at a spot on the floor as the events of the last twenty-four hours started to come back.

The car. The shack. Lucy's Lake.

Fires. Joe. The dog. Max.

Tessa.

knockknockknockknockknock

And a visitor to boot. Who would come looking for him all the way out there? He glanced at his watch: ten o'clock in the morning.

"I'm telling you, dog, I don't know where home is for you, but if you ever think about going back, take my advice: Don't."

The dog stared at him, cocked its head sideways, and gave a small huff of a bark.

knockknockknockknockknock

"All right, all right," he said, throwing his legs over the side of the cot and yanking his flannel shirt on over the jeans and T-shirt he'd slept in. He ran his hand through his hair and shuffled to the door, pulling it open to see a blonde girl staring up at him.

Christ.

"Okay," he said. "One box of Thin Mints and two Samoas, but that's all you're squeezing out of me."

"Finn?" she said, her voice tentative. She sounded just like Tessa, only younger and less pissed off. He squinted.

"Oh, man," he said, amazed as he realized who he was looking at. "Izzy?"

She smiled. "Yeah. You remembered?"

"Yeah." He laughed, trying to mesh his memory of the

scabby-kneed kid he knew with the pretty young girl in front of him. "Wow. Look at you, all grown up."

Izzy beamed. Man, if only it was as easy to make Tessa that happy . . . Well, there was one way he knew of, but the chances of Tessa letting him do that were very small indeed.

"I need to talk to you," Izzy said, pushing herself into the room.

"Come on in," Finn said, shutting the door behind her.

"Oh!" Izzy said, clapping her hands and bending over to pet the dog, which was wagging its tail and playing the cute angle to the hilt. "What a cutie! What's his name?"

"It's a him?" Finn asked. Izzy shot him a look over her shoulder. Finn shrugged. "I dunno. Not my dog."

"Yes, it's a him," Izzy said, standing upright. She let her backpack drop to the ground, then looked around.

"Nice digs."

Finn reached down and picked up the sleeping bag, tossing it onto the bed. "Thanks. I was going for rustic with a hint of squatter."

Izzy surveyed Finn carefully, a light smile on her face.

"She said you were a wiseass."

"Who? Tessa?"

Izzy shrugged. "Yeah. She doesn't say much about you, but I remember her saying once that you were a Grade-A wiseass."

"I prefer social commentator, but potato, po-tah-to," Finn said. "Speaking of your lovely and mildly dangerous sister, does she know you're here?"

Izzy remained silent, and Finn nodded, reaching for his pack.

"Mind if I smoke?"

Izzy shook her head. "No. Can I have one?"

"No," Finn said, pulling out his smokes and lighter.

She put on a slight pout. "Why not?"

"One, quitting's a bitch, so don't start. Two, your sister would hunt me down and kill me twice if she found out I even let you in here, let alone gave you a cigarette. So pardon my rudeness . . ."

He put the cigarette in his mouth and lit it. The dog gave a small huff. Finn pulled out a folding chair and set it down for Izzy. He sat on the edge of the cot, took a drag of his cigarette, and exhaled.

"So, how'd you find me here?"

"There are only two bed-and-breakfasts in town, and you weren't at either of those." She shrugged. "It was just a guess."

Finn took another drag. "Good guess. Second question: Why are you here?"

Izzy hesitated for a second, then sat up a little straighter. "I'd like to hire you," she said finally.

Finn had to raise an eyebrow at that. "To do what?"

"You're a private detective, right?"

"So I'm told."

"Well, I need you to privately . . . detect something."

Interesting. He watched Izzy for a moment. "How much?"

"Hmmm?"

"How much are you willing to pay me?" he asked.

"Um . . . ," she stammered, "don't you want to hear the details of the case first?"

"There's only one detail I'm interested in," he said. "How much?"

"Okay." She nibbled at her lip and reached into her bag,

pulling out a clear Ziploc bag with some bills and change in it. "I have eighty-nine dollars and seventy-three cents that I can put down now. And then, when I turn eighteen, I'll get my half of the money from Mom's life insurance."

He kept his face impassive. She shifted on her seat.

"I have an after-school job," she said, wringing her hands in the way young girls did when they asked a favor. "Maybe I can pay you on an installment plan or something, then give you the balance next May?"

Finn took another drag of his smoke. Whatever she wanted, the kid was serious about it. Which, when you're talking about a sixteen-year-old girl, usually meant only one thing.

A sixteen-year-old boy.

"Hope you didn't smash your piggy bank getting that money out," Finn said, "because it's all going back."

Izzy's eyebrows knit together, and she looked down at the bag in her hand. "But . . . but . . . don't you want to hear the details of the case first?"

"Nope," Finn said, "because whoever he is, he's not worth it."

"What? Who are you talking about?"

"Whatever little punk has got you so in a tizzy that you're willing to part with the whole of your allowance money and then some to find out if he likes you or if he *like* likes you." Finn took another drag. "Trust me, whoever he is, he's not worth it."

"I want you to find the person who killed my mother," Izzy said.

Well. That'll teach me to underestimate a Scuderi sister.

"Your mother died in a car accident." He leaned forward, watching her carefully. "Didn't she?"

Izzy bit her lip, then pulled her backpack into her lap, unzipped it, and presented Finn with a small wooden box, decorated with stickers and newspaper and dried flowers under shellac. Finn took the box, turned it over twice in his hands, and looked up at Izzy.

"Look inside," Izzy said. Finn slid the top off the box and pulled out a picture of three women at the beach, taken some time ago, judging from the bent corners and general wear and tear.

Izzy leaned forward. "That's Mom in the middle." Finn nodded, recognizing Karen. Izzy pointed to a blonde on the right side. "That's Margie Fletcher." Her finger moved to the other side, indicating a tiny woman with dark curly hair. "And that's Vickie Kemp."

Finn flipped the picture over. Nothing on the back. He took another glance at the box. Nothing unusual there. He handed it back to Izzy.

"Great. A box and a picture of your mom and some friends. You using the new math? Because I don't follow how this adds up to murder."

Izzy took the box back. "This is a worry box. My mom used to make them and sell them at the craft store. You write down your worries, put the paper inside, sleep with it under your bed, and in the morning, your worries are gone."

"Really?" he said. "People actually bought that crap?"

Izzy gave him a harsh look, reminding him more of Tessa than ever. "Yes, they did, and it's not crap."

Finn held up his hands. "I take it all back."

Izzy let out a sigh, gave him a grudging yet forgiving look, and went on. "Anyway, after Mom died, I found this under her bed."

"So, she was worried about her friends?" Finn asked.

"The newspaper clippings on the box," she said, handing the box back to him. "Do you notice anything weird about the clippings?"

Finn looked at the box again and saw that Izzy was right. The clippings weren't complete, mostly covered with the other decorations, but Finn did notice one thing.

They were all about accidental fires that had happened in town. From what he could gather, there had been three in the seven years prior to Karen's death.

"Well," he said, "this is a little quirky, I'll grant you that. But your mom died in a car accident."

Izzy took a deep breath. "Running from a fire."

"And you think her fire was related to these other fires? Lucy's Lake has been around for a while. Lots of old buildings with lots of old fuse boxes."

Izzy scooted forward on her chair. "Look at the box again."

"Izzy," Finn said, holding the box out to her, "I'm not playing games here. If there's something to see, just tell me what you think it is."

Izzy gave him plaintive eyes. "Please. Just look closer. I want to make sure it's not my imagination."

Finn took another look at the box. Flowers. Stickers of little girls in fluffy dresses. Something registered and he looked closer.

Everywhere the word "accidental" appeared in print, the shellac was just a little bit thicker, a little browner. Kinda like a subtle highlighter.

"Do you see it?"

Finn looked up at Izzy. "You think your mother thought these fires weren't accidents?"

Izzy relaxed and sat back. "You see it."

"I see it," he said. "What's it mean?"

"I don't know," Izzy said. "But here's some more weird. I was working for Vickie Kemp last summer, and one day she asked me to go pick up something for her at her house, and I found an identical worry box in the far corner of her closet."

Finn raised an eyebrow. "She sent you to get something from the far corner of her closet?"

Izzy rolled her eyes. "No. I snooped, okay? Don't tell Tessa. Anyway, I found one, just like Mom's, only it had a Catholic saint medal in it, Saint Catherine of Siena."

"Yeah? So what?"

"I looked her up. She's the patron saint for fire prevention."

Finn looked down at the box, then back up at Izzy.

"It's all clear, then," he said flatly.

"Well, duh," Izzy said. "They knew who was setting the fires and they wanted to protect themselves."

Finn put the box down on the bed and rubbed his eyes. "Look, kid. I'm not gonna tell you there aren't some questions here, but I think you're connecting dots that might not be there."

"I'm looking for more dots," Izzy said. "That's why I've been snooping. I thought if I could find Margie's box, you know, there might be another clue. I searched her car, her shop. I even broke into her safe—"

"You what?" Forget underestimating Izzy; Finn made a mental note never to turn his back on this kid for a second.

"—and there was nothing," Izzy went on. "I know she's gotta have a box, and there's only one place I haven't searched—her house. It's gotta be there, and if we can just get to it, her box might have another clue . . ."

"Why are you so sure she has a box?"

Izzy looked at him like he was stupid. "Because the three of them were best friends."

Finn waited for the rest. Instead, Izzy just looked at him. "Yeah. So?"

Izzy huffed. "You don't know a whole lot about women, do you?"

"Apparently not," Finn said, and couldn't help but smile.

"Look, best friends share everything. If Vickie and Mom had a box, Margie has a box. I just need to find it."

"Um, no," Finn said. "You *need* to eat and sleep and breathe. You *want* to find this box. Big difference, as in, drop it."

"But if I could just find Margie's box—"

"Okay, fine," Finn said. "Let's say Margie had this box ten years ago. She might have thrown it out. She might have lost it." Izzy made a rude face at this. Finn ignored it and talked over her. "And your mother died in an accident."

"Caused by the fire," Izzy said.

"Maybe. Maybe not. But everything has been deemed an accident so far, and I think the best thing for you to do is let this go."

Izzy leaned forward, maintained eye contact. She wasn't backing down, which meant this wasn't about getting attention, or stirring up trouble. The kid really believed everything she was saying.

"Joe said the fire at Mom's might have been suspicious."

"He told you that?" Finn asked. That wasn't like Joe,

being the big, strong, silent, protect-the-womenfolk type that he was.

"I overheard him say it to Max once a few years ago," Izzy said. "And there's one more thing."

She paused. Finn let her, just waiting. This was the big reveal; no need to rush it.

"My mom . . . she had this locket. A little heart, a picture of me on one side, a picture of Tessa on the other. She always wore it, but they didn't find it. It wasn't at the shop, it wasn't on her, and it wasn't in the car."

Finn took this in. For a big reveal, it was on the smallish side, but it obviously meant something to Izzy. He shrugged. "Maybe she wasn't wearing it that night."

Izzy shook her head. "She always wore it."

"Maybe it burned up in the fire."

"It was pure gold."

"Maybe an investigator pocketed it. Maybe a member of the cleanup crew swept it up and threw it away. Maybe your mom lost it before any of this happened and just didn't want to tell you. At any rate, you got a lot of maybes and not a lot of facts."

Izzy sighed. "I know. It doesn't make sense. But I've got a gut feeling on this. I really think there's something here."

Her eyes were earnest and desperate. Getting bigger. And a little watery.

Shit. If the kid started crying, he was a goner. Crying women were hell on him. He never knew what to say or do, usually ended up patting them on the shoulder and saying something lame like, "There, there."

"I know it was a long time ago. I know the fire was deemed an accident." She sniffled. "I know there might be reasonable explanations for everything. But what if the reasonable explanation is that someone out there is responsible for my mother's death? How can I just pretend these big questions aren't there?"

Her eyes brimmed with tears. Finn patted her on the shoulder. "There, there."

She swiped at her eyes and sat up straighter. *Thank God.* Finn lowered his hand.

"I don't know if any of this means anything," she said, "but it's driving me crazy. I can't sleep at night. I just . . . I need to know. I just need to, and I don't know how to follow up on something like this. I don't know what to do."

"Have you talked to Tessa about it?" Finn asked.

"Oh, pffft," Izzy said, rolling her eyes. "I can't tell Tessa. She'd pull a freak-out of mammoth proportions if she found out I snooped around Vickie's house, and my case kinda rests on that second box. I can't go to the police. They'd just call Tessa. Can't go to Joe, he'd just go to the police."

She looked up at Finn. Her eyes had somehow managed to get even bigger. How the hell did she do that?

"But you," she said, pleading, "you're a detective. All certified and bona fide and . . . whatever. You could do this. You could help me."

Finn sighed and took another drag of his cigarette, not quite having the heart to tell her that the only thing he knew about detectives was how to avoid getting caught by one. Besides, whatever Tessa had been telling people, he knew she had a reason. He wasn't going to be the one to rat her out.

"Look, Iz," he said, trying to figure out how to let her down easy. He didn't know what had happened to Karen

Scuderi, but Izzy made a compelling argument. Not to mention the unsettling fact that Vickie's pet shop got a fresh coat of soot yesterday morning. Izzy's snooping could have made someone nervous, and a nervous arsonist can easily result in charred shih tzu.

But he was no detective. He couldn't take the case if he wanted to.

Of course, because of Tessa's lies and his decision to keep them, he couldn't tell Izzy that.

As it turned out, it didn't matter. In the grand tradition of frying pan/fire, the door to the shack opened up, and in walked Babs Wiley McGregor, in all her Annie Hall-looking glory.

"We've found him," she said, and before Finn could wonder who exactly comprised the *we,* Tessa stepped into the shack. Izzy jumped up, stuffing the box into the backpack in one swift, deft movement.

Tessa's eyes went from Izzy to Finn to the cigarette and then back to Finn, where they flashed murder. Finn nudged Izzy with his elbow and leaned over to speak quietly in her ear.

"Guess this means no Samoas for me."

Chapter Eight

Tessa blinked, stunned. Even though her antennae had gone up when she'd seen the old Mazda she and Izzy shared parked by the lake, she still wasn't prepared for what she was seeing.

Izzy. In the shack.

With Finn.

During school hours.

Smoking.

"Well," Tessa said. "I think I'm speechless. It doesn't happen very often, so let me see." She held up one finger, tried to think of something to say, then nodded. "Yep. Speechless."

Izzy took a step forward. "I just came here to say hi. It's been a long time since I've seen him."

"You don't even remember him," Tessa said.

"Sure I do. He used to give me piggyback rides to school. And he fixed my bike once."

Finn leaned toward Izzy a bit and spoke in a quiet tone. "Roller skates."

"Right." Izzy snapped her fingers. "Right. Roller skates."

Tessa crossed her arms over her chest and stared at Finn. "You are best off if you say nothing."

"Actually, I'm pretty much screwed no matter what," Finn said, tossing his cigarette into the open woodstove behind him, "so I figure I might as well be chatty."

"Dermot," Babs said. "I think you want to shut up now."

Tessa sighed, looked at Izzy. "You go straight home and call the school and tell them you're sick. Shooting everything out both ends. The more disgusting the details, the less they'll want to know. And then you wait for me. And you're calling in sick at Margie's, too."

Izzy huffed. "Tessa—"

"Now."

Izzy shot a look at Finn, which Tessa couldn't read, then slipped out past Babs. Tessa crossed her arms over her chest and stared at Finn.

"And you—"

"You know," Babs said quietly from behind her. "I didn't get a good enough look at that gorgeous lake. It's all just so charming."

Tessa waited for Babs's footsteps to retreat, then looked at Finn. They held eyes for a while, the silence only serving to feed her frustration. Even more infuriating was the fact that not all of her fury stemmed from protectiveness.

"So," she said finally, "since it's okay for you to hang out in the shack smoking with my baby sister—"

"I was smoking, she wasn't."

"—maybe next we can take her to Riker's and get her piss-ass drunk and teach her how to hustle pool. What do you think?"

"It's not like that," he said. "She came looking for me because she wanted to talk about something."

"Talk to *you*? About what?"

Finn let out a breath. "That's her business to tell you, not mine."

"Whatever," Tessa said. "There's nothing she doesn't tell me. Nothing."

"That's a dangerously naive belief system you got there, Tess."

Ow. Tessa took a breath and put her hand to her chest. There were so many emotions in there, all of them unpleasant and tied up in such a whirling ball of bad that she couldn't distinguish one from the other.

What could Izzy tell Finn that she couldn't tell me?

Finn's face softened a touch and he sighed.

"Look," he said. "She just wanted to talk. Nothing happened of which you would disapprove, except possibly the secondhand smoke."

"Possibly?" Tessa said, her voice taking on some volume. "You were in here smoking in front of my sister. What the hell were you thinking, Finn?"

"I was thinking she's sixteen," Finn said. "I'm sure she's been around a burning cigarette before. Jesus, when did you become so uptight?"

Uptight? Tessa blinked. She was uptight?

"I'm not uptight," she said, her voice weakening because even as she said the words, she knew he was right. She was uptight. She was raising a kid on a tightrope. She had to be uptight, damnit.

"Oh, God," Tessa groaned. "I'm uptight."

Finn smiled. "Looks good on you, though."

Suddenly deflated, she walked across the room and sat on the edge of the cot. A little black-and-white mutt stuck its nose in her lap and wagged its tail.

"Cute dog," she said.

"Not my dog," Finn said.

The dog wagged its tail a bit more, huffed, and walked away, settling on the floor next to the woodstove and giving a dramatic shiver.

"Dog's cold," Tessa said.

"It's not my—"

"Fine, then *I'm* cold," she said. "It's freezing in here. Build a fire, would you?"

Finn gave a little nod and tossed some logs into the stove. She watched him as he lit it, his strong hands, the curve of his back, the spiky redness of his hair. There was a time when they were so close that she always knew what was running through his head. Now, she had no idea, and despite the familiarity of the characters and setting, everything felt foreign to her. When he was done, he grabbed a yellow backpack from where it sat next to the bed and fished out a pack of cigarettes. He pulled one cigarette out for himself and held the pack out to her.

"I figure you quit," he said, "but you know how I hate to be impolite."

"No. Thanks," Tessa said. Part of her really wanted one, but she hadn't had a cigarette in ten years, and she wasn't about to give in to temptation now.

"Suit yourself," Finn said. He sat down next to her on the bed, lit his smoke, leaned his elbows on his knees, and looked up at her, his blue eyes locked on hers and meaning business.

"This might be a good time to give me the full scoop on what the hell is going on here," he said.

Tessa's anger was still simmering, but at the same time, she felt overcome with a potent desire to share everything with the one person who would understand why she'd done what she'd done.

"Well," she said finally, "you remember the night we stole the town bell?"

"Yeah." He smiled at her and she felt her lungs tighten. *Must be the secondhand smoke.*

"After you relieved me of my virginity and stole my car—"

"Don't pull any punches," he said, letting out a short laugh. "I can take it."

"Good," she said. "You're gonna have to."

Their eyes locked for a moment, and Tessa felt her face start to warm.

"Anyway," she said, "later that night, there was a fire."

Finn nodded, and she could see a twinge of sympathy in his eyes that threw her a bit.

"I know."

"How?"

"Talked to Joe," he said. "And Izzy." He watched her for a moment, a sad smile lurking at the edges of his eyes. "I'm sorry about your mom. I always liked her, even when she was beating the hell out of me with that two-by-four."

Tessa smiled, remembering the sight of Finn being chased down the aisle of the school theater with her mother on his tail, waving that huge chunk of wood. "God. I'd forgotten about that."

"Not me," Finn said. "Got the scars and everything."

Tessa let out a small laugh, then felt her smile fade as she let the rest of the story come out.

"That night . . . ," she said, her heart seizing up at the memory. She tamped down the emotion and kept going.

"That night was so awful. I've blacked most of the details out. I remember being down on the porch, waiting for you to come back, and Matt Tarpey coming to the house . . ." She shook her head. "The rest is a blur, except that numb sense of falling and being unable to move at the same time."

She shot a glance at Finn, who was staring at his shoes, his expression dark.

"Anyway, a week or so later, the cherry on top of the misery sundae: They took Izzy from me."

Finn raised his head and looked at her. "They what? Who?"

Tessa sighed. "Mary Ellen Neeley. Social worker from Brattleboro. Izzy's caseworker. Evil little troll of a woman." She exhaled. "I hate her."

Finn smiled. "You hide it well."

"I'd only just turned eighteen," Tessa said, "and Mary Ellen said I couldn't have Izzy back until I was twenty-one. If then. She'd interviewed some people in town who told her about the trouble we used to get into and she said she couldn't be sure living with me was in Izzy's best interests."

Finn's eyes flashed with anger. "What? That's crazy."

Tessa shrugged. She'd spent most of that fury ages ago. "Mary Ellen basically told me that even though I didn't have a real criminal record, just the pranks and stuff we did, she had to take everything into account. I was eighteen, I hadn't even graduated yet, I didn't have a job, and if anything was ever traced back to me . . ."

Finn's eyes squinched shut. "Like stealing the town bell."

". . . like stealing the town bell, then it'd be over. I'd never get custody."

"God. Tessa." Finn's hand landed on hers, the tips of his fingers running over the back of her hand, and *God*, just that small touch felt so good. Suddenly she felt like crying, and there was no way in hell that was going to happen. She'd stayed strong too long to let Finn bring her down now. So she pulled her hand back and gripped her own knees, wishing now that she'd taken him up on the cigarette. Sure, they killed you dead, but they were magic when you needed a distraction.

"I was such a mess when they took Izzy. I think I just shut down, you know? I finished high school. Max hired me on so I'd have a record of employment. But then, later that summer, the town bell showed up, just sitting by the road on a street in Manhattan . . ."

Finn smiled, but she could see the self-recrimination in his eyes. "Can't knock me on my timing."

"I would have liked to," she said, twisting her mouth into a small smile.

"Bright side: I made the Guinness for being the first person to fail to fence an item in New York City." He gave her a mildly chagrined look. "How bad was it?"

"Bad," she said. "They put it right back into the town hall building, right across the street from Max's, and the stupid thing chimes every half hour on the half hour."

"Sorry," he said.

She gave him a small smile. "That's when they started the big investigation. *What happened to the town bell? Who took the town bell?* I freaked. I thought if they traced it to you, then they'd trace it back to me, and I'd never get Izzy back."

Finn's face went serious. "I wouldn't have ratted you out, Tessa. You know that."

"I know. But if they found out you were the one who took it, it would just be a matter of time before Mary Ellen Neeley came knocking on my door. . . ." She trailed off, sighed. "So, I told everyone I'd heard from you. That you were in Las Vegas, had been there since you left. I don't know why. I was just panicked, and . . . eighteen. You just . . . you don't see things clearly at that age, you know?"

"Yeah," he said. "I know."

She looked up to meet his eyes, and he held her gaze. Tessa knew he wasn't just being sympathetic. She could see the regret in his eyes, and for a powerful moment, she felt him, the way she used to. That odd connection that linked them back in the day surged between them again, and she could feel his sadness, his regret. His love for her. She felt it all, and knew him in that moment the way she'd known him all those years ago.

Then it was gone, and his eyes were the same unreadable blue pools they'd been since he'd returned. Tessa took a deep breath, pressed her nails into her palm to give herself a new sensation to cling to, and blamed her imagination. There was no point in thinking otherwise.

Finn released her hand and cleared his throat. "So. I'm still not sure how I went from asshole to hero in ten years flat, though."

"Oh. That." She chuckled and felt a swell of relief to move the conversation to safer ground. "After I turned twenty-one, Mary Ellen was still fighting my getting Izzy, and I had to go to court. It took a while but I won. Well, mostly. I got custody with state supervision until Izzy reaches the age of eighteen. Anyway, I guess Mary Ellen took it personally. She was all fakey nice about it, but she made it clear that she'd be watching me like a hawk, and if I slipped up, even a little, she'd move to have Izzy taken away."

"So, she's a crazy bitch, then?" Finn asked, his eyes twinkling at the edges.

Tessa gave a short laugh. "You said it, not me."

She met his eyes, and for a moment she felt connected to him again, but again, it was only for a moment. She glanced down at her hands, realized she'd been wringing them, and let them fall flat in her lap.

"Then, not a week later, someone came back from New York and said they thought they'd seen you there and I freaked. At the same time, Alton Summers's truck died, right before Gloria was about to give birth to their seventh kid. So I took out some cash, stuffed it in an envelope, and put your name on it."

"Wait a minute." Finn's smile faded. "You used your own money . . . ?"

"Mom left me life insurance. I have a full-time job so I look responsible on paper, and the house is paid for. It's not like I needed the money for college tuition."

"Yeah," he said, although his expression was still troubled. "I guess I can understand that."

"Well, it worked. People started talking about you, and stopped talking about the bell."

Finn rolled his eyes. "Fucking bell. They got it back, what the hell else did they want?"

"Preaching to the choir, mister," Tessa said. "Anyway, I sweetened the gossip pool with a few minor details. Told them I'd heard that you became a private investigator." She smiled, shrugged. "It sounded like something you might do, if you ever went straight." She turned to look at him. "Did you ever go straight?"

He quirked one eyebrow. "Far as I know, I never strayed, although there was this one time at Scout camp . . ."

She tightened her lips against the smile forming there and shook her head. "Forget it. My fault for asking. Anyway, every now and again when someone in town needed something, I'd tuck some cash in an envelope. Made you look like the kind of guy who wouldn't steal the town bell, you know. Mr. Upstanding Citizen Guy. Then, after a while it became . . . I don't know. Fun. When people had little problems, needed some help, I could help them, and no one knew it was me. It was like my little secret, my little bit of personal deviance. And it sorta kept you . . . I don't know. Alive, I guess."

She stopped talking and looked up at him. She hadn't admitted to herself that part of the secret charity thing had been about keeping Finn around, but it had. The realization made her feel suddenly off balance.

"Anyway," she said, "that's pretty much the story."

"Good to know," Finn said, "seeing as I might be here for a while."

"What?" Her throat went dry. "Why?"

"The fires. One on the night I left, one on the day I come back. Looks kinda bad. Joe said it might be a good idea to hang around until it all gets straightened out."

Tessa felt her stomach turn. "But . . . the fire at Mom's business . . . that happened . . ."

"While we were out stealing the town bell." He smiled at her. "It's okay. It happened a long time ago, the investigators deemed it an accident, but Joe kinda has a point. I run out now, it could look bad. And it won't kill me to stay a couple of days."

Tessa took a deep breath, resisting the strong urge to toss herself back on the bed and throw a raging fit. "So. Crap. They're asking questions about Mom's fire now?"

Finn shook his head gently and let out a sigh. "I don't know. Joe seems to think there's something there, but that could just be Joe." He leaned his head into her line of vision until she looked at him. "Tessa, don't worry. If it comes to it, we'll just lie about where we were."

"Yeah, and if we get caught in a lie, I'll get in trouble, and they'll take Izzy away. I can't lose her, Finn, you don't understand—"

"Shhh." He reached up and gently touched his thumb over the worry crease forming between her eyebrows, quickly withdrawing his hand. "No one's gonna take Izzy away from you again."

He let his hand slide down to her cheek, and Tessa wanted to tell him to knock it off, but she couldn't. She knew it was a moment of weakness, and she knew it would pass. For the moment, however, Finn had the *zing,* and it had been so long since she'd *zinged* with anyone. Right now, she could use a little damn *zing,* and a moment or two of indulgence couldn't hurt, right?

Only, he didn't indulge her. He pulled his hand away, took one last drag of his cigarette, and stamped it out on the bottom of his shoe.

"So, that's everything?" he asked.

Tessa blinked at the sudden change in direction. "Pretty much."

"Except the how much," he said quietly.

"How much what?"

He angled his head to look at her. "How much of your inheritance did you spend trying to make me look like a decent human being?"

"Oh." She looked down at her fingers in her lap. "Not much."

"How much is not much?"

"None of your business is how much," she said, her annoyance rising. "It's my money to do whatever I want with, and I didn't do it for you, I did it for me, so this is the end of this conversation."

His smile quirked at the side of his mouth, and her heart went *zing,* and . . . damnit.

"All right," he said. He stood up and started toward the door. "You don't have to tell me. I'll find out."

She stood up as well. "How?"

He turned to face her, his expression light and playful. "I have my ways."

"Gonna flirt with the bank teller, huh?" Tessa said. They were now just inches apart, and her smile was fueled by such a strong wave of genuine good feeling that she felt almost dizzy. She wanted to be mad at him. She should be mad at him. Why didn't she want to slap him? She really should be slapping him.

"What is it about you?" he whispered as though reading her mind, his eyes going soft-focus as their bodies moved closer together. She didn't answer, merely relaxed as he raised his hand and wove his fingers through her hair. He leaned toward her and she closed her eyes, letting him graze his lips gently over hers. Softly, she fell into the kiss with him, accepting everything for the moment, even though she knew it was just for the moment.

Never make the same mistake twice.

Oh, shut up.

She let the kiss deepen, let her fingers glide over his face. He pulled her into his arms and it felt so good. Like coming home. Like getting a damn break. It was Finn, and even though she would have committed hara-kiri before admitting it, this was the moment she'd wished for in the shadow of her heart all these years, and it felt damn good to finally have it.

But still. Real life and reason were just inches away, and it only took a moment for them to catch up to her. She ended the kiss, pulled back, and looked up at him.

Finn.

"Oh, man," she said. "I'm stupid."

"Really?" he said, reaching for her again. "You feel fine."

She smacked at his hands. "Knock it off. I'm not kidding. Whatever this insanity is between us, it ends here."

Finn's head cocked gently to the side, and he unleashed that damn smile that made her get all stupid and *zingy.*

"You're right," he said after a minute. "No more insanity. Although, I have to tell you, you're not helping matters any."

She crossed her arms over her chest. "Oh, so, what? This is my fault now?"

"A little." He shrugged, his eyes sparkling and playful. "You could help by quitting it with the pretty."

Tessa rolled her eyes at that one. "Ten years, you'd think your lines would improve."

"I'm serious," he said. "I'm only human. You could make an effort, you know."

"Oh, yeah?" she said, not wanting to smile but doing it anyway.

"Sure. You could go a few days without showering. Grow a big wart on the tip of your nose. Or, hey, one of those moles with a long hair right there on your chin."

She gave him a playful pout. "You wouldn't think I was sexy if I had a big hairy mole?"

"Well." He kept his eyes on hers, gave a short laugh. "How'd this conversation get dangerous again?"

"I don't know." She swallowed. "I think we just do that."

"Yeah," he said. "I think we do."

She nodded, staying where she was as he moved forward toward her. In an unexpected twist, though, he simply opened the door for her.

"You'd better go," he said. "Gotta get cracking on that mole."

Tessa ignored the cold air wrapping around her and looked at him.

"Where have you been?" she asked.

He let out a small laugh and shook his head. "Las Vegas. Private investigator."

"Right," she said.

She held one last lingering look with him, emotions tangling in her chest. She wanted him, and she didn't want him. She wished she could curl up here with him and forget everything else, and she wished he would go back to wherever he'd come from and leave her alone. Only one feeling was coming through clearly, and it was the realization that she'd missed him so much more than she'd ever suspected, even in her most private and honest moments.

And that just wasn't fair.

Tessa pulled her eyes away from him and walked out of the shack into the frigid winter air. She took long deep breaths, hoping the cold air would freeze the feel of Finn's kisses right off her lips, taking with it her decidedly inconvenient yearning for more.

It didn't work, but it was worth a shot.

Chapter Nine

Finn stared at the door, the image of its wooden planks burning into his eyes as he tried to figure out what the hell was going on. All he'd wanted to do was return the car, shake the karma, get the mess out of his head so he could go back to his uncomplicated life and move on. When he'd planned the trip to Lucy's Lake, he hadn't even planned on seeing Tessa, let alone kissing her.

Twice.

And those kisses had nearly knocked him over. He never thought that she'd still have such a hold on him, after all this time. He released a breath and ran his hand through his hair. She was still there. He could feel the softness of her face in the palm of his hand, smell the scent of her when he breathed in.

Hell. Between Babs and Izzy and Tessa, he was about ready to appreciate some time with Joe. At least Joe was straightforward, even if he was straightforwardly accusing Finn of arson and murder.

It was the women in his life who were truly dangerous.

You ain't kidding.

Finn blinked, looked down at the dog sitting next to the fire. "You got something to say, dog?"

The dog smacked its lips and rested its snout on its paws. *The name's Wallace.*

Finn eyed the dog for a minute. While working birds, he'd been shot at, knocked out, stiffed, and beaten up—most of them more than once—but none of the birds had ever taunted him telepathically.

Well. There was a first time for everything.

The door flew open and Babs stepped in, smiling brightly.

"My ride seems to have run off," Babs said.

"Huh?" Finn turned to face her. "Oh. Yeah."

"I assume it was something you did?"

Finn nodded. "That'd be the smart bet."

"Oh, Dermot," she said. "For such a charming young man, you can be such an abominable putz."

Suddenly Finn felt bone-tired, and the last thing he wanted to do was discuss his life with a Manhattan Presbyterian who used the word "putz."

"Where's my car?"

Babs reached into her purse, pulled a set of keys out, and handed them to Finn. "It's at the diner."

He took the keys and motioned vaguely around the shack.

"It ain't the Ritz, but you'll survive for an hour," he said. "I'm gonna hike into town and get the car."

Babs gasped and leaned down over the dog. "What an adorable little creature! Is he yours?"

"No," Finn said.

"Oh, you are a cute little fellow," Babs said, scratching Wallace on the head. Wallace shot a look of victory up at Finn.

"She's all yours, dog."

"Hmmm?" Babs said, looking up at Finn.

Finn sighed and focused on Babs. "When I get back, I'm taking you down to Brattleboro and putting you on the next bus back to the city. Then, after I'm done with the Boston job, I'll bring the car back with me to New York. That's the plan."

"Hmmm," Babs said, with just a hint of judgment in her voice.

Finn tightened his grip on the keys. "You got something to say?"

"Oh, nothing. I just thought you might stay, you know, for a little while. Take the opportunity to reunite with your family." She smiled innocently. "Your uncle seems lovely."

"Lovely, huh?" Finn said. "We talking about the same guy? Because as I remember, *lovely* isn't a synonym for *cranky old fucker,* but then, I left my copy of *Roget's* at home."

Babs sat down on the edge of the bed. Wallace wedged his head between her knees and lolled his head back, his neck exposed for her to scratch.

Suck-up.

"You know, I was estranged from Dana for a long time," she said. "Not quite as long as you and your uncle, but still. I will never get those years back. Neither will you."

"Babs, I appreciate your concern, a little, but you don't know anything about me and Max, okay? So butt out."

"I know he raised you," Babs continued. "I don't need to know anything else. When you're a parent to someone, Finn, it doesn't make you infallible. It just makes you vulnerable. Everything they do, everything they say can break your heart. And if Max is anything like you—stubborn, closed-off, emotionally stunted—then I can see why he might have said those things to you. It doesn't mean he meant them."

"Emotionally stunted?" Finn took that in. "What the hell does that mean?"

Babs sighed and stood up. "I've never met your father . . ."

"Dangerous territory, Babs," Finn growled. "Watch your step."

She continued to talk over him. ". . . but I know your character well enough to know you're nothing like a man who would abandon a sick wife with two young children."

"You don't know anything." He didn't want to talk about his father, or Max, or any of it. Anyone with an ounce of sense would be able to see that.

Unfortunately, he was dealing with Babs.

"Max knows it, too," she went on. "I'd bet everything I own that he didn't mean a word of what he said to you that night, but you'll never know unless you talk to him."

Finn watched Babs for a second as a thought, which had been forming at the back of his head, jumped up front and center.

"There is no Boston job, is there?"

Babs scoffed. "Of course there's a Boston job."

"You manipulated this whole situation to get me stranded here. I can't believe it took me this long to figure it out." He reached to the floor, grabbed his pack, and tossed it over his shoulder. "Emotionally stunted, my ass. Mentally stunted, that's what I am."

"I had to do something," Babs said. "I had a responsibility."

"You have a personality disorder. Why is everything your business?"

"Why is it not? I think this nonsense about 'my business, your business' is just another way to keep people at arm's length."

"If we're ever in a church together, remind me to douse you with holy water. Just a test."

"You confided those things to me on your deathbed."

"It wasn't my deathbed. I fell from a fire escape."

"And you called *me* to come to your aid. That meant something to me, Finn."

"I called to let you know that one of your stupid favors damn near killed me."

"The point is, you confided in me."

"I was doped up on painkillers. I didn't know what I was saying." He closed his eyes. This was why he didn't drink. The slightest mind-altering substance, and his brain went soft and he got all . . . talky.

"You confided in me," Babs repeated, "thus making it my responsibility to help you, as it's apparent you're too stubborn to help yourself."

"Just say the words," Finn said. "There is no Boston job, is there?"

Babs pursed her lips and shrugged noncommittally.

Finn let out an I'm-gonna-kill-you laugh and stared her down. "And how long were you gonna string me along here?"

Babs shrugged. "I would have told you by Saturday."

"Saturday." Finn took this in for a moment. "You were going to string me along here for three more days?"

"And now I don't have to," Babs said, grinning. "You're

suspected in that fire. You can't leave town. See how perfectly everything is working out?"

"I can leave town," Finn said. "I'm not officially a suspect."

"But you'll look like a suspect if you leave," Babs said. "I heard your brother say so himself at the diner this morning. Seems like such a nice young man, by the way."

Finn was about to comment on Joe's nice-young-man-ness when another suspicion hit him.

"Babs, tell me you didn't start that fire."

Babs laughed. "Oh, goodness, no. It was a brilliant move on the part of Fate, though, don't you think? Just convinces me all the more that I did the right thing."

Finn ran his fingers over his eyes until they pinched the bridge of his nose.

"Okay. You know what? Talking to you is pointless. I know this. So I'm done. I'm gonna go get the car, and you're getting on the next bus back to New York. I'll figure out the rest later."

"Oh, don't be silly," Babs said. "This town is absolutely charming. I'm not going anywhere. All I require is a nice little bed-and-breakfast, and I think I'll turn this into a much-needed vacation. Do you know I've never been to Vermont before?"

Finn released a breath. "You can't stay here."

"Sure I can," Babs said. "And I think you know how pointless it is to argue with me. Now, do you have a place to recommend, or shall I hunt down a set of yellow pages?"

Finn took a moment. She was right about the pointlessness of arguing. Firing squads were more compromising than Babs once she'd made up her mind. And who knew? She might come in handy if things got sticky for him.

Babs was a major pain in the ass, but he'd never met anyone more fiercely loyal in his life, and the woman had a
knack for getting her way. Whether he liked it or not, she
was a good friend to have around, and he was in short
supply of good friends.

"Fine," he said. "You wanna stay? Stay. But no more
screwing with my life."

"Absolutely."

"You stuck me here; you did your part. From here on
out, no matter how badly you think I'm handling things,
you stay out of it, understood?"

"Of course."

He paused for a moment. "And there's something else."

"For you? Anything."

"It's not for me, it's for Tessa, and it's a long story, so
don't ask questions, just do what I say, okay?"

Babs smiled, her face open and receptive. Finn took a
deep breath.

"I'm a private detective from Las Vegas. You work for
me. We just came from there, and in a few days, we're
going back. Anyone wants to know anything else, be eva-
sive. No making up grand stories, nothing I might have to
back up later. If they pry, then claim client confidentiality
and shut up about it. Okay?"

Babs let loose with a small laugh. "Wow. She's really
been telling some whoppers, huh?"

Finn opened the door. "You have no idea."

Tessa pushed through the door to Max's Diner. She'd
stopped briefly back at the house, made sure that Izzy was at
home and staying there, threatened her with various forms
of television/computer/telephone/allowance restrictions,

and rushed back to the diner. She was already tired, distracted, and cranky; by the time she finished her shift, things were bound to get really ugly.

"Hey, Tessa," Joe said, meeting her by the counter. He was wearing an apron tied around his waist and had a pencil tucked behind his ear. The place was fairly dead, just a few stragglers from the breakfast crowd.

"Thanks for picking up the slack," Tessa said.

"No problem," Joe said. "Brings me back to my high school days."

"Lot of that going around," Tessa mumbled.

"Hmmm?"

"Nothing. Sorry I took so long. Things kinda got"— she puffed her bangs up with a sharp release of breath— "complicated."

"It's okay." Joe sat down at the counter, drummed a beat on the surface with his fingers before continuing. "So. He's still here."

"Huh?" Tessa ducked under the counter, grabbed a rag, and popped back up. "Oh. Finn. Yeah."

"You look upset."

"I do?" She relaxed her face. "I'm not."

Joe's face went hard. "He upset you?"

"Oh, God, Joe, not now, okay? Yes, having Finn here is intense, but I'm a big girl, and I can take care of myself."

Joe went quiet. Tessa felt something torque inside. Joe felt so much like a big brother that sometimes she forgot he was an ex, and the rules were different for how you treated an ex.

"Thank you, Joe, for being concerned, but it's not a big deal. We were in the shack . . ." She paused. "In the shack" was Lucy's Lake High's euphemism for having sex; easily a quarter of the student body had lost their virginity in the shack. It was one of those phrases you couldn't use within town boundaries without it sounding dirty. "Not like that. You know what I mean. Just talking. It was no big deal, really."

"Well," Joe said, getting up from the counter and untying the strings on his apron. "Everybody's pretty much just finishing their refills on coffee. Max is in the back, but be warned—he's in a bad mood."

"And this is different from every other day how?"

Joe gave her a dark look and Tessa understood instantly.

Finn.

"Well," Joe said, "I should probably go."

Tessa reached out and grabbed Joe's hand, giving it a squeeze. "Thank you. Really."

Joe gave her a small nod, then headed to the front to grab his coat. Tessa sighed. Joe was so . . . *good.* So noble. Always did the right thing. Too bad there was no one in Lucy's Lake worthy of him, including her.

"Tessa?"

Tessa blinked and looked up to see Margie Fletcher standing at the counter, holding her bill and some cash.

"Oh, hey, Margie. Sorry. Spaced out there for a moment." Tessa punched the numbers into the cash register. "How was your meal?"

"Great," Margie said. She settled on a stool and leaned in. "I actually wanted to ask you . . . is everything okay with Izzy?"

"Define *okay*," Tessa said flatly.

"It's just . . ." Margie looked around. No one was in the place except Digger Hodges, who was sitting at the back attacking a plate of eggs, and he was deaf in one ear anyway. Margie sighed, relaxed in her seat, and smiled tentatively at Tessa. "I'm a little worried about her."

Tessa took a moment to remember the flu story she'd made Izzy call in sick with. "Oh, she's fine. It's just a little bug."

Margie shook her head. "No, I'm sure she'll be fine. What's concerning me is that . . . well . . ." Margie nibbled on her lip, an oddly juvenile habit for a woman in her late forties, but then Margie had always been really youthful. "She broke into the safe in my office yesterday."

Tessa froze. No, it wasn't possible. Izzy would never . . . she wouldn't . . .

Oh, hell. She *so* would.

"What did she take?" Tessa asked, her heart pounding and her mind racing. "Whatever it is, she will be bringing it back as soon as I can get over there and kick her little—"

"Don't get mad," Margie said. "She didn't take anything, as far as I can tell. I think it was just a . . . I don't know. A prank, I guess? But it worries me. It's not like her."

Tessa kept quiet about that. "She will be over to apologize first thing tomorrow."

"That's not necessary," Margie said. "I just thought you should know."

"Okay," Tessa said, her lungs tightening in her chest as the panic hit. "So . . . um . . . you're not going to press charges, then?"

Margie smiled warmly and put her hand on Tessa's. "God, no. Are you kidding?"

"You'd have every right," Tessa said, wondering why she wasn't just shutting up while she was ahead.

Margie reached over and grabbed Tessa's hand. "Your mother was one of my best friends, and one of the biggest troublemakers I've ever known. That's why I loved her so much. I just don't want to see Izzy pick up those traits before she's eighteen or that horrid social worker is dead." She released Tessa's hand and smiled. "Whichever comes first."

The panic subsided, replaced by intense relief and a frustrating sense of helplessness. Tessa wished not for the first time that Max had a liquor license.

"Thank you," she said.

"Pffft." Margie waved her hand in the air dismissively. Then her smile faded a bit. "I just wanted you to, you know, keep an eye on her. I don't want to see her get into trouble."

"Oh," Tessa said, slamming the register shut and holding out Margie's change, "trust me, I will."

Margie got up from the stool and closed Tessa's hand over the change. "You keep that."

Tessa smiled. "I'll make sure Joe gets it."

"Yes, do that," Margie said. "Joe's a really good man."

"Yeah," Tessa said. "He is."

Margie pulled her purse over her shoulder and shot a thoughtful look back at Tessa. "I hear his brother is back in town."

"That seems to be the case."

"Did he really save the animals at Vickie's?"

"Yeah," Tessa said, feeling a strange swell of pride. "He did."

Margie nodded and leaned over the counter. "Well, a little advice, woman to woman?"

Tessa tried not to let her surprise register on her face. Margie Fletcher wasn't a gossip, or the type to give unsolicited advice, so if she had something to say, it was probably worth listening to.

"Sometimes people only seem like they've changed," she said. "You can't be too careful."

Tessa let out a short laugh. "Heard about me and Finn by the drugstore, huh?"

Margie blushed a bit. "Flower shop and gossip. They go together like chocolate and peanut butter." She smiled softly at Tessa. "I just want to make sure you're okay. You can tell me to butt out and I will."

"Thank you. But Finn and me? We're not, uh . . ." She flashed back to the kiss in the shack and her shoulders tensed. "I don't know what we aren't. But don't worry. I'll be fine."

"I know you will." Margie smiled, gave a small wave, and left. Tessa watched her go, took a deep breath, picked up the phone, and dialed. She waited through three rings, then listened to her own voice instructing her to leave a message.

"Izzy, I assume you're home pretending to be sick and not answering the phone. Continue to do so, because when I get home tonight, you and I are gonna have a very special episode of *Blossom*, kid."

She slammed the phone down, closed her eyes, and imagined a line of Mary Ellen Neeleys on a carnival duck shoot game. She mentally aimed her rifle and shot every one.

"For Pete's sake!" an old, rusted voice shouted out from the back of the diner. Tessa opened her eyes and saw Digger holding his cup out. "Who's a guy got to kill to get a damn refill around here?"

Tessa grabbed the carafe off the warmer and headed over.

"You just bought yourself a switch to decaf, mister."

Chapter Ten

Joe Finnegan raised his hand, hesitated, then tapped lightly on Matt Tarpey's office door.

"Yeah," Tarpey barked from inside, his way of saying, "Come on in."

Joe pushed the door open and walked in. Tarpey, a big hulk of a man with fists reminiscent of cinder blocks, was huddled over a tiny office golf setup, preparing for his putt.

"Joe Finnegan," he said. "Why am I not surprised to have a visit from you today?"

"Your gift of prescience?" Joe glanced at the papers on Tarpey's desk as he sat down. On top of an open manila folder was a spread of Polaroid pictures of Vickie Kemp's charred back office. There also appeared to be something that came off the fax, although Joe couldn't read it from where he was standing.

"Yeah, I'm known worldwide for my ability to predict the obvious," Tarpey said, wiggling his hips back and forth in a way Joe could have been perfectly happy going his entire life without seeing. Tarpey whacked the ball and sent it rolling somewhere three to four feet to the left of the hole.

"Damn warped floor," he grumbled and went after his ball. "The wife says playing golf is supposed to relax me, lower my cholesterol. I think it's a big crock, but you know women. You can argue, or you can sleep in the bed."

Joe shrugged at that. What he understood about women was limited, at best. But that wasn't something he particularly wanted to discuss with Matt Tarpey.

"So," Matt said, shooting a look at Joe, "let me guess why you're here. You need new gear?"

"Nope, gear's just fine. Thanks."

Tarpey raised his eyebrows, but didn't look the gift horse in the mouth. "Your uncle needs Grace to hook him up with some more of her brother's cod?"

Joe smiled. "No. Believe it or not, the cod didn't move that well last summer."

Tarpey scoffed. "Oh, yeah. I believe it." He settled his grip on the club and lined up his shot.

"Actually," Joe began, but Tarpey made *I'll get it, I'll get it* noises to shut him up.

"You're here because"—he did the wiggle thing again—"you want another look at the Scuderi file." He gave the ball a prodigious whack. It went straight for the hole, bounced up off the edge, knocked into the wall, and skittered down the hall.

Joe smiled. "Feeling relaxed?"

Tarpey straightened up. "Stupid fucking game." He tossed his putter to the floor, walked around his desk, and sat down.

"Have a seat," he said, motioning to the wooden chair opposite his desk. As Joe settled, Tarpey reached for his coffee, which rested on his green desk blotter in a mug that read, *Firemen do it with a big hose*.

Joe smiled. "Aren't you supposed to be avoiding caffeine?"

Tarpey raised an eyebrow. "Yeah, *Grace*, thanks for reminding me," he said flatly. He took a large swallow. "So, what's making you second-guess the Scuderi fire this time?"

"Nothing in particular," Joe said. "Just wanted to take another look."

Tarpey allowed a small grimace that passed for a smile. "What for? I'd expect you to be able to re-create it from memory by now."

"Thought maybe I missed something."

"You didn't miss anything. Neither did the investigators who ruled it an accident in the first place." Tarpey leaned forward, his old eyes smiling at the edges as he talked. "Look, I know you were close with Karen Scuderi. You used to work at her place a bit, didn't you?"

Joe shrugged. "I helped out there sometimes."

Tarpey leaned back. "You're not the first guy to start volunteering after having a personal experience with a fire. That's how I get a lot of my guys. And you're one of the best on my team, Joe. But there comes a time when you've gotta let it go. The Scuderi case is closed."

"Then who does it hurt if I have another look?"

Tarpey chuckled. "You ever think about maybe getting a hobby? Grace is dragging me out to the mini-golf place over on I-91 this weekend. You could go in my place. She probably wouldn't even notice right away."

"Thanks. I'll pass." He leaned forward, jerked his chin

to indicate the pile of papers on Tarpey's desk. "Those your pictures of Vickie's?"

Tarpey sighed. "Yeah. Snapped a few before the county guys came in and took over."

"Did they find anything?"

"Lot of charred tail feathers." Tarpey raised his eyes. "Good thing that brother of yours got there when he did."

"Yeah." Joe tapped his fingers on the arms of the chair. "Good thing." He paused for a moment, nodded toward the pictures on Tarpey's desk. "You think it was arson?"

Tarpey shrugged. "Could be. Investigation's still active."

"But you think it might be arson?"

"Everything might be arson until it's not." Tarpey slid the papers and pictures into a manila folder. "At any rate, it's out of our hands now. The county Cause and Origin team is on it, and we'll know when we know."

Joe nodded. "I understand."

Of course, understanding didn't do much to ease the tension in his gut. Tarpey didn't shoot Polaroids on his own unless something struck him as suspicious. As fire chief, he knew that any evidence not taken by the official county team would be inadmissible in court. So if he was taking pictures, it was because of his own curiosity. And Tarpey, as a rule, was not an overly curious guy.

Something was wrong here. Joe could feel it.

And he was very possibly related to it.

"So, you think you can call County for me, then? I can run down there this afternoon and pick the files up myself."

Tarpey plunked his coffee mug down on his desk, clasped his hands together, and leaned forward.

"Did I ever tell you that Grace's cousin died in a suspicious fire?"

"No. When did that happen?"

"Twenty-five years ago, before we were married. Hell, we hadn't even started dating yet. I was determined to solve the mystery, be the big hero. But I didn't have anything, really, other than a gut feeling. One day, Grace asked me to stop looking into it. Said she'd rather I help her move on than stay stuck on something we'd never know the answer to." Tarpey gave Joe a brief nod. "You understand what I'm saying?"

Joe leaned back in his chair. "I don't understand what it has to do with the Scuderi files, no."

"Joe, Karen Scuderi died in a car accident."

"Running from a suspicious fire."

"The fire was also accidental. It was a bad convergence of events, nothing more."

"Maybe."

"And there's nothing in those files now that wasn't there the last five times you looked at them. Cause and Origin ruled it was an accident, and I'm inclined to trust their judgment."

"Then why did you take your own pictures of Vickie's?"

Tarpey sighed. "Look, Joe, if you've got a thing for Tessa Scuderi, get her some flowers. Don't dig up her dead mother. It isn't romantic."

Joe watched Tarpey for a moment, then spoke. "This isn't about Tessa."

Tarpey tapped his big beefy fingers against the desk blotter as the wheels in his mind cranked.

"No skin off my nose," he said finally. "But I think you're better off just taking her out to dinner. Somewhere out of town. Or maybe to mini-golf on I-91. We could make it a double."

Joe smiled, tapped the flat of his hand on Tarpey's desk, and stood up. "Call me when I've got clearance to go get those files?"

Tarpey gave a slight shake of his head, then waved one hand in acquiescence.

Joe smiled. "Thanks, Tarpey."

"Hey, while you're here," Tarpey said, "you find someone else to take that damn bird yet?"

"The macaw? You don't like it?"

Tarpey shook his head. "No, I like it fine. But Grace has allergies. She keeps sneezing and hacking and the thing is making her crazy, and she's making me crazy. Bird's likely to come to an untimely and violent death, it stays at my place much longer."

"I'll come by and pick it up later." Joe paused. "Hey, has anyone talked to Vickie?"

"Beats the hell out of me," Tarpey said. "Last I heard, no one had been able to get a hold of her."

"She didn't leave any contact information with anyone? No cell phone number, no e-mail? The hotel where she was staying?"

"What can I say?" Tarpey leaned back, put his hands behind his head, and smiled. "Woman knows how to take a vacation."

"No," Finn said, wrenching his hands around the steering wheel of the car.

"Oh, come on," Babs said. "I'm hungry. I'm homeless. I'd like a nice slice of apple pie from the local greasy spoon. Is that too much to ask?"

Finn shot her a look. "You're not homeless. You've got a perfectly good home in New York. And since all the rooms in town are filled—"

"All *six* rooms," Babs said. "What kind of town has only six rooms for visitors?"

"It's the middle of winter, the middle of the week. It's not exactly the hot tourist season."

"Well, it's very frustrating. I think the least you can do is take me to the diner and get me some pie."

Finn shot her a sideways glance. "Fine. I'll take you to Max's—"

Babs clapped her hands together, her face lighting up like a little girl's on Christmas morning.

"—and you can go on inside and get your pie while I wait."

Babs rolled her eyes and slumped back in her seat. "Now that just doesn't make any sense."

Finn turned the car onto Main. "No, it doesn't give you what you want. It *makes* perfect sense."

"You're just going to wait outside. In the cold?"

"Yep."

"You're not hungry?"

"Not hungry enough."

Finn pulled into the parking lot at Max's. Babs shot a look at the backseat. "Talk some sense into him, will you, Wallace?"

At the sound of his name, Wallace gave a short huff from the backseat. Finn watched him for a second in the rearview, but the dog didn't say anything.

Which was good.

'Cause dogs don't talk.

Finn pulled around the side of the diner to the employee lot, parking next to Tessa's Thing. As Babs let herself out of her side, he opened the back door and looked at Wallace, who refused to move from his curled-up position on the backseat.

"I'm not paying for this car to be detailed from you marking your territory," Finn said. "Out. There's a fire hydrant around here somewhere just waiting to be abused, I'm sure."

Wallace huffed again, then pulled himself up and hopped out of the car. Finn turned toward the diner, listened as the *clack-clack-clack* of Babs's heels came up behind him.

"You're just going to let him off like that?" Babs said. "Aren't you afraid he won't come back?"

"Nope," Finn said. He scooted himself up on the trunk of the car and pulled out his pack of smokes. Babs tightened her grip on her shoulder bag and sighed.

"I thought you said you were quitting," she said.

"I said I would quit when I turn thirty." He flicked his lighter and lit the smoke. "That's not for another eight months."

Babs watched him. He took a long drag, exhaled, flicked the ashes to the ground, and met her gaze.

"Better go get that pie," he said. "Tick tock, lady."

As if to prove his point, the town bell struck the half hour. Babs let out a heavy, dramatic sigh, then turned and headed into the diner. Finn stared at the brick on Max's side wall and felt like he was seventeen again, out sneaking a smoke on his break. Didn't help having Tessa's big, flowered Thing sitting there. It was like a damn time machine, and for a moment he even had an impulse to run inside, grab an apron, and start bussing tables.

Except he'd sworn after that last argument with Max that he'd die before setting foot back in that diner again, and he meant it.

He tossed the cigarette down on the ground and hopped off the trunk to smash it out with his boot. As he did, some movement toward the back of the lot caught his eye, and he glanced up to see Izzy skirting through the parking lot in the direction of her house, arms crossed over her stomach, head down. It wasn't until she'd passed him that he saw the soot on the back of her white coat.

"Just what the doctor ordered," he muttered as he walked after Izzy. "A healthy dose of distraction."

Chapter Eleven

Izzy scrubbed at her hands in the kitchen sink, creating a mound of soap bubbles that came halfway up her arms, but still, there was soot under her fingernails.

"Crappity crap crap shit," she muttered.

"Well, hello, sailor."

Izzy's body jolted backward as she let out a violent scream. Suds hit the wall of the kitchen. She finally gained her balance, leaned back against the counter and turned to see Finn smiling at her.

"Holy cats," she said, putting her hand over her chest.

"Now, that's better." He picked up the Mickey Mouse snow globe on the kitchen table and gave it a shake. "You have to watch your language. People will think you have no fucking class."

"What are you doing here?" she said. "Don't you knock?"

"I did. You must not have heard me."

Izzy took a deep breath. "Oh."

"Actually, that's a lie. I didn't knock. But imagine if I

had. I would have missed the whole Macbeth act. Couple of witches and a cauldron, you could take that on the road."

Izzy stared at him. He gestured toward her with the snow globe. "Someday, you're gonna get that joke, and man, are you gonna laugh."

Izzy snatched a towel off the oven handle and dried her hands. "I get it. *Out, damned spot.* It's not funny."

"Oh, it so totally is," Finn said, mocking teen-speak in a way that somehow wasn't as annoying as when Tessa did it. He set the globe back on the table and eyed Izzy for a moment. "So, I thought you were smart."

"I am," Izzy said.

"Really?" he said. His face went dark. "Because I don't think smart girls break into crime scenes thinking they're gonna catch something the cops didn't."

Izzy's eyes widened and a chill went through her. She swallowed. "How . . . how did you . . . ?"

"Just this morning you told me about Vickie and your mom. Doesn't take a detective to see you covered in soot and put two and two together. Just takes not being brain-dead." He gave her a confident smile and crossed his arms over his chest. "And for that, would you believe I just squeak past the qualification round?"

Izzy sighed. "Well, I had to do something. You weren't going to help me."

"Don't make this my fault, kid. You crossed the border into Delinquentville all on your own. Besides, I never said I wouldn't help you."

"You said to put the money back in my piggy bank," she said. "Which, by the way, I don't have."

It was a Hello Kitty bank. Which was way, way cooler. Finn pulled out a chair at the table and nodded toward it.

"I think we need to chat," he said.

Izzy slumped, resisting the impulse to give the floor a petulant kick.

"Fine," she said in resignation, dramatically turning toward the refrigerator. "Want something to drink?"

"A shot of your finest single malt."

Izzy shot a look over her shoulder at him. She wasn't sure what a single malt was, but it sounded gross. He smiled at her, and she got a little tingle, a glimpse of what it was about this guy that got her sister all in a twist. She pulled two Diet Cokes out of the fridge and walked over, handing him one. Finn inspected it, one eyebrow raised.

"You girls and your damn diets," he said.

Izzy popped the top on her soda. "It's how we stay beautiful for you men."

"Oh, please," Finn said, flipping the chair opposite Izzy and straddling it. "First of all, guys like curves, and anyone who tells you different is trying to sell you something. Second, it would take a thousand whacks with the ugly stick for you girls to lose your looks, and even then . . ."

He stopped, stared down at the Diet Coke can in his hand, and shook his head. Izzy knew he was thinking of her sister—everyone was always thinking of Tessa—but she blushed all the same.

"Anyway." He set the can down on the table and leaned his arms against the back of the chair. "What'd you find?"

"Find?" Izzy let out a frustrated sigh. "Nothing."

"Okay. We'll assume for the sake of argument that I'm buying that crock of crap. What were you looking for?"

Izzy shrugged. "I don't know."

"Sure you do," he said, his expression flat. "Think about it. Why would a nice girl like yourself violate a crime scene? Certainly not looking for the latest issue of *Teen Beat*."

Izzy gave him a black look.

Finn grinned at her. "*Seventeen*?"

"Quit making fun of me."

His face went serious. "An empty gasoline can and a pack of matches with the bad guy's name and phone number scribbled inside?"

Izzy sat up straighter. "No." *Kinda*. "But it doesn't matter, because I didn't find anything. It was a total waste of time."

"I'm sure your warden will agree," Finn said, popping his soda open.

Izzy felt a chill go down her spine. "What?"

"Oh, yeah, baby. You're big-time now. You just violated a potential crime scene, and based on those dirty little mitts of yours, you probably left a mother lode of prints for anyone who's interested to find." He took a sip of his soda, grimaced, and checked out the ingredients list on the side of the can. "Hey, turpentine has no calories. Who knew?"

"But . . . they already did all that stuff yesterday," Izzy said, her heart starting to pump madly. "They wouldn't go back . . . would they?"

Finn shrugged. "Maybe. Maybe not. But I think you should brush up on your prison break movies just in case. I hear *Stalag 17* really defines the genre."

"Oh." Izzy swallowed against the panic forming in her gut. "Oh. Man. Oh, God. Tessa's gonna kill me."

"Deader'n a doornail."

Izzy figured she must have looked as panicked as she felt, because Finn's face softened, and he leaned forward.

"Hey. Don't worry about it, okay?"

"How can I not worry? If I get caught—"

"It's not *if* you get caught, babe," he said. Izzy couldn't help but warm to the term of endearment. "It's *when*. Even in a town like this, there are people and technology that can track you. If you're gonna be breaking into places, you have to be smart about it."

Izzy leaned back, tried to look casual. "Yeah. Like how?"

"Nice try." He watched her for a moment, and when he spoke again, his face was serious. "Do you want to be put back in foster care?"

"No." Izzy felt her chin start to tremble at the thought. *Don't cry don't cry don't cry.* She'd already cried in front of him once today. Finn would think she was a total baby if she did it again, and she was *not* a baby.

"Really? Because you're acting like a kid who wants to be taken away from her sister."

"No!" Izzy took a deep breath, clenched her jaw, stared at her hands. The tears backed off. "I know I should leave it alone. I know I shouldn't be doing these things, but . . ."

She swallowed hard and met Finn's eye.

"Someone out there killed my mother," she said. *Don't cry don't cry don't cry.* "How can I just ignore that?"

"By pretending it's not there. If not for your sake, then for Tessa's. She's given up everything for you. What do you think losing you is going to do to her? I'll tell you. It'd kill her."

Izzy rolled her eyes, slumped in her chair, and grumbled, "Big difference."

Finn's eyes narrowed at Izzy, and for a moment she thought he was gonna yell at her. Instead, his voice was still and quiet. "What's that supposed to mean?"

Izzy focused on her fingernails as she tapped them on her Diet Coke.

"It's just, she never laughs. She never cries. I remember when I was a kid, she used to draw and paint a lot, enjoy life. Now she just gets angry and tries to be perfect." She finally met Finn's eyes. "Do you know she never even cried over Mom? She never talks about it. She never talks about you, or what happened with that. It's weird. She needs to get her own life instead of trying to live mine all the time."

Finn raised his eyes, and she could tell she'd pissed him off. The guilt started to seep in. Izzy gnawed on the inside of her cheek and blinked hard.

"Sorry," she muttered.

"You should be. You have no idea what Tessa's gone through for you." He stopped talking, and Izzy thought she saw something flash over his face, but it was gone before she could tell what it was. He sighed, then gave one brief nod. "All right. Go break out that piggy bank, kid. You just hired yourself a private detective."

Izzy sat where she was, frozen, not believing what she was hearing.

"Really?"

"Don't start jumping up and down yet. I've got one condition: When Tessa comes home tonight, you tell her everything you told me. Start to finish. No secrets. I'll work for you, but I'm not gonna lie to your sister. Understood?"

Izzy swiped at the moisture in her eyes. "Okay. Okay. Will you . . . can you stay here until she gets here? I don't know if I can face the firing squad alone."

Finn smiled, and her heart melted. He was supercute, with that spiky red hair and the blue eyes and being all grown-up and everything. She sighed before she realized she was doing it.

"Go get that money, honey," Finn said. "I don't work for free."

Izzy nodded, pushed herself up from the kitchen table, and headed up to her room. Once there, she closed the door gently behind her and reached into her front pocket. Slowly, she pulled out the item she'd found in Vickie's mailbox.

It was a plain white envelope, now smudged from Izzy's handling. She reached inside, her fingers shaking a bit as she did. The first thing she pulled out was a piece of notepaper with three words written in all caps.

LEAVE IT ALONE.

Izzy fished out the last item, a gold heart locket with a broken clasp, as though it had been torn off the wearer. She fingered the heart, but couldn't open it. She knew she should probably give it to Finn, but he'd open the locket and Izzy wasn't ready for that. Either it was her mother's locket, and everything was as awful as it seemed, or it wasn't, and she'd have to feel that loss all over again.

At any rate, either way, she knew she was right. There was nothing accidental about the fire at her mother's shop. Somehow, that knowledge wasn't as much of a comfort as she thought it would be.

•   •   •

Babs put another bite of the apple pie in her mouth. It was heavenly, just heavenly.

"Did Max make this pie?" she asked Tessa, who sat across from her sipping a cup of coffee on her break, staring out the window, no doubt looking for Finn.

Poor girl. She had it bad. Worse, she didn't appear to know it. Very sad.

"Hmmm?" Tessa said, then blinked. "Oh. No. Charlie at the bakery. It's really good, isn't it?"

"Heavenly," Babs said, and smiled.

"So," Tessa said, leaning forward and keeping her voice low, "what exactly do you and Finn do together? I mean, professionally?"

Babs smiled. "Why, we run an investigation agency in Las Vegas." Babs winked at Tessa, then glanced around. There were only two other customers there, and they were involved in a discussion on the other side of the diner. It was probably okay to take pity on the poor girl. Babs leaned forward, also speaking in low tones.

"We do charity work," she said.

Tessa's eyebrows knit together. "Finn? Does charity work?"

"Hard to believe, isn't it?" Babs laughed. "Well, he could hardly spend the rest of his life being a bird thief, could he? Can you imagine?"

"He was a bird thief?" Tessa's face registered dark surprise, and Babs wondered briefly if she was telling too much, then shooed the feeling away. Tessa would learn about Finn eventually, anyway.

"Yes," Babs said. "He was a bird thief. A damn fine

one, too. That's how we met, actually. He was breaking into my penthouse to steal my bird."

Tessa looked confused. "You hired him to work for you after he broke into your house?"

"Well, yes, but not until after he'd saved my daughter's life."

Tessa's eyes widened. "He . . . what?"

Babs sighed. Time to stop dancing and get to the heart of things.

"He's a good man, Finn. It's a shame he doesn't know it, but what are you gonna do, right? But the truth is, I'd trust him with my life and every belonging I have." She took another bite of her pie. "This pie really is delicious. My compliments to Charlie."

Tessa leaned forward a bit more. "So . . . I don't understand. What exactly is it that you two do?"

Babs smiled. If she had a nickel for every time she had to explain this . . .

"It's all a little complicated. I'm a widow, which is boring beyond the telling of it. There are only so many benefit luncheons one can organize before one wants to stick one's head in one's oven. So, I started doing favors for various people in my circle, who tend to be the eccentric wealthy, and in turn they donate large sums to the charities of my choice. When the favor requires any skills I don't possess or breaking any laws I don't wish to break, I call Finn in, give him a cut, and he helps me."

Tessa sat back. "So, he . . . breaks the law? For charity?"

Babs reached over and patted Tessa's hand. "Oh, it's not as bad as it sounds. For instance, one girlfriend of mine received a truly hideous diamond brooch from her husband for Christmas. Oh, it was awful. All shaped like . . . I don't even know what. Looked like a small intestine. Anyway, she asked us to break in and steal it, make it look like a burglary, so she wouldn't have to wear it when he took her to the opera. That sort of thing."

Tessa blinked. "Oh."

"Yes, it sounds odd, doesn't it? But it's what we do, and it really can be a lot of fun. And it's all for the greater good, you know. Have you ever heard of St. Jude's?"

"The children's hospital?"

"Yes. Last year, Finn was responsible for over half a million dollars in donations to St. Jude's."

A small smile spread over Tessa's face. "Really?"

"Yes." Babs grinned. "Really."

Tessa went quiet, and Babs didn't have to ask to know what the girl was thinking. It was clear on her face. She was proud of Finn. As well she should be; Babs meant it when she said Finn was a good man. Under all his smart talk and bluster was a genuine goodness, whether he cared to accept it or not. And Babs could tell that Tessa knew it, too. That smile wasn't just pride; it also held a hint of vindication. And, if Babs wasn't mistaken, which she rarely was about these things, there was a dose of genuine affection in the mix as well.

Babs thought for a moment about how she could get Tessa and Finn back together. The two of them obviously weren't going to get the job done on their own, what with Finn all racked with stupid guilt and Tessa . . .

Hmm. She didn't know what Tessa's problem was, but she made a mental wager with herself that she'd be able to uncover it in a few days' time. If there was one area in which she was eminently skilled, it was getting to the heart of things.

"So, tell me, Tessa," she began, but then her cell phone rang.

"Pardon me," she said, fumbling around in her bag. "I know it's supposed to be rude to talk on the phone in a restaurant, but honestly, what's the difference between talking to your companion and chatting on the . . . Hello?"

"Is Tessa there?"

Finn. Of course. Babs swore the boy would never learn proper phone etiquette. "Yes. And hello to you, too. How are you?"

"Tell her she needs to come home. Now."

Babs put her fingers over the mouthpiece. "It's Finn. He says come home, now."

Tessa's eyes widened. "What? Why? Is it Izzy? Is she okay?"

Babs removed her fingers from the phone. "What? Why? Is it Izzy? Is she okay?"

"She's fine."

"She's fine?" Babs smiled at Tessa. "Now that wasn't nice. You scared poor Tessa half to death. She's got her hand on her chest and she looks like death." She nudged her untouched water glass to Tessa. "Drink some water, dear."

Finn huffed on the other end of the line. "Just tell her she needs to get here as soon as possible."

Click. No good-bye. Honestly. For such a funny, smart, and handsome young man, he really was beyond hope sometimes. Babs tucked the phone back into her bag.

"He needs you at your house."

Tessa finished a gulp of water and put the glass down. "What's he doing at my house?"

Babs shrugged. "Either causing some measure of trouble or stopping it, I imagine. It's usually one or the other."

Tessa ran her fingers through her hair. "Oh, crap." She looked at her watch. "Dinner starts in an hour. I can't just leave Max to handle it by himself."

Babs stood up. "Well, then you won't. Point me to a uniform and an apron, and I'll take your shift."

Tessa blinked. "You don't work here."

"I do now," Babs said, excited at the prospect of an evening spent taking orders at a greasy spoon. "Do you know I've never worked in a diner before?" She took Tessa's arm and pulled her up. "We'll just go speak briefly with Max and I'm sure it'll all be just fine."

A man raised one finger at them as they passed. Babs smiled at him.

"Just one minute, dear," Babs said. "We've got a minor personal crisis at the moment, but I will be with you in just a moment, and when I get back, that coffee's gonna be free."

She winked at him. He smiled and nodded. "You bet. Thanks."

"See, I'm a natural already," Babs said, her chest swelling with excitement at the opportunity to try something new.

"Babs, there's no way Max is going to let you—"

They pushed through the kitchen door. Max stood at the range, spatula in his hand. He turned and Babs could see a flash of recognition and slight interest in his eyes when he saw her. She'd been around the block too many times to pretend she didn't know interest when she saw it. She smiled.

"Hello, Max. I'm Babs. We met briefly earlier today."

Max nodded, looked to Tessa, then back to Babs. "Yes. How are you?"

Now, see, *there* was a man with manners.

"Just beyond lovely. And yourself?"

Max again looked to Tessa. Tessa sighed.

"Look, Max, something's come up with Izzy and—"

"Get out of here," Max said.

"Pammy can't cover, but maybe you could call Joe—"

"I'll be fine. Go on, get out."

Babs smiled at the way Max put Tessa and Izzy ahead of his own needs. It was an intriguing side of the man to see, considering that everything she'd heard from Finn had been less than flattering.

This was going to be an interesting job indeed.

Tessa pulled at her apron strings and crossed the room to the coatrack. "Babs, you can come with me."

Babs waved her hand at Tessa. "Thank you so much for the invitation. I'll be there the moment my shift ends." She grinned at Max, who stared at her blankly. "I'll require a uniform. Do you have a size eight?"

"You ever worked in a diner before?" Max asked. His face was unsmiling, but his eyes . . . now that was a different story.

"No, but I used to run a winery."

"'Used to run a winery' is not a résumé," Max said.

He was gruff. Babs smiled. She liked gruff men. They were honest, and honesty was a virtue she could get behind.

"There's much more on my résumé than that, you can be sure."

He smiled. It was a small smile, but it was there. A few days, the man would be putty in her hands.

Well, here's hoping, anyway.

"Babs—," Tessa said, shrugging into her coat.

Babs went to full wattage on her smile, looking at Max as she spoke to Tessa.

"Nonsense, child. Run along. We'll take it from here."

Chapter Twelve

Tessa blew through the front door, coming to a skidding halt in her living room to find her sister and Finn sitting on the sofa, chatting and laughing. They both quieted and looked up at her, as though she was the one who was crazy.

"What . . . what . . . what?" she said, unable to form a full sentence. She took a deep breath and looked at Izzy. "You're okay? No bleeding. Not on fire. So, what the hell, Iz?"

Izzy had on her guilty face. Tessa knew it well, and it never meant good news. Tessa put her hand to her forehead. She needed a drink. She needed a drink bad.

"What did you do?" she asked, not really wanting to know. She pulled her hand down and looked at her sister. "And what is Finn doing here?"

Izzy and Finn exchanged glances, and Finn motioned for her to take the question. Izzy straightened up and put on a nice front of confidence.

"He works for me."

Tessa laughed. She couldn't help it. "What?"

Finn stood up, walked over to her, and held out his hand. "Hello, Miss Scuderi. I'm Dermot Finnegan. I'm your sister's private detective." He grinned. "You can call me Finn."

Tessa stared at him blankly. This couldn't be happening. First, Finn wasn't a private detective. She didn't know exactly what he was, but he wasn't a private detective. Second . . .

"What the hell do you need a private detective for?"

Finn curled his fingers in, dropped his hand, and he and Izzy exchanged a different, more serious look.

"Oh, man. Izzy, what did you do? You were supposed to stay in the house and feign gastrointestinal distress. How hard is that?"

Finn touched her arm. "Sit down, Tessa."

Tessa wrenched her arm away. "Don't tell me what to do." She looked at Izzy. "How bad is it? What did you do? Why do you need a private detective?"

Izzy dropped her eyes. Oh, God. Whatever it was, it was bad. Tessa could feel it. She walked over and sat down next to Izzy.

"You need to tell me what's going on."

Izzy looked at Finn. Finn nodded. Izzy focused back on Tessa.

"It's about Mom."

Tessa took a deep breath. "Mom? What . . . ?"

Izzy began her story, starting with the night their mother died, moving into Joe's suspicions, then with the worry boxes, then with the snooping around Vickie's and Margie's. By the time she got to the part where she'd trespassed on the site of a potential arson, Tessa felt the numbness descending over her. She knew she'd process it all later; right now she just had to take it in and let it sit.

"So . . . ," Izzy finished up, "that's why I was at Finn's this morning. And that's why he's here now. I can't do anything else with this." Izzy rolled her eyes, shamed. "Obviously. But he's a professional. He knows what he's doing."

Tessa chuckled, ran her fingers over her eyes. *Dr. Frankenstein, meet your monster.*

"Tessa?" Izzy said nervously. "Tessa? Say something. You're scaring me. You can yell, that's fine, but you're really scary when you're quiet."

Tessa put her hands on her knees and pushed up from the sofa, looking at Finn.

"Can I talk to you privately for a moment, please?"

Izzy stood up. "Don't be mad at him, it's not his—"

She shot her evil eye at Izzy. Izzy shut up.

"Iz," Finn said, "why don't you go upstairs, take a shower, get the soot out of your hair?"

Izzy ran her hand over her hair and made a face. "I have soot? In my hair?"

Tessa gave her a look. A moment later Izzy was upstairs. Tessa remained quiet until she heard the shower running, then looked at Finn.

"You know you can't take this case," she said.

Finn crossed his arms over his chest and shrugged. "Your sister has eighty-nine dollars and seventy-three cents that says I can."

He smiled at her with that infuriating twinkle in his eyes, the one he got whenever he wasn't taking things seriously, which was most of the time. Tessa took a few steps closer and lowered her voice.

"You are not a private detective," she spat in a harsh whisper.

"Yeah, but I'm damned good-looking." He grinned. "That's gotta count for something."

"It doesn't," she said.

"Ah, but you do admit that I'm damned good-looking. And people say you're not observant."

"Stop it," she said. "This is serious. My little sister just told me she thinks our mother might have essentially been murdered. This is not a joke."

His smile faded, and he gave her a small nod. "You're right. It's not." He paused, looking at her for a moment, then put his hand on her arm. "You okay?"

She let out a breath, scuffed her toe on the wood floor. She wasn't exactly okay, but she was numb enough at the moment that she could fake it pretty well.

"I'm fine."

"No," he said, leaning his face into her field of vision until she allowed her eyes to meet his. "Are you okay?"

"Yeah," she said, tamping the sadness down as it welled in her chest. "Thanks."

He lowered his hand, and his expression went all business. "Good. Then understand something. My condition for taking this case was that Izzy tell you, not that she get your permission. This is between me and her."

Tessa stared at him, her anger rising. "Wait a minute, you can't just blow into my house and tell me how it's gonna be."

"Tessa, if I don't start looking into this, Izzy won't stop, and if there's something bad to find, I'd rather it be me than her that finds it. Wouldn't you?"

"There's nothing bad to find," Tessa said. "It's just her

imagination in hyperdrive. She's sixteen. She's incapable of being rational about this." The words sounded good as they came out. If only they weren't followed by a niggling bit of doubt . . .

Finn eyed her for a minute, his expression serious. "You don't think there's a connection between all these fires?"

"Over the course of some seventeen years?" Tessa felt a tug in her chest, but ignored it. "No."

"Well, Izzy does," Finn said. "And I don't think she's gonna stop poking around just because you said so."

"And I don't think it's your problem. She's my sister."

"She's my client."

Tessa threw her hands up in the air. "I don't know why I bother talking to you."

"Because you need to talk to me," Finn said. "Because I'm the only person in your life who knows how full of crap you are."

Tessa narrowed her eyes at Finn and dug her nails into the palm of her hand. "Excuse me?"

Finn sighed. "Tessa. This isn't you. You're not the kind of girl who does this. Ignores reality, cowers in corners afraid of social workers—"

"Excuse me? Protecting my sister is cowering now?"

"You're letting this social worker completely bully you until there's no you left, and you're burying your head in the sand over this fire thing, which I personally think might just hold some water. This isn't like you."

Tessa felt the rage swell up and over her. *How dare he?*

"Yeah, well, people change when they lose everything that means anything to them in a single night." Her voice cracked and she took a deep breath, blinking wildly against the tears threatening to come. She was not going to break.

Not now. Not now.

Finn's face was tight, his eyes hard and unreadable. They stared at each other for a moment, neither one of them backing down. Finally, Finn spoke.

"Get over it."

Tessa blinked, surprised at the verbal slap. "What?"

"I said get over it." He shook his head, looked at her, his eyes suddenly plaintive. "You were dealt a shit hand, sweetheart. No one's gonna argue that. I'm not gonna tell you what I did wasn't total bullshit because it was. I'd give my right arm to take it back, but I can't. And nothing is going to bring back your mom, or give you back those years without Izzy. But shutting down inside because of all that . . ." He released a deep breath. "Baby, you lose. Everyone loses when you're not here."

"I'm here," she said tightly. "I've been here. I'm not the one who ran off."

"Oh, yeah, you did," he said. "Maybe not in the same way, but you did."

"Oh, so because you managed to talk me out of my underwear in the back of a Volkswagen, you think you have some kind of insight into my soul, is that it?"

"No," he said, not flinching, not looking away. "That's not why."

Tessa rubbed her hand over her face. She didn't want to go there. Not with Finn. Not with anyone. "Get out of my house."

Finn went quiet, stared out the window for a minute, then turned his eyes back on her. "I'm going, but I'll be coming back. Izzy's my client, and I'm going to figure this out for her."

"Yeah, best of luck with that, Magnum," Tessa bit out.

He took a step closer, gesturing angrily up the stairs. "You keep pushing her, babe, she's gonna push back. She's a kid. You wanna live in a glass box, that's your choice, but she is gonna shatter everything all around you if you don't start listening to her."

Tessa folded her arms over her chest, embracing the numbness that was finally washing over her. "I thought you said you were leaving."

Finn shook his head and let out a mirthless chuckle. "Good to see some things don't change. You're still stubborn as hell."

"Let me get the door for you." She turned and headed to the front door, pulled it open, and stepped back. Finn walked over and stopped in front of her.

"First, I need you to do something for me."

Tessa felt her mouth drop open. "What, are you kidding me?"

"No," he said. "I think Babs and Wallace should stay here with you guys."

Tessa blinked. *Hello, left field.* "What?"

"If, on the off chance that there's a bad guy out there setting people on fire, I'd rather there were more eyes here keeping an eye out."

Tessa opened her mouth to tell him to get out, but paused. She didn't know what she thought about Izzy's theories. But she knew she liked Babs, a lot, and the idea of having her there was oddly comforting. And if Izzy was right . . . well, it wouldn't hurt to have someone else around.

"Okay," she said. "Um, Babs can stay in Mom's room, I guess."

Finn's face softened. "Thank you. What about Wallace?"

"Who's Wallace?"

Finn put two fingers in his mouth and whistled. Tessa jumped back. A sound of scurrying came through the bushes at the front of the property, and the little mutt from the shack shot up the steps, past her, and into the house. She looked up at Finn.

"Still not my dog," Finn said, a smirk curling up on the edge of his mouth. Tessa fought an urge to smile, knowing that if she did, he'd win. Instead, she leaned back against the doorway for support.

"Where are you going?" she asked.

"Has Izzy ever had her fingerprints taken?"

Tessa felt a stab of alarm. "What? Why?"

Finn shrugged. "Just making small talk."

"No. Not that I know of. Why?"

"Like I said. Small talk." He put his hands in his pockets and glanced out at the street. "I should get moving, though. Is Babs still at the diner?"

Tessa tried to shrug the uneasiness out of her shoulders. It didn't work. "Um, I guess so. She, uh, insisted on taking my shift."

"Sounds about right," he said, smiling. "Something else. In about fifteen minutes, I need you to call Joe and tell him that I was asking questions about the pet shop, and now you can't find me. Try to sound a little concerned, but not too much."

Tessa gave him a sharp look. "Why?"

Finn shrugged, started toward the steps. "Been a while

since he's jumped to any conclusions. Man's gonna need a fix."

Tessa watched as Finn jaunted down the steps. What had just happened? She remembered ordering him out of her house. Things had seemed about right at that point. Now she was putting up his business partner and his dog and doing him favors. Why?

What is it about you? she heard him saying, an echo in her memory.

She had to wonder.

He was almost to the street when she called his name. He stopped and looked at her, waiting for her to speak. She didn't say anything. She wasn't sure what she wanted to say, if she wanted anything other than just to look into his eyes for another moment. For some reason, there was comfort there, and she was running low on comfort at the moment.

After a while, he smiled, touched his fingers to his lips, and tossed her a kiss, then turned and headed down the street.

Tessa watched until he was out of sight, then went inside to have a drink and call Joe.

Chapter Thirteen

Finn ducked under the tape at Vickie's and gave his eyes a moment to adjust to the darkness. He'd already wiped the railing, the doorknob, and one of the outer windows where he'd seen some smudges that may or may not have been Izzy's work. He figured the chances were slim that Izzy'd ever had her fingerprints taken. It was a small town; Tessa would have known about it. But still, when it came to the Scuderi girls, Finn knew he was better safe than sorry.

Which was why he needed Joe.

After a moment, the room started to come together. The office door, charred within an inch of its life. Empty cages lining the south wall. All manner of pet food lining the north. Cash register. Counter. There wasn't a whole lot of soot in the store itself, definitely not enough to get Izzy's hands so dirty. Finn made a beeline for the office.

"Ten years," he muttered. "Ten years breaking and entering all over New York City, and I'm gonna get caught in a pet store in Lucy's Lake, Vermont." He knew that investigation teams very rarely returned to a scene once they'd processed it, but sometimes they did. He wasn't in the mood to roll the dice on their finding any evidence of Izzy if this was going to be one of those times.

He clumsily handled the doorknob and pushed into the office. Thanks to the full moon and windows that had apparently exploded outward in response to the heat, there was enough light for him to see the basics of the office. The blackest area was the corner, and a little investigating showed a series of three-way extension cords melted and mangled into a jumble of electrical cords leading to the coffeemaker, the computer, the small microwave, the printer, etc.

Well. Nothing suspicious about that, except that it pointed to an absurd level of stupidity on Vickie's part. In the day of power surge strips, there was no excuse for that kind of electrical setup, but it certainly wasn't rare by any standard. People did it all the time, took their chances. It certainly looked like an accidental fire so far.

His eyes adjusting more to the limited light, he started looking for places where the soot had been disturbed by Izzy's snooping fingers. Vickie's desk drawer. The filing cabinet in the corner. The knob on the back door. Finn went around touching every place where Izzy might have been, then went through the back door and up the outside steps to Vickie's front door, where he found sooty prints on Vickie's mailbox, but not on the doorknob.

Interesting.

Finn carefully wiped the mailbox, then checked out the door lock so he'd know what tools to bring when he returned to pick it.

The store's front door opened. Showtime. Finn headed down the steps and back into Vickie's office just in time for Joe to open the door, his hand carefully swaddled in a handkerchief, then scope the place with a flashlight until it landed on something interesting: Finn. On cue, Finn opened the drawer to Vickie's desk.

"Hey, good thinking. Can you point that thing over here?" Finn said, shutting the drawer and ducking his head under the desk.

"What the hell are you doing here?" Joe said. "This is still an active investigation."

"Really?" Finn popped back up from under the desk. "So you think it was arson, then?"

Finn couldn't see Joe's expression, but suspected it was dead serious. "Why don't you tell me?"

Finn shrugged. "Beats the hell out of me. I'm just a guy looking for his keys."

He moved past Joe out into the store. Joe, of course, followed.

"Do you know if anyone found a set of keys during the investigation?" Finn asked. "One deadbolt key, one outer door key, one mail key? All on a Marvin the Martian key ring?"

"You'd have to call the county and ask them."

Finn turned to face his brother. "You work for the fire department, right?"

"I volunteer."

"Think you could get me access to the files?"

Joe eyed Finn suspiciously. "Once they're done with the investigation, it's possible I could go through channels—"

"Oh, Jesus," Finn said. "I'm not talking about channels. I mean, can you get me access to anything? Pictures, information, anything?"

Joe crossed his arms over his chest. "Why do you want access?"

"You obviously have no idea how hard it is to find a Marvin the Martian key chain."

"What are you up to, Finn?"

"Me? Nothing. So you really haven't looked?"

"For your keys? No."

"Not for my keys. How would you know my keys went missing as I was heroically rescuing itty-bitty furry things? No, I mean, you haven't tried to get access to the investigation? Not even one little peek? You're not curious about it at all?"

"My curiosity isn't the issue," Joe said. Amazing he didn't choke on all that sanctimony. "It's classified information. Investigative team only."

Finn took a moment to absorb this, then huffed out a laugh.

"You're kidding."

"No."

Finn paused. "You're *kidding*."

Joe didn't respond.

"Are you for real? Here you have a possible sister crime to the one that may have caused Karen Scuderi's death, both of which you suspect your brother of committing, and you haven't even taken a peek at the files?"

"I'm not on the investigative team."

"So . . . what? You're saying the only reason you haven't taken a look is because you're not *allowed*?"

Joe said nothing. Finn let out a little whistle.

"Wow. You are amazing. If you have that kind of self-control in bed, you're gonna make some nice librarian very happy someday."

"What are you doing here, Finn?"

Finn took another look around the store, let out a sigh of disappointment. "Not finding my keys, looks like." He looked up at Joe and grinned. "Well, see ya, bro. It was great having this little chat."

"I never said I suspected you," Joe said.

Finn let his grin fade. "Never said you didn't."

They stared each other down for a moment, and Finn felt the anger rise. Despite his better judgment, he gave in to it. "So, just out of curiosity, why do you think I would burn down Karen Scuderi's place?"

Joe sighed. "I don't think you meant to hurt Karen."

Finn had to laugh at that. "Of course not. What's the harm in burning down a woman's livelihood? Still, I can't come up with a motive for myself. Can you?"

Joe shrugged. "She didn't like you dating Tessa. She attacked you with a two-by-four."

"Oh, hell, Joe. If being chased with a two-by-four by a woman who wanted to put some distance between me and her daughter motivated me to burn places down, then 1860s Atlanta would have nothing on this place."

Joe didn't so much as crack a smile. "You used to mess around with explosives. You've got experience with flammable materials."

"What, you're talking about the nativity scene? I was sixteen and that was a prank. A prank is not murder."

"I never said murder," Joe said.

"Just arson with a side of manslaughter, then?"

This was followed by a long silence. Joe, carefully choosing his words. Which meant that Finn had pretty much hit the nail on the head.

"You were a kid. Maybe you didn't know Karen was in

there." Joe took a step forward. "I can't help you if you don't tell me what happened."

"You really are a piece of work, you know that?" Finn said. "You're just determined to believe that I'm no good."

"About as determined as you are to prove me right."

Finn let out a sharp breath. "Well, hey. I may be a murderous good-for-nothing, but I do have a knack for knowing when a conversation is over."

He turned and started toward the door.

"If they need to come back here for anything," Joe called after him, "I'm going to have to report that I saw you here."

Finn didn't stop moving.

"I'm counting on it, bro."

Tessa scrubbed the last plate with yellow rubber hands and looked up at the clock. Nineteen minutes to ten. The living room was clean. Bills all ready to go in the mail tomorrow. The only thing she hadn't done was wash the windows, but she wasn't about to do that. She was desperate to distract herself, but not that desperate.

Everybody loses when you're not here. She'd heard his voice in her head all night, and it was really pissing her off. Where did he get off judging her? She'd done what she needed to do. She hadn't shut down. She'd moved forward. It was what her mother would have wanted her to do, and she did it, damnit.

The *click-clack* of dog nails sounded softly on the linoleum behind her. She smiled, turned, and looked down at Wallace as she pulled the rubber gloves off her hands.

"There's nothing wrong with me, right, Wallace?" She

dropped the gloves on the counter, then crouched down to his level. "I'm cute. I'm a good dancer. I know how to have fun. Right?"

Wallace wagged his tail and wedged himself between her legs, resting his snout on her left knee. She scratched him behind the ears, then snuggled her face next to his.

"Wanna go to Vegas and get married, Wallace?" She pulled her face up and scratched under his chin. "I could use a guy like you in my life. Silent and loyal."

Wallace raised his head and lapped at her face. Tessa laughed lightly, pushed herself up, and wandered into the living room, where she stopped and stared out the window. Wallace followed her and sat at her feet. She looked down at him and smiled.

"You gonna be my protector, big guy?"

There was a knock at the front door and Wallace turned around three times and thunked himself down on the rug.

"Guess that answers that question," Tessa said as she pulled the door open to see Babs, cashmere coat draped casually over a waitress uniform. She had a suitcase tucked under one arm and a plastic bag holding the clothes she was wearing earlier in the other hand.

"Good evening!" Babs's face broke out in a wide grin as she stepped inside and set her suitcase down in the foyer. "Finn tells me we're to be roommates. I'm so thrilled to be staying in this lovely town for a while longer. Thank you."

"No problem," Tessa said. She shut the door behind Babs and wrapped her arms around her stomach. "So, when did you see Finn?"

"I didn't," Babs said. "He called while I was working. Told me to tell Izzy he'd check in with her later." Babs smiled, glanced around at the foyer and the living room, then patted Tessa's arm warmly. "Your home is lovely, just lovely."

"Thank you," Tessa said. "And thanks for taking the shift with Max. How was it?"

Babs giggled. "It was wonderful! Do you know how long it's been since I've actually worked for a wage? I'd forgotten how much fun it could be. And tips! I have never been on the receiving end of tips before, and I have to say, I quite like it."

Tessa laughed. "Yeah, it's not bad." Tessa glanced up the steps. Although Izzy had claimed exhaustion and gone to bed an hour ago, Tessa knew it was better to assume eavesdropping. "So, did Finn tell you everything that's going on here?"

Babs nodded. "Yes. And don't you worry about a thing. We'll keep your girl safe and out of trouble. I may not look like it, but I'm quite used to dangerous situations. Remind me to tell you about the time I got kidnapped at gunpoint." Babs sighed and glanced up the stairs. "But not right now. It's been a very long day, and if I don't lie down soon I'm pretty sure I'll fall over. Where will I be sleeping?"

Tessa took Babs's suitcase and led her up the stairs to her mother's room. It had been empty for years. Neither Tessa nor Izzy ever wanted to move into the big room, but when Tessa had made up the bed earlier, it was comforting to think of Babs sleeping there, although she wasn't sure exactly why.

"The bathroom is right through that door," Tessa said as she set Babs's suitcase on the bed, "but be sure to lock the hall door when you're in there. Izzy tends to just bust in in the mornings."

Babs nodded, sat on the bed, and patted the spot next to her.

"Come sit, dear," she said. "I'd like to talk to you for a moment."

Tessa moved over and sat next to Babs, who took Tessa's hand in both of hers.

"I know that I seem a little silly," Babs said. "I don't tend to take things too seriously because there are plenty of people out there taking things far too seriously, and someone needs to balance that scale."

Tessa gave a small laugh. Babs smiled warmly at her.

"But if you ever need to talk, about anything at all, and you choose to talk to me, I would honor that. I would take that very seriously."

Tessa swallowed against the lump forming in her throat. It was the same thing that happened to her whenever Max expressed pseudo-parental concern for her, and it always shook her confidence in the fact that she was just fine despite having been orphaned at the age of eighteen. "Thank you, but I'm fine. Really."

Babs gave Tessa's hand a pat and released her. "Of course you are, dear. Me, on the other hand, if I don't visit the little girls' room immediately, your carpet might never forgive me."

Tessa stood up. "I'll let you get some rest. See you in the morning."

"Yes, you will," Babs said. She grabbed a travel toiletry bag and headed to the bathroom, turning back to face Tessa when she reached the door. "Just out of curiosity, dear, what's the name of this horrible social worker Finn was telling me about?"

Tessa blinked. "Mary Ellen Neeley. Why?"

Babs smiled. "I have a psychic friend in New York who does numerology readings. I just thought it would be interesting to see if we can't get some guidance on that situation. That's Neeley with an 'e'?"

Tessa laughed, feeling affection for this woman bloom in her chest. "Yep."

Babs nodded. "Very well, then. Good night."

Tessa gently let herself out of her mother's room, pulling the door behind her until it shut with a gentle click. From the bathroom, she heard Babs turn on the water, then start singing the theme to *Laverne and Shirley*. Tessa chuckled to herself and headed down the stairs to wait for Finn in the living room.

Finn pulled the rental to a stop in front of Tessa's and sat back in the driver's seat, staring up at the house. It was exactly the same as it had always been. Colonial style, blue paint, white trim. He'd been five when he'd first seen it, on a walk through the neighborhood with Uncle Max, not long after his mother had gotten sick and his parents had moved the family up from Boston. He remembered thinking how nice it looked compared to the apartment above Max's Diner where they were staying. It looked like a real home for a real family.

That was when Tessa had come running out of the house, buck-ass naked and wet, dark hair flailing wildly about her face as she evaded her mother. Foamy chunks of bubble bath fell from her body as she ran. Max helped Karen race after Tessa, but being a gentleman, he wouldn't actually touch her. Finally, Finn yelled, "I gots Tootsie Rolls!" from the sidewalk where he stood watching. Tessa froze in her spot, staring at him, transfixed. Finn remembered that moment so clearly, their eyes meeting and locking like that, as though they both knew it was an important moment.

Then Karen swooped Tessa up into a big, fluffy towel, yelled her thanks, and carried her daughter inside, breaking the moment. Max walked Finn back to the diner and gave him ice cream.

The next day, Finn stole a bag of Tootsie Rolls from the corner market and went to Tessa's house, where he found out she was four years old and that her favorite color was yellow. They'd been friends ever since.

And look how well that turned out.

He checked the rental's dashboard clock: 12:14. He'd been driving around Lucy's Lake for five hours. No wonder the tank was nearly empty. Of course, at least one of those hours had been spent parked at the lake, staring at the glossy surface of the ice, thinking about Izzy and Tessa. Joe and Max. The fire that led to Karen Scuderi's death and the possibly related fire at Vickie's that had sucked him back into everything he'd been avoiding for so long. All of it made him want to take that rental and run, just take off and never look back. He'd gotten as far as I-91 before turning around.

You're just like your father.

Max's voice echoed back to him from that night ten years ago, after Finn had gotten caught once again sneaking out after curfew.

You have the smarts, and you don't use them. That makes you stupider than anyone. You could be somebody, but all you do is screw around and make trouble. That makes you trouble. You think you're ever going to be good enough for her? You won't. You will drag her down with you until it kills her, or at least kills her spirit.

That makes you nothing.

Finn sighed and shook his head. He had two good reasons why he didn't like to sit and ruminate about the past: There was no point, and it made his ass twitch. He looked down at the bag of dog food on the passenger seat and debated for a moment, but in the end, he knew the dog was going to need to eat, and the last thing he wanted to do was lay one more responsibility on Tessa. He grabbed the bag from the passenger seat and got out of the car, feeling every heavy footstep as he made his way to the front door. He tried it gently.

It was locked. Which was good. There was very possibly someone in town with an itchy lighter finger and if the door had been unlocked, Finn would have been furious.

Now, locked out of Tessa's house and her life, all he felt was disappointment.

Get used to it, he thought. He laid the food next to the front door and took a step back. He was just about to leave when the foyer light flicked on and the front door unlatched and opened.

And there was Tessa. One eye was half-closed, and the left side of her hair had this strange gravity-defying thing going on.

"Hey," she said, rubbing one side of her face with the flat of her hand.

"Sorry," he said. "I didn't mean to wake you."

"I fell asleep on the sofa," she said, vaguely gesturing toward the living room.

"I see," he said, smiling. "I was just dropping off some food for Wallace."

"Okay." She squinted up at him. "Come on in."

"No," he said. "It's late. You go to sleep. Tell Izzy I'll be by in the morning."

"You don't have to go," she said. "Sofa's lumpy, but it beats the shack."

Finn watched her for a moment, and decided they were both too worn-out to argue.

"Okay," he said. "Thanks."

"You're welcome."

He picked up the dog food and headed in. Wallace raised his head from where he was lying by the door.

"He's a great watchdog," Finn said.

Wallace gave a little huff and rested his snout back on his forepaws.

"Hmmm. Very vicious." She glanced down at the bag. "Hey. Dog food."

Finn smiled. "Yeah."

"Good." She stretched out one arm, scratched her head with the other. "We're gonna need a collar and a leash and . . ." She blinked and looked at the bag of dog food. "Why is the bag covered in soot?"

Finn shrugged. "Afterthought."

"Oh." Tessa crossed her arms and stared at it for a minute. Finn watched her. Her shirt was crinkled and she had a little mascara burn under one eye, but damned if she wasn't more beautiful than she'd ever been.

You got it bad, man, the dog said.

"Shut up," Finn said.

"Huh?" Tessa snapped to attention from her trance.

"You should get to bed." Finn smiled down at her. "You're gonna need your rest."

"Yeah." She started toward the stairs, then turned, came back, and passed by him. He caught her by the arm.

"If memory serves, your room is upstairs."

"Yeah, but you need sheets and a pillow and a blanket. They're in the—"

"Linen closet by the laundry room," he said softly, taking her shoulders and turning her toward the stairs. "I can find it. Go to bed."

She twirled in his arms to face him.

"It'll just take me a minute," she said, then stopped and looked up at him. His hands rested on her shoulders, and he was too beat to fight the instinct to slide them down her arms, finally settling them on her hips. She moved closer, resting her cheek against his chest as his arms circled her waist.

"I don't want to fight with you," she said softly.

"Are we fighting?" He let his fingers brush against the small of her back. "Because if we are, we should do it more."

She smiled and closed her eyes. "I'm still mostly asleep. I'm just saying what's in my head. It doesn't necessarily make sense."

"Oh. Well. In that case, keep going."

She raised her head a bit and blinked sleepily at him.

"I missed you," she said.

He reached up and moved a lock of hair away from her forehead. A strange pressure clamped down on his chest, and all he could say was, "Yeah."

Slowly, she rested her head back on his chest. He felt her body relax, melting into his. He raised one hand and put it on the back of her head, gently trailing his fingers through her hair. It was impossibly soft. She inhaled deeply, and her arms slid down again, snaked around his waist, and she sighed. Finn rested his cheek on top of her head and was amazed at how something so simple could feel so good.

A moment later Tessa released him, stepping back with a lazy smile on her face.

"See?" she said. "I'm fun."

How was it legal for one person to be that beautiful?

"There's no one funner."

He felt like he could stand there and look into her eyes for the rest of his life.

"Damn straight."

One side of her mouth twitched up in a semismile, and it literally took his breath away. He didn't realize time was passing until she cocked her head to the side.

"You okay?"

No.

"Yeah." He smiled and touched her face, then leaned down and kissed her lightly on the forehead. "Time for bed, sweetheart."

She took a step back, then turned and headed up the stairs. He stood at the bottom of the steps and watched her go, wondering if she'd get the reference if he brought her a package of Tootsie Rolls in the morning. He immediately scrapped the idea on account of extreme sentimentality and overall lameness.

This isn't what you came here for, he told himself. *You're not doing her any favors with all this.*

Wallace raised his head and looked up at Finn. *You really are an idiot, you know that?*

Finn glanced down at the dog. "You got something to say?"

The dog quirked one eyebrow at Finn. *Seems to me I said it.*

Finn squatted and looked Wallace in the eye. Wallace stared back, licked his chops quickly, thumped his tail twice against the floor in anticipation of nothing in particular. Just like a normal dog.

"So, you think you're the big dog, with all the talking?" Finn said.

I'm about average size, Wallace said. *But you know what they say—it's not the size of the ship, it's the motion in the—*

"Oh, for Christ's sake," Finn interrupted. The dog said nothing. Finn stared at it for a while. It was a regular-looking dog, nothing special. All of this was probably just Finn's subconscious trying to get his attention.

Or, he'd picked up a talking dog. Which, given the grand range of weird shit that happened to people on a daily basis, wasn't something Finn was going to get too worked up about. He narrowed his eyes at it and leaned down lower, his eyes level with the dog's.

"You were there yesterday morning," he said. "Who started that fire?"

It was a chick.

Finn considered this for a second. "What did she look like?"

I don't know. Wallace yawned. *You all look alike to me.*

Finn stood up, ran his thumb and forefinger over his eyes. "I can't believe I'm talking to a fucking dog."

Whatever, man, the dog said. He looked at the package

of dog food, then back up at Finn. *You planning on using that as a doorstop, or were you gonna feed me eventually?*

Finn grabbed the food and stood up. Wallace hopped up and followed him, tail wagging, panting happily, just like a normal dog. Finn got a bowl from the cupboard and filled it with food. Wallace dug into it happily.

Just like a normal dog.

Which meant that if anything here was abnormal, it was probably him.

Which came as no surprise.

Chapter Fourteen

Tessa rolled over in her bed, her arm flopping over the other side, which was empty. Confused, she opened one eye.

Nope. Definitely empty.

She rolled over onto her back, closed her eyes again, and in a moment, he was there again, next to her in the bed. He kissed her gently, his hand running through her hair and sending shivers through her.

"You know I love you, don't you?" he said.

She pulled back and looked at him.

"You stole my car," she said.

"I brought it back."

"After ten years."

He nodded. "Yeah. What does that tell you?"

He moved his hand down her shoulder, over her breast, down to her stomach. She sighed.

"That you're the world's worst procrastinator?" she said.

He laughed, picked up her hand, kissed the palm. She felt waves of heat break over her down to her toes.

"I need you to know," he said, staring into her eyes. "That I love you."

"Why?" she asked, her voice quivering, but she knew the answer before he said it.

"Because I can't stay with you," he said. "We both know that."

"Why not?" she asked.

He pulled his hand away from her. She reached for him, but the bed seemed to grow bigger, the space between them too wide.

"Five tomatoes for a dollar," he said.

"What?" she said. She pushed herself up, tried to crawl across the bed, but it was too big. He laid on his back, his hands behind his head, and stared blankly at the ceiling.

"Finn," she said. "Don't go away again."

He turned to look at her. "I'm already gone, babe."

And then the fire alarm went off and she shot up in bed to find it was its normal size, and empty. She blinked a few times, the shock of the sound and the smell of something burning wrenching her from her dream into the real world. It took another moment before her brain processed all the signals.

Fire.

She jolted out of bed and ran across the hall to Izzy's room. Empty. She ran into her mother's room, where Babs was staying.

Empty. But the bed was made. Points for Babs.

She ran down the stairs, the air getting smokier as she went. Her heart calmed when she heard voices in the kitchen and recognized the smell: burned bacon.

Izzy must have tried to cook again.

She threw the front door open and pulled open the window in the living room before going into the kitchen. There, she found Babs standing on a stool, trying to turn off the smoke detector.

"You have to hit it with something," Izzy yelled over the screaming alarm.

Babs nodded and looked around. Tessa grabbed an old can of SpaghettiOs out of the cabinet and tossed it to Babs. Babs caught it in one hand, and smashed it against the smoke detector, which screeched out one final wheezing complaint before the face popped off and swung lazily from exposed wires. Izzy hooted and clapped as Babs gracefully stepped down from the stool and tossed the dusty and dented can into the garbage.

"Well, it seems my family curse is still in full effect," Babs said, glancing behind her at the hissing pan in the sink. Tessa leaned over and saw a few blackened pieces of bacon floating in oil-slicked water. Babs clapped her hands together and grinned. "No matter. I'll beat it eventually. What do you girls say I take you to Max's for breakfast?"

Tessa looked at the clock on the wall; it was 7:18 in the morning. "You know, if you could take Izzy, that would be great." She tugged at the hem of her oversized Spin Doctors concert T-shirt. "I really need to take a shower, and then I've got to get in for the lunch and dinner shifts—"

"No, you don't, actually," Babs said, putting one arm around Tessa's shoulders. "Max and I decided that I could take your shifts for a few days. Well, I decided more than he did, but I think he'll take the news just fine." She shared a conspiratorial look with Izzy. "And I believe you have some shopping to do."

Tessa looked back and forth between them. They were both smiling. This couldn't be good.

"Shopping?" she said. "For what?"

"The Come As You Aren't Ball, of course." At Tessa's blank look, Babs gave her a squeeze. "Saturday night. It's the benefit for the library."

"Or the ducks," Izzy said.

Babs grinned. "Oh, the ducks. Now, who doesn't want to help the ducks?" She linked her arm through Tessa's. "You should come with us. I'm going to go as a Goth chick, can you imagine?" She threw a wink at Izzy. "It was Izzy's idea."

Tessa shook her head. "I think I'll pass."

Babs and Izzy shared another look, with Izzy's clearly saying, "I told you so."

"Well, okay, darling. If you insist, it's your choice." She released Tessa and stretched out her hand to Izzy. "Looks like it's you and me, kid."

Izzy stood up and let Babs guide her out of the kitchen. Tessa watched them walk out together, her throat tightening with conflicting emotions as Izzy happily headed out with Babs. On the one hand, it was a relief to have someone else taking care of Izzy. On the other hand, how come it was so easy for Babs? Why didn't Izzy argue with her? Why did they get to share conspiratorial winks when Tessa was only partially friend, mostly warden?

How was it that Babs was there for one day and already she was mothering Izzy better than Tessa had in the past ten years?

Tessa flew out after them, catching them in the foyer just as they opened the door. She grabbed Izzy's backpack and held it while Izzy finished shrugging into her coat.

"Don't forget to be at school by 8:05. If you're late—"

Izzy grabbed the pack and made a face. "I know, I know."

"Don't worry, Tessa," Babs said. "I'll take her in myself."

Izzy grabbed Babs's arm. "Oh! Oh! Can I drive?"

Babs raised one eyebrow at Tessa. "Can she?"

Tessa smiled at Babs, appreciating the deference. "I hope you're insured."

Izzy squealed and bounced down the front steps. Babs tucked Tessa's arm in hers and leaned her head against Tessa's.

"She's a lovely girl," she said. "You've done an incredible job." She pulled back and looked at Tessa. "You enjoy your day off." She started out, then turned suddenly.

"Oh! I almost forgot; there's a note for you on the sofa," she said, her eyes twinkling for a moment before she followed Izzy down the porch steps.

Tessa watched until they pulled out of sight. Slowly, she shut the door, then went to the sofa and picked up the folded piece of paper with "Tessa" scribbled on the front in Finn's handwriting. She ran her fingertips over the scrawl, and déjà vu fell over her as she remembered all the notes he'd written her when they were kids.

But that was then. This was now. And they weren't kids anymore. Squelching the warm feeling, she unfolded the note and read it.

T—

Hope you slept well. I had to go see a man about a horse. Or something like that. I don't really know what that means. If it's something bad, let's pretend I never said it.

Tessa smiled.

*Thanks for letting me crash. I'll be back to confer with
my client after she gets home from school, assuming she's
managed to go that long without getting into any major
trouble. If she has, give her some milk and cookies, on me.
Samoas if you have 'em.*

As for you, get to work on that mole, damnit.

Always,

F.

Tessa let out a light laugh and pressed the note to her
chest before she realized that she was acting like a love-
struck teenager. Which was ridiculous. She folded the note,
walked over to the coatrack, and tucked it in her purse. At
that moment, the doorbell rang, and she gave a startled
yelp and jumped back.

"Oh, no," a high-pitched, saccharine voice came through
the door. "I hope I didn't startle you."

You've gotta be kidding me, Tessa thought, then pulled
the door open. She blinked twice, not believing her eyes
at first.

But no. It was definitely Mary Ellen Neeley, social-
working troll from hell, standing on her porch, clutching
her brown leather padfolio to her chest and looking like
righteousness warmed over.

"Tessa!" Mary Ellen stepped inside and gave Tessa one
of her big, pseudo-warm hugs. Pseudo-warm because
Mary Ellen was all of ninety-eight pounds and couldn't
manage a body temperature of over sixty degrees in the
middle of July, and also because Mary Ellen Neeley, with
all her bright smiles and white teeth and curly blonde
froth hair and soft-spoken manner, was possibly the most
insincere person ever to walk the planet.

Still, Tessa hugged her back because Mary Ellen was her lifeline to keeping Izzy, and if that meant faking affection for the popsicle-stick troll, then that's what she'd do.

"Oh, you look . . ." Mary Ellen paused, her eyes slowly grazing down Tessa's T-shirt to her exposed thighs, then slowly back up again. Of course, Tessa knew damn well that Mary Ellen had noted her attire already; this show was for show.

". . . comfortable," Mary Ellen said, finishing off her sentence with a smile that deepened her dimples back into the black pit of hell from whence they sprang.

"Thank you," Tessa said, snatching her trench off the coatrack and shrugging into it. "I just woke up."

"Oh, don't you worry about it," Mary Ellen said brightly. "You should see me first thing in the morning. Goodness, I'm a fright!"

Tessa made a noncommittal noise, then ran her fingers through her hair.

"Speaking of first thing in the morning," she said, trying to keep her voice polite, "you usually call before you visit."

Mary Ellen gave a fake look of contrition. "I know. I'm so sorry. But I just came into town for a visit—I have an old friend in town—so I thought I'd drop in and see how you were."

"Who's your friend?" Tessa asked.

Mary Ellen gave a dismissive wave of her hand. "No one you'd know. So, are you going to the Come As You Aren't Ball on Saturday? I hear it's going to be very fun. A benefit for a day-care center, right?"

"I know everyone in town," Tessa said, trying to keep her smile friendly.

"Hmmm?"

"It's impossible for you to be visiting someone in this town that I don't know, because I know everyone."

"Yes." Mary Ellen's smile faded. "Can we talk?"

She pushed past Tessa into the house. Tessa let her smile fall like a brick as she kicked the front door shut and followed Mary Ellen into the living room, then forced the smile back to full wattage just as Mary Ellen turned around.

"May I?" Mary Ellen said, nodding toward the sofa.

"Of course," Tessa said, holding one arm out in invitation, trying to keep the disdain out of her face. *Lifeline to Izzy, lifeline to Izzy,* she repeated in her head.

"So," Tessa said, situating herself as far from Mary Ellen as she could get while still sitting on the sofa, "how long will you be in town?"

"Hmmm," she hummed vaguely, turning a concerned expression to Tessa. "Actually, I told a little fib."

"A little fib?" Tessa repeated, trying to figure out what kind of person spoke like that.

Little fib. Jesus.

"I'm also in town because, well, I'm a little concerned. I received a phone call yesterday." Mary Ellen leaned forward, speaking in a low tone and patting Tessa's hand with her icy fingers of death. "About Izzy's repeated absences from school."

Tessa felt her muscles stiffen. "Yes. There's a stomach bug going around, and Izzy—"

Mary Ellen laughed that high-pitched, tinkling laugh that grated on every nerve Tessa possessed.

"Oh, I know, I know." Mary Ellen's face went serious.

"But, you know, it's my job to check in when things start looking dire."

Tessa raised one eyebrow. "Dire?"

"You see, it's my job to make sure that this environment is the best possible one for Izzy." Mary Ellen smoothed her hands over her knees, and then her eyebrows quirked together and she sniffed. "Is something burning?"

"Um, no," Tessa said, tugging at the hem of the coat to keep herself from scratching the woman's eyes out. "We had a little bit of a kitchen disaster this morning."

"Oh, goodness!" Mary Ellen put her hand to her chest. "A fire?"

"No, just smoke. Mostly."

Mary Ellen's eyes widened. "Mostly?"

Tessa stood up. "Thanks for stopping by, Mary Ellen. I really need to get started on the day."

Mary Ellen stood up as well, clutching her padfolio to her nonexistent breast. "That's fine, Tessa. I totally understand. I'd like to drop in maybe a little later and see Izzy, if that's okay? It's been so long, and you know how I feel about that little girl."

"She's not a little girl anymore," Tessa said. "She'll be graduating from high school at the end of next year."

Mary Ellen sighed and headed toward the front door. "Let's hope."

Tessa stomped out after her. "Excuse me?"

"She dropped half her classes."

"Just the AP ones. She wanted to graduate with the kids her age. And there are many studies from noted psychologists that show—"

"And then there's the chronic truancy . . ."

"I'd hardly call it *chronic*," Tessa said, but she could hear the lack of conviction in her own voice.

". . . and the trouble she's been getting into at school."

"She played a prank on the principal. Big deal. Kids do that."

"I've heard from the Robinsons," Mary Ellen said. "They've expressed an interest in taking Izzy back, just until she finishes high school and comes of age."

Tessa could swear her heart stopped beating. "You mean, the family that had Iz when she was six?"

Mary Ellen nodded. "Yes. And I think you should consider—"

"I'm not considering anything," Tessa said. "Izzy stays with me. Period. The judge said so."

Mary Ellen's eyes went dark, and Tessa felt all her suspicions locking into place as truth. She'd beaten this woman in court, despite all her passive-aggressive bullying, and Mary Ellen would never forgive her for it. This wasn't about Izzy's best interests. It was about Mary Ellen's pride and her overblown sense of her own power.

Mary Ellen pursed her lips. "Tessa, my only concern is for Izzy. I'm here to make sure that her best interests are met."

Tessa felt her heart start up again, with a raging boom in her chest. "I have done nothing but see to Izzy's best interests. I don't have a life because of her best interests. I am nothing but a hollow shell of who I used to be because of Izzy's best interests."

"Children can sense resentment, Tessa," Mary Ellen said, sanctimony curling around her like a swirling pool of evil.

"I don't resent her," Tessa said. "How dare you?"

Mary Ellen raised one eyebrow, flipped open the pad-folio, and jotted something down, then sighed and raised her little beady eyes back to Tessa's. "I see I've upset you."

"You haven't upset me!" Tessa snapped.

"Well," Mary Ellen said, tucking the padfolio under her arm. "I'm going to check in with my friend. I'll give Izzy a call later. And in the meantime"—she grasped Tessa's hand in her talons—"I want you to really consider what's best for Izzy. Okay?"

Tessa ripped her hand free of Mary Ellen's and pulled the door open.

"I never consider anything else," she said. Mary Ellen's smile was finally gone, and she slipped out the door into the frigid air. It was all Tessa could do to keep from slamming the door behind her.

The Robinsons have expressed an interest . . .

Bullshit. Mary Ellen had hunted them down and asked them if they'd take Izzy back. Tessa was sure of it. The woman was crazy, and vindictive, and horrible, but she had the power to put Tessa and Izzy through another big court battle. She had the power to make their lives hell.

Again.

Tessa sighed and closed her eyes. All these years, she'd been dancing to Mary Ellen's tune, trying to avoid just this situation. She'd inflicted limitations that were suffo-cating Izzy, and she'd played the good girl to the point where her only deviance was doing good deeds in Finn's name and lying about it to the whole town. And that was just twisted.

And all that, for what? Nothing. *Nothing.* What she'd

been trying to avoid had just slinked into her living room and all but demanded she relinquish custody of her sister.

"Well, screw the hell out of that," she muttered, then trudged up the stairs, hoping a long shower and some fresh clothes might help her figure out the new rules of the game, because it was for damn sure things were going to change.

Immediately.

Chapter Fifteen

Finn leaned over the sage green counter at FLOWERS, ETCETERA and tapped the bell lightly twice. It was a little after eight, and the only sign the place was open was that the front door was unlocked. He sighed and leaned back against the counter, staring blankly at a table filled with violets while he waited.

He felt a wave of fatigue, and rolled his shoulders to allay it. Sleeping last night had been impossible. No matter how he tossed and turned, he could still feel Tessa's hair soft under his fingers. Could still smell her. It was as if touching her had altered his nervous system, and now she'd always be there, a phantom under his skin. Even after giving up the fight at five in the morning, taking a shower, doing his laundry, and hiking out to Margie's, she was still there with him.

So, does someone have to hit you over the head with a two-by-four or what?

He looked down and saw Wallace at his feet, the little furry face looking up at him, eyes deeply sarcastic and totally unimpressed with Finn. The dog had insisted on following Finn out that morning, and Finn hadn't resisted the company, but trying to get the dog to wait outside the flower shop had been a battle of wills Finn had quickly lost.

"Dermot?"

Finn turned around to see Margie Fletcher coming into the shop through the back. She pulled off her coat and hung it on the rack by the door. Finn assumed his most charming grin.

"Morning," he said. "Door was unlocked. I rang the bell."

She crossed her arms over her chest and stood where she was, watching him with an expression of extreme prejudice. Finn stood up straighter and let the charm fade. Obviously, Margie was part of the relatively small but justified camp of Lucy's Lake residents who didn't think Finn was a big hero.

Good, he thought. *I can work with that.*

"I hope it's okay to have dogs in here," Finn said, nodding down at Wallace. "He's not mine, but he's been kinda following me around."

Margie's eyebrows knit, and she slowly moved into the shop, peering around the counter to look down at Wallace. Her face instantly brightened and she bent down and took Wallace's face in her hands, scratching behind each of his ears.

"Oh, Bitsy!" she said.

Finn quirked an eyebrow. "Bitsy?"

"Yeah," Margie said. "I know he's a boy, but when he first showed up begging at Vickie's, I thought he was a she. Unfortunately, by that time, we'd already named him Bitsy."

Finn raised an eyebrow at Wallace. *Bitsy?*

Wallace struggled against Margie's enthused petting to meet Finn's eyes. *Bite me.*

Finn grinned. "I guess that explains why he was at Vickie's that morning. Didn't look like her typical pedigree dog."

Margie straightened, her smile fading a bit.

"I heard you saved Vickie's," she said, her voice tight. "Thank you."

Finn shrugged. "Wrong place, wrong time. My specialty. Where is Vickie, anyway? I would have thought she'd come back, considering her business almost burned down."

Margie shook her head, her expression unreadable. "I don't think she knows. She left for Bimini last Friday, and I don't think her cell phone has roaming."

Bimini, huh? This was the first he'd heard of that. "And no one knows what hotel she's in?"

"Guess not," she said. "She usually tells Stella those things, but . . ."

"I'm just kind of surprised she didn't tell you," Finn said. "Aren't you two close?"

"Yes, we are," Margie said. Finn waited for her to elaborate, but she didn't. Instead, she reached over the counter, pulled a dog biscuit out of a fishbowl, and tossed it to Wallace, who snapped it up as though he was starving, despite the fact that he'd been gorging himself on dog food since Finn brought it home the night before.

"So, is there anything I can help you with?"

"Yeah," Finn said. "I actually came by to get some flowers."

Margie's smile completely disappeared, and she raised one eyebrow. "For Tessa?"

"Actually, no," he said, leaning his hip and elbow against the counter. "But don't feel you have to mask your disapproval on my account."

Margie's face softened. "I'm sorry. I don't mean to be rude. I know you've done a lot of wonderful things for the people in this town. But ever since Karen passed . . ." She sighed, and her pale blue eyes brimmed with tears. "Well, I just feel very protective of those girls."

Finn smiled. "I'm glad to hear it." He nodded toward the display cooler by the wall. "Can I get that bunch there in front?"

Margie turned and glanced at the cooler. "The Gerbera daisies?" She shot a look at Finn. "Do you know what daisies say?"

"What, the daisies are talking now, too?"

Margie's eyebrows knit for a moment, and a small smile played on her lips. "They have meaning, yeah. Daises say, 'My love is loyal and pure.'"

Finn pulled out his wallet. "Works for me."

Ten minutes later, Finn was cutting fresh footprints through the snow of Lucy's Lake's only cemetery, shared by all religious factions of the town, and kept pristine by said factions on ten acres of land just south of town. He wound his way through the maze of gravestones, Wallace keeping time behind him, until he found the stone he was looking for.

He knelt down in front of Karen Scuderi's grave and cleared the snow out of the steel vase on the side of her tombstone. He peeled the plastic wrap off the flowers and tucked them into the vase, then crouched down before the grave.

"I hope you like the flowers," he said. "I couldn't find a two-by-four on such short notice." He laughed lightly at his own joke, then stood up, started to walk away, and turned back.

"There isn't much about me that's loyal and pure." He took a deep breath of the cold air. "And I know you're probably hating that I'm back. If it makes you feel better, you're not alone. But I swear, I won't let anyone hurt her. Either of them."

He stood for a moment longer in silence, then gave Karen one last nod and turned back toward town.

"I really think you should call your sister," Sosie said, her whisper barely audible, even though she was huddled up close to Izzy in the bathroom stall.

"I can't," Izzy said, holding the locket, bundled in tissue paper, out in the palm of her hand. "I have to know, and I can't do it." She extended her hand toward Sosie. "Please. Just open it."

Sosie bit her lip and tucked a long strand of brown hair behind her ear. She stared down at the tissue, then opened the stall door again to make sure no one else was in the bathroom.

"Sose, if someone had come in since the last time you checked, we'd hear them." Izzy pulled the stall door shut again. "Please. I need you. If this is what I think it is, I swear, I'll run out and find Finn right now and give it to him."

Sosie blinked. "What? Cut school? Again?"

Izzy shrugged. "Yeah. Big deal. Everyone cuts."

"Yeah, but didn't your sister say—?"

Izzy rolled her eyes. "Tessa's totally paranoid. I'm sixteen. No one's gonna take me away. Everyone cuts. And if you don't open that soon, my five-minute pass is going to expire and you know Mr. Dudley. He wrote Shinae up for cutting class when she took too long in the bathroom last week." She grabbed Sosie's right hand and slapped the bundle into her friend's palm. "You wanna keep me out of trouble? Help me."

Sosie let out a heavy sigh, then slowly unwrapped the paper. Izzy closed her eyes. There was the sound of tissue crumpling, then a small silence before the click of the locket opening. A little more silence. Another click as the locket closed. More tissue crumpling.

Izzy opened her eyes. "What?"

Sosie's eyes were moist. "Tell me what was in your mother's locket again?"

"A picture of Tessa with a beach ball on one side. A picture of me as a baby on the other."

Sosie put the bundle back in Izzy's hand.

"It's your mother's," she said quietly.

It was so strange, the way Izzy felt nothing at the words. She didn't really know what she should be feeling—sadness, anger, confusion—but she expected she'd feel something.

Instead, she was perfectly calm, completely untouched. *This must be what shock feels like,* she thought. Although she had suspected these things, part of her had been convinced that it was just her imagination, that the Nancy Drew bit would end in a benign cul-de-sac of reason, and she would look back on it years down the line and laugh at her own silliness.

She hadn't really, truly expected she'd be right. Part of the reason she'd gone to Finn had been to get him to prove her wrong.

But she wasn't wrong. Her mother's locket proved it.

Numb, she put the bundle back into her pocket, then opened the door to the stall and let herself out.

"Iz?" Sosie called from behind her as Izzy touched up her lip gloss in the mirror. "What are you gonna do?"

"I'm gonna go back to trig," Izzy said, feeling weirdly separate from her own voice. "Mr. Dudley will write me up if I don't get back."

She gave Sosie a tight smile, then headed out the door. She felt like she was floating, like her feet weren't connecting with the ground. As she moved through the hallway, she was only aware of the thought running through her head.

Someone killed my mother. She shook her head to push it away, but it stayed, repeating, like an automated message.

Someone killed my mother. Someone killed my mother.

It felt like it took a year to get back to trig class, but when she walked in, Mr. Dudley only nodded briefly at her as she took her seat. So her entire life had completely changed in just under five minutes.

Weird.

Tessa tossed herself on the couch and settled the bottle of gin beside her. She liked this. This was good. This felt good. And hell, it was five o'clock *somewhere*. Moscow, maybe. She picked up the bottle and took another drink, then held it out to see if she could tell how much she'd had.

It was below the tippy-top of the label now, but only just. She hadn't had much.

"Jesus, what a lightweight." She giggled at the sound of her own voice, having no idea why it was funny but enjoying the feeling of lightness the giggling gave her.

The front door opened and she heard the *clack-clack-clack* of little doggy toes on the hardwood floors.

"Wallace!" she said, and leaned forward a little too fast. Bad idea, that. "Whoa."

Wallace hopped up next to her on the sofa and licked her face. She patted him on the head and sat back, pulling the gin with her. It wasn't until she tipped her face up to take another swig that she noticed Finn standing in front of her, watching her with an amused expression.

"So, I guess the dog is allowed on the furniture, then?" he asked.

Tessa finished the swallow—so much smoother than the first swallow had been—and simply smiled and nuzzled Wallace closer to her. She'd already forgotten the question Finn had asked. A moment later, Finn was on the sofa next to her, although she couldn't exactly recall him moving there. Gently, he pried the bottle from her fingers and she let him, because she was fairly certain she'd had enough.

"Seventy proof," he said, one eyebrow quirking up in a way that was so freakin' cute Tessa had to giggle.

"And it's lime-twisted," she said, pointing to the lime on the bottle. "You don't even need limes. I ask you, how freakin' convenient is that?"

Finn laughed, and it sounded so nice. He had such a nice laugh, all tickly down in his chest.

Tickly. Tickly. Man, that's a weird word.

Finn rested the bottle in his lap, then glanced casually at the clock on the wall before turning his attention back to Tessa, which, quite frankly, was where Tessa liked his attention.

"So," he said, "I'm willing to bet cash money that I missed something today."

"Oh, you did," Tessa said. Her head was leaning on his shoulder, and she didn't remember letting it fall there, but what the hell? "You missed the big show, in which I realized that I've been busting my ass for a big, fat zero. You know what I learned today?"

She lifted her head to look at him and he looked down at her and *damn*.

He was cute.

"I learned," she said, pushing herself away from him a bit so as not to be distracted by all the cuteness, "that it doesn't matter how hard you work, or how good you are, how many envelopes full of cash you slide under people's doors just when they need it most, you'll never be safe from assholes with padfolios. You know?"

Finn gave a noncommittal hum and nodded. "Sounds like you've had an eventful morning."

Tessa sighed. "Hmmm. But, you know, whatever."

She reached for the bottle, but he was too quick, holding it just out of her reach.

"It's five o'clock somewhere," she said.

"Yeah," he said, chuckling. "In Moscow, maybe."

"Hey," she said softly, "that's what I said."

She pulled back from him a bit so she could focus on his eyes. They were so blue. And so, so pretty.

"I fear that I'm a lightweight," she said.

He lifted his arm up and over her, resting it behind her

on the back of the sofa, his hand playing lazily with her hair.

"I think that's a reasonable fear," he said. "Maybe you should go upstairs and sleep it off."

She closed her eyes and let her head slump to the side, flattening his hand against the sofa. She heard his laugh—tickly, tickly—and smiled, eyes still closed.

"I don't want to sleep it off," she said. She opened her eyes to see him with his head resting against the sofa, his face just inches from hers.

Man. He really was good-looking. Why was she resisting his charms again?

Oh, yeah. Took her virginity. Stole her car. Abandoned her when she needed him most. Completely untrustworthy. Used to be a bird thief.

Blah blah blah . . .

She raised her head.

"You know what I want to do?" she said, awkwardly pushing herself up from the sofa. The cushions seemed softer and more sucky than usual, but she managed to get to her feet on her own, which was good.

"I want to go skating," she said. "Will you take me skating?"

Finn stood up. "Aside from the issue of you landing face-first on the ice, I don't have skates."

"No problem." Tessa walked over to the hall closet and rummaged through all the crap at the bottom. Worn-out shoes, discarded purses that she frankly couldn't believe were ever in style, something that looked kinda like an old candy bar that she decided to ignore for the moment, and finally—bingo. She grabbed the men's hockey skates and stood up too fast.

"Whoa." She blinked until her vision returned and held the skates out to Finn. He eyed her with a suspicious grin for a few seconds, then took them from her, turning them upside down to check the number printed on the bottom.

"My size." He smiled at her. "How did you know?"

"Bought them for Joe a few years back, he didn't like skating, though, so . . ." She motioned vaguely toward the closet. "They just sort of stayed here."

"They're Joe's?" he said flatly.

"Oh, for Pete's sake," Tessa said. The words were coming out exactly as she thought them. No editing. Nothing. Man, she liked gin. "This thing with you and Joe is really stupid, you know that?"

Finn raised his eyes to meet hers. "What about the thing with you and Joe?"

"There is no me and Joe," she said. Wait. How did he know about her and Joe? "How did you know about me and Joe?"

It was like an echo. Cool.

"Forget it," Finn said. "I'll wear the skates. It's no problem."

"Did he tell you about us? He told you, didn't he?"

"He might have mentioned something," Finn said. "I don't know. I wasn't really paying attention."

"Pffft," Tessa said, sending her bangs flying. "Look, the thing about Joe—he's a great guy."

Finn held up his hands. "You know what? I don't want to hear this. Sorry I asked. Let's skate."

"No," she said, waving her finger in the air. "No. You shut up and listen to me."

One side of his mouth curved up in a grin. "I like it when you take charge."

"Shut up," she said again. "Joe is a great guy. He's honest, he's honorable, and he's really good-looking. And yes, we dated. Briefly. But he wasn't . . ."

She stopped, knowing in her gut she'd regret it if she opened up on this one, but she couldn't quite get up the motivation to lie about it.

"He wasn't what?" Finn asked, looking down at the skates in his hand.

"You." Tessa's heart gave a little flip as she said it, but what the hell? "He knew it and I knew it and we broke up and he was really great about it and I don't think either one of us has given it a second thought since."

Finn didn't say anything, just looked at her, at a loss for words.

Will wonders never cease?

"Well, now that we've got that out of the way," she said. She walked toward the front door and felt as though her head might be clearing a bit. That was no good. She turned suddenly and slammed into Finn's chest, which threw her equilibrium all to hell, and she stumbled. Finn caught her wrist with one hand and balanced her. She looked up at him and wobbled a bit.

"I was gonna go get the gin. I don't want to sober up."

He released her wrist and put his hand on her neck, his thumb running over her face. "You have to sober up, babe. Izzy's gonna be home from school—"

Tessa shook her head. "She works at Margie's today."

"Then she'll be home from Margie's. That gives us, what, maybe five hours to indulge whatever this is, and then we've gotta be grown up again. Okay?"

Tessa nodded, feeling the warmth from his hand seeping into her neck.

It felt so good. *So good.*

"Fine," she said. She took the skates from his hand and tossed them at the closet. She missed by about five feet and they took a small chunk out of the wall before rattling to the floor. Whatever. Tessa put both arms around Finn's neck and pulled herself up against him.

"Let's indulge, then," she said quietly.

He laughed lightly, his eyebrows quirking together in a way that was really, well, cute.

"Tessa . . . ," he started.

"Shhhh," she said. She placed a finger on his lips and didn't know if the *thump-thump-thump* she felt was coming from her heart or his, but either way, it was time they did something about it. She lowered her finger from her lips, then stepped up on her toes and tilted her head slightly. All he had to do was lean down just the tiniest bit and meet her.

Which he wasn't doing. She felt the hardness of him below, so she knew he was feeling something. She slowly lowered down on her heels and looked up at him.

"Okay," she said. "Well, I feel stupid, which means I'm definitely not drunk enough."

"Tessa . . ." He trailed off and she could see the tension in his face. Didn't make her feel any less stupid, though.

"No, it's no big deal," she said. "Let's go skating."

She took a step toward the front door, but he caught her arm and stopped her.

"You think this is easy for me, having to shut this down? It's killing me, Tess."

"Then here's a thought. Don't. Saves your life. Saves my dignity. Sounds like a win-win to me."

He slowly released her arm. "You're drunk. You don't really want this."

"Don't tell me what I want," she said. "I'm not a child."

"If you knew . . ." He stopped talking, shook his head, breathed in deep, and started again. "If you knew all the facts, you wouldn't want this."

"What?" she said. "If I knew you used to steal birds for a living?"

He blinked and eyebrows lifted in surprise. "You know about that?"

"Babs told me yesterday. Pffft." She waved her hand in the air in a dismissive gesture. "Big whoop."

Finn's expression transitioned from surprise to anger, and yet he was still so cute. How did he do that?

"You know what?" he said. "This is the thing. Never trust a woman to keep a confidence."

"She also told me that you were responsible for half a million in donations to St. Jude's last year."

Finn's face was unreadable. "She did, huh?"

Tessa nodded. "Yes. She also said you were a good man. She said she'd trust you with everything she owned. She said—"

He held up his hand to stop her. "I get it."

"She said you saved her daughter's life."

"Did she tell you that I was the one who put her daughter in danger in the first place?" he said, his voice hard. "There's a difference between being a hero and not being a total asshole, Tess. I'll cop to one, but not the other."

"Why can't you just accept that you might not be as worthless as you like to think?"

"I'm not the one having trouble accepting reality."

"What is that supposed to mean?"

"You know what it means."

He grabbed her hand and pulled her closer to him in one swift motion, and her breathing quickened.

"It means this. What happens to us when we're together." He reached up and brushed his thumb over her bottom lip. Tessa felt her skin grow hot, and her imagination was just about to take her to the very good place when he pulled his hand away.

Crap.

"You're letting all that confuse you. It doesn't change the facts of who and what I am. I'm not the kind of person you should have in your life, Tessa, for a million reasons, not the least of which is you keeping Izzy."

Oh. God. Izzy. Mary Ellen Neeley. Crap.

"Funny you should mention that, actually," she said, "since it really doesn't matter anymore."

He released her arm slowly. "Yes, it does. You just don't care now because you're drunk, but—"

"They're gonna take Izzy away," she said, surprised when the words came out. The room went dead silent, and when she finally looked up, Finn was staring at her, his expression dark.

"Who's gonna take Izzy away?" he asked.

"Mary Ellen Neeley thinks that living with me is not in Izzy's best interests. She came by this morning. She—"

Tessa swallowed, fighting off the tears. She did not want to cry.

Finn reached out and touched her arm and his compassion sent a shocking wave of hurt through her. She pulled away from him.

"Look," she said. "My buzz is beginning to wear off and I don't want to feel this."

"Feel what?"

"*This*," she said, waving both hands by her face in a weak attempt to stave off the inevitable torrent to come. "Izzy is everything, Finn. She's my whole life. I don't have a life without her."

"Hey," he said, his voice soft, "sure you do."

"No. I don't. And it's okay. I'm not upset about that. Everything I've given up, everything I didn't do . . ." She felt her breath catch in her chest as their eyes met. "I'd give it all up again. She means that much to me. And if they take her away again . . ."

"They're not going to take her away."

"How do you know? How can you tell me that?"

He shook his head and put the palm of his hand gently on her face.

"They're not going to take her away." His voice was rough and scratchy, and she couldn't see his expression clearly through the tears suddenly welling in her eyes.

"I don't want to feel this," she said. "It'll kill me, I swear it will."

"Shhhh," he said, pulling her into his arms. One arm held tight around her waist, and his other hand cradled her head. She rested the side of her face on his chest and closed her eyes, letting the tears fall where they may.

"I can't do it," she said. "I got through everything else but I can't get through this."

He kissed the top of her head, and she allowed herself to lean into him. She had more she wanted to say, but the sobs were choking her, and she couldn't get it all out. She couldn't tell him how much she missed her mother, how much she wished her mother could be there to tell her what to do and how to take care of Izzy. She couldn't tell him how many times she'd wanted to find him, just for the peace of mind of knowing he wasn't dead in a ditch somewhere. She couldn't tell him how much it meant to her that he was there, or how terrified she was of waking up one day and finding him gone again.

Instead, she just folded herself into his arms and cried until everything around her softened and went black.

Chapter Sixteen

Finn lowered Tessa onto her bed. She sniffled a little, then rolled onto her side without waking up. Finn let out a breath and sat on the bed next to her. He unlaced his boots as quietly as he could, slipped them off, then slid into bed next to her, spooning her from behind, one arm draped over her waist and the other supporting his head as he watched her.

She hiccuped out a half sob. He shushed into her ear and gently kissed her face. Her eyes didn't open, but she seemed to calm down a bit. He reached up and nudged her hair away from her face. Even all red and puffy-eyed, she was still the most beautiful thing he'd ever laid eyes on, and if he ever doubted for a moment that he was beyond in love with her, he knew better now. His chest felt as if it were cracked right open, and he would have moved heaven and earth if he thought it would just make her smile.

As fate would have it, though, the only thing he could really do for her would be to go away. Even though he'd never gotten caught during his bird thieving days, the only employment he'd had in the last ten years was a part-time job at a pet shop in Manhattan. Everything else, even his jobs with Babs, were all under the table. On paper, he was a loser and a freeloader and that was the last thing Tessa needed in her life.

He could stay a few more days, just long enough to put Izzy's concerns about her mother's death to rest, and then he'd have to go.

There was just no other way.

He lowered his face down onto the pillow next to her and inhaled the scent of her. Her hand lazily came up over his, pulling his arm even tighter around her waist. He kissed her cheek, then settled in next to her, trying to live fully in that moment for as long as it lasted.

Tessa opened her eyes to find herself in her bedroom, bright with sunlight. Disoriented, she blinked a few times before realizing it wasn't morning.

She'd already had morning.

And, whoa, what a morning. Vague images flew at her. Mary Ellen Neeley. The padfolio. The gin. Finn.

Finn.

"Oh, God," she groaned, and put her hand over her eyes.

She'd thrown herself at Finn.

Better still, she'd thrown herself at Finn *and been shot down.*

"Oh, *God,*" she groaned again, wishing she could just pull the covers over her face and forget everything that happened.

But she couldn't. She was an adult. She'd gotten drunk at ten o'clock in the morning, and whatever the consequences were for that kind of crap, she'd have to face them.

She rolled over in bed and looked at the spot where she thought Finn had been. Maybe she'd dreamed the part where he'd snuggled with her. Maybe he was on his way back to wherever he'd come from. Maybe she'd so thoroughly freaked him out that he caught the first bus out of town.

She reached out and ran her fingers lazily over the space next to her, remembering how kind he'd been to her, even while shooting her down. She remembered the feel of him holding her together while she fell apart, safe in his arms. All these years, the people in her life had been there for her and supported her and kept her sane, but no one had ever made her feel safe.

How did he do that?

The front door slammed downstairs, startling her.

Izzy.

She closed her eyes. *Izzy.* A stab of dread shot through her, and then she took a deep breath and pulled herself together. Izzy wasn't lost yet. There was still a fight to be had, and goddamn if Mary Ellen Neeley and her freakin' padfolio weren't going to get just that. She heard Izzy's voice downstairs, followed by the rumble of Finn's voice.

He's still here, she thought. *Thank God.*

She pulled herself out of bed, went to the bathroom to brush her teeth and drink a little water, and then headed down the stairs. As she appeared on the landing, both Izzy and Finn looked up at her. Izzy had an expression of serious concern on her face, and moved toward the bottom of the stairs to meet Tessa.

"What happened?" Izzy said.

"Nothing." Tessa exchanged a warning look with Finn.

He nodded and she knew they were on the same page: *Don't tell Izzy.*

"Fine," Izzy sighed. "Don't tell me. I don't care. There's something . . ." Izzy nibbled at her lip and looked nervously from Finn to Tessa.

Oh, crap, Tessa thought. *What now?*

She sat on the bottom step and ran her hands over her hair.

"Okay," she said. "I'm sitting. What's up?"

"I have something I need to . . . um . . ." Izzy reached into her pocket and pulled out a bundle of tissue paper. Tessa's eyebrows knit as Izzy handed it to her.

"What is this?"

Izzy sniffled. "It's Mom's."

Tessa looked at her for a minute, then unwrapped the tissue paper, gently pulling a familiar locket and chain from the bundle.

"Oh, my God," she whispered as she looked at it. She hadn't thought about the locket in a long time, but she recognized it instantly. Her mother had never left the house without it. "Where did you find this?"

Izzy didn't answer. Tessa pulled on the locket and it opened easily in her hands, revealing pictures of her and Izzy that she hadn't seen in ten years.

"The clasp is broken," she noted, staring at it in wonder.

"Is that what you pulled from Vickie Kemp's mailbox yesterday?" Finn asked, his voice quiet.

Izzy glanced at him, nodded. "Along with this," she said, handing him an envelope. He pulled out the paper inside, read it, and handed it to Tessa.

LEAVE IT ALONE. Along with her mother's locket. Someone was trying to send a message.

Someone had killed her mother.

Tessa felt a coldness run through her, and hugged herself to ward it off.

"You found this in Vickie's mailbox?" she asked Izzy. "What was it doing in Vickie's mailbox?"

Finn settled on the stairs next to Tessa. "Whoever put it there probably wanted Vickie to find it when she got back. It's a good place to put it; the fire investigators have no reason to go into her mailbox."

"Okay." Tessa nodded, trying to take it all in, then looked up at Izzy. "You found this yesterday? Why didn't you tell me?"

Izzy sighed. "I didn't want to say anything unless I knew for sure that the locket was Mom's, and I was too afraid to open it. I made Sosie do it for me."

Finn's face darkened. "Who's Sosie?"

"Her friend from school," Tessa said.

"You told your friend about all this?" Finn's voice was angry, and Izzy bristled.

"Yeah," she said, looking at him like he was stupid. "She's my best friend. Duh."

Finn looked at Tessa. "What is it with women and the best friend thing?"

Tessa sighed. "It's a girl thing. The best friend is a sacred relationship. You keep nothing from the best friend."

"That's insane." He paused for a second, his focus on Tessa. "Do you have a best friend?"

Tessa raised an eyebrow and said flatly, "Used to."

She could tell by Finn's expression that he got the stinger end of the comment, as intended. Part of her felt bad, but part of her didn't.

Finn turned his attention to Izzy. "You need to make sure she doesn't tell anyone, for her sake and yours."

"She won't," Izzy said, irritation seeping into her tone. "She can keep a secret."

Finn stood up. "Let's hope so. Izzy, it's really important that you understand what this means."

"I'm not remedial," Izzy said. "It means I was right." She looked down at Tessa. "It means someone killed Mom."

Tessa felt her heart clutch at the thought. Finn glanced down at her, then back at Izzy.

"Not so fast, Grasshopper," he said. "Someone scared your mom, and she got in a car."

"Which means they killed her!"

Finn put one hand on Izzy's shoulder. "Which means they're responsible. But we don't know if they meant to kill her. You're connecting a lot of dots that might not be there, and you need to take it down a notch if we're going to do this right. We don't want to screw this up, okay?"

Izzy calmed and nodded. Finn gave her shoulder a quick squeeze, then let go.

"Okay. So let's connect the dots we've got." He glanced down at the locket in Tessa's hands. "Someone put this in Vickie's mailbox to intimidate her into minding her own business. Whoever that someone is knows the significance of the locket, and expects Vickie to know, too."

Tessa put one hand on the banister and pulled herself up.

"So we find Vickie and ask her what the connection is."

"Or," Finn said, "we go to the police and give them everything and let them deal with it."

"What?" Tessa shook her head. "No, we can't—"

Finn held his hand up and Tessa went quiet.

"I think we've got some damn compelling evidence that there's a bad guy out there," he said. "The police can protect you."

"No," Tessa said, shaking her head. "Izzy's broken into safes, she's violated crime scenes. I'm not taking the chance of that getting out."

Finn's face flooded with understanding, and Izzy threw her hands up in frustration.

"Oh, for God's sake, Tessa, would you quit worrying about what the stupid social worker will think for once!"

"The social worker can bite my ass," Tessa said. "If there's someone out there lighting things on fire, I don't want them wondering what you might know."

Izzy blinked. "Did you just say the social worker could bite your ass?"

Izzy smiled and Tessa smiled back, but when she looked at Finn, he didn't look as amused by the whole "bite my ass" thing as they were.

"I think it's a mistake not to involve the police, right now," he said. "This guy has already gotten away with murder once."

"Since when are you such a big fan of the police?" Tessa asked.

"Since now," he said. "Since someone started setting things on fire. You need protection."

"And we have you," Izzy said. "You're a private detective, right? Can't you protect us?"

Finn sighed, and Tessa reached over and gave his hand a subtle squeeze. He looked at her, but didn't say anything.

"Yeah," Tessa said, keeping her eyes locked on Finn. "He can."

Finn didn't look happy, but he didn't argue. That was something.

"Well," Izzy said, picking up her backpack from where she'd dropped it by the door. "I'm gonna hit the homework and let you two fight this out."

She started toward the stairs, stopping when Tessa pulled her in for a hug.

"Thanks for telling me," Tessa said. "About Mom's locket. About everything."

Izzy smiled. "Yeah. Of course."

Tessa kissed her on the cheek and released her, watching her sister with a strange mix of pride and affection. Babs was right. Tessa *had* done an incredible job with Izzy. By any scale other than Mary Ellen Neeley's, Izzy was a spectacular kid. Why did it take all the drama to make her see that?

"You need to take this to the police," Finn said.

She turned her attention to Finn. "Boy, now who's uptight?"

He stepped closer to her, glanced up the stairs where Izzy had gone, and spoke in lowered tones.

"I'm not a private detective," he said.

Tessa smiled. "I've got eighty-nine dollars in my sister's piggy bank that says different."

Finn gave a brief nod acknowledging the skillful turnabout, but looked unamused. "I can't protect you, not as well as someone who's trained in dealing with this kind of thing."

Tessa tried to consider what he was saying, but her instinct was screaming "No," and it was just louder.

"And what are the police gonna do, huh? We have a vague threatening note and a broken locket, all related to an accidental death that happened ten years ago. If we go to the police now, everyone will know—including this bad guy. I'm not taking a chance with this person finding out Izzy knows something."

"Or the social worker finding out that Izzy broke some laws."

Tessa felt her bite-my-ass bravado start to slip. Best friends, man. They always knew.

She shrugged. "Look, I'm done kissing up to Mary Ellen Neeley. Wench wants a fight, she'll get one. But . . . yeah. It won't help at all if any charges are pressed against Izzy."

Finn watched her for a long moment, then ran his hand through his hair and sighed.

"Okay. No police. But I think I should stay here, then."

Tessa blinked. "You were going somewhere?"

"I thought . . . well." He shrugged. "I didn't want to assume . . . you know. Just because I crashed on the couch for one night, that's not an open invitation. But now, with the insane arsonist and everything, I think maybe it's a good idea. And I'm glad to see you agree."

Tessa couldn't help but smile at that one. "You're glad to see I agree?"

"You making fun of me?" he said, a trace of indignation in his voice.

Tessa moved closer, placing her hand against his chest as she sidled up next to him, enjoying the *thump-thump* she felt under her fingers.

"Little bit," she said, angling her head up to look at

him. "You're just always so quick with the verbal. It's kinda fun to see you off your game."

He looked down at her and smiled, letting his arms circle her waist. "I am not off my game."

She could hardly believe how good it felt just to relax in his arms.

One side of his mouth quirked up in a smile. "How did this conversation get dangerous again?"

"I think we just do that," she said.

"Yeah," he said. "I think we do."

With that, he kissed her chastely on the nose and released her, clearing his throat as he walked toward the dining room table.

"So, uh," he said, "I guess we need to work on tracking down Vickie Kemp, then."

Shot down twice in one day, she thought. *Has to be some kind of record.*

She watched as he grabbed a pad of paper and a pen from the hutch in the dining room, and couldn't help but smile at how businesslike his demeanor was. She knew he was just playing it safe, and she had to respect that. She'd been doing that herself for quite some time.

The only thing was, playing it safe got you a whole lot of nowhere. It had taken a long time for that lesson to make its way through her thick skull, but now that it had, Tessa knew she was all done with safe.

Finn looked up at her.

"You gonna come in here and help me figure this out, or are you just gonna watch me with that stupid grin on your face?"

"I beg your pardon," she said with mock indignation as

she headed toward the dining room. "This just happens to be the smartest grin I own."

Vickie Kemp sat on the olive green beanbag chair in Margie Fletcher's basement and drummed her fingers against her arm. She'd been down there for almost a full week, and there was no sign she'd be leaving anytime soon.

And, as much as she loved Margie, the woman's cooking was really atrocious. But, bright side, Vickie thought she might be losing some weight. She glanced down at her middle-aged middle, sucked it in, let it go.

Eh. Maybe not.

"Sorry I'm late," Margie said, traipsing down the basement stairs carrying a pizza box, paper plates, and a two-liter bottle of soda.

"That better be pepperoni," Vickie said.

Margie gave her a look as if to say "Duh," then settled down on the futon and put the pizza and soda on the old glass coffee table. Vickie pushed herself up from the beanbag— no mean feat for a forty-eight-year-old woman—and walked over to the minibar in the corner.

"Oh, no," Margie said, hand on the flat stomach Vickie tried hard not to envy. "No rum for me tonight."

"So, what then?" Vickie glanced at the stock of liquor. "Vodka, scotch, or that awful homemade cranberry wine Astrid made last year?"

There was a slight pause. "Vodka."

Vickie retrieved the other bottle, then sat on the futon and mixed alcohol and soda while Margie settled the pizza slices on the paper plates. It was the picture of twenty-first-century domesticity—two middle-aged divorcées getting blitzed over pizza on a Thursday night.

"So," Vickie said, grabbing a slice, "what's the news?"

Margie's face registered disappointment. "No news. Although Finn did visit me at the store today."

Vickie paused midbite and pulled back from the pizza. "That's news. Did you tell him anything?"

"No." Margie's expression was pensive. "I'm just not sure we can trust him yet. I think he's staying at Tessa's."

"That's good; he can protect them," Vickie said.

"I guess." Margie's eyebrows rose in reluctant approval. "He bought daisies."

Vickie put her hand to her chest. "Ohhhh! His love is loyal and pure!"

"Eh. Maybe." Margie dropped her pizza on her plate. "I just don't trust him. After what he did to Tessa, I wanted to kill him. And now here he's back after all these years, and . . ." Margie took a big swallow of her drink. "I don't trust him."

"You don't *forgive* him," Vickie said. "Give him credit where credit's due. He did save my store."

Margie rolled her eyes.

"And he bought daisies."

Margie gave a grudging shrug. "And he took in Bitsy."

"Oh, honey." Vickie winced. "You've gotta stop calling that mutt Bitsy. It's got a penis. Give it some dignity."

Margie took a bite of her pizza, chewed thoughtfully for a moment, then spoke. "If that boy hurts Tessa again, I'll hunt him down and kill him, I swear I will."

"Oh, please. You will not. You'll do exactly what you did last time—be there for Tessa." Vickie paused for a moment before saying what she had to say next. "Besides, I think we've got bigger things to worry about."

Margie's eyes met Vickie's, and her face darkened.

"What are we gonna do now?"

"I don't know. I've been trying to formulate a plan B, but considering how stupid plan A was . . ."

"It wasn't stupid," Margie said. "He did try to burn your place down. We just didn't catch him."

"Which was the whole point of plan A, if I recall," Vickie said. "The part where we catch the bastard."

"Look, I said I was sorry," Margie said. "I realize now I'm too old to be doing stakeouts." She shrugged. "But at least we know he got in there between the hours of three and six. That's something."

Between the hours of what? "I thought you said you only fell asleep for twenty minutes."

Margie refused to meet Vickie's eyes. "Are we gonna argue about details, or are we gonna figure out a way to catch that asshole? People are beginning to seriously wonder where you are. And I'm getting nervous. I told Finn you were in Bimini."

"Bimini?" Vickie had to laugh. "Why the hell would I go to Bimini?"

"I don't know," Margie whined. "I was under pressure, and he was looking at me like he didn't believe me, and I'm a terrible, terrible liar. You know that. I wasn't supposed to be getting questioned by people. That was not in the plan. Now, if he looks into it, he'll find out you're not there and . . ."

"Finn's the least of our problems." Vickie downed another swig of her drink. The vodka went right where it was supposed to, and she smiled. "Do you think it's possible we're not catching Matt Tarpey because we're getting drunk every night?"

Margie paused with her drink half lifted, raised an eyebrow and smiled, then sallied forth and downed a large swallow.

"You know," Vickie said for probably the tenth time in the last two days, "Finn *is* a private detective. And we're both too old and too drunk to pull this crap off on our own. I think we've pretty much proven that." She paused, then swung for the fence. "I really think we should consider bringing Finn in on this and letting him nail the bastard."

"Maybe," Margie said, looking unconvinced.

Vickie sat back. A "maybe" was progress. Every night prior, Margie had responded to Vickie's sensible suggestion with rounds of creative cursing. Man, that woman could hold a grudge like no one Vickie had ever known.

"You know we're gonna need help," Vickie said. "I can't hide out in this basement forever."

"I know." Margie paused for a moment, her expression troubled. "Izzy was acting weird again today at work. I don't know what she's up to, but I'm worried about her. If Matt Tarpey realizes it's Izzy and not us who's been snooping around—"

"He won't," Vickie said. "We'll just have to keep his attention on us, and draw him out before he can suspect Izzy knows anything. And if Finn's staying with Tessa and Izzy, it's even more reason to let him in on everything. It'll be easier to protect them if he knows who he's protecting them from."

Margie made a face and took another bite of pizza. There was a long moment of silence as Vickie remembered back to a night a lot like this one, when she and Margie and Karen Scuderi all sat around a pizza box, throwing out theories on who had started the mysterious string of fires in Lucy's Lake, spanning seven years. Karen had suggested Matt Tarpey as a joke. After all, anyone who'd ever read a pulp novel would know it had to be the fire chief behind everything. However, even after the fire at Karen's, they weren't sure. And at that point, they didn't care. Their best friend had died, and they decided it was time to let the amateur snooping go and make up for their stupidity the only way they could—by keeping eagle eyes on Tessa and Izzy.

Until, that was, Izzy started snooping around. She'd asked both Vickie and Margie casual questions about the fire that took her mother, and then Vickie's worry box went missing for a day or so before mysteriously returning to her closet. It was then that Vickie and Margie had retreated to the basement with a bottle of scotch and came up with the plan of smoking Tarpey out with a classified ad placed in the *Lucy's Lake Weekly*.

M. I know what you did. V.

And it worked, better than Vickie ever thought it would. Unfortunately, all she had to show for it was a charred office. No proof.

Vickie sighed. She'd done too much thinking in the past few days, and it was beginning to give her a headache. She needed to let it go for a little while.

She pushed up from the futon and plodded across the room to Margie's laundry closet. From the top shelf, behind the Bounce dryer sheets, she pulled out a small wooden box. On her way back to the futon, she caught Margie's eye, and they shared a knowing look. Margie grabbed a pen and a small pad of notepaper from the small table next to the futon and began scribbling. She snapped one page off and handed it to Vickie.

Izzy. Vickie folded it and tucked it in. Margie handed her another page.

Tessa. Vickie stuffed it in the box, then looked to Margie, who had stubbornly set the pen and pad of paper down on the coffee table. Vickie rolled her eyes and picked up the pen.

"You and your stupid grudges," she grumbled, scribbling the last name down.

Finn.

She folded the last paper up and put it in. She closed the box, said a private prayer over it, and tucked it under the futon.

Margie pointed the remote at the television, flicking through the channels until they landed on the BBC production of *Pride and Prejudice* playing on A&E. The two friends shared a knowing smile, sat back, and quietly let Darcy take them away.

Just another day in the basement, Vickie thought, *as two middle-aged women pass the time waiting for a psycho to strike.*

Chapter Seventeen

Joe sat at his kitchen table eating a bowl of Wheaties and stared at the spread before him. He'd looked at the pictures from Karen Scuderi's fire so often during the years that he probably wouldn't see anything new even if there was something to see. He pretty much had every detail memorized by now: the charred craft supplies, the curled wallpaper, the barely recognizable defective coffeemaker that was at fault for the whole thing. It had been recalled just a month before the fire, but Karen had apparently never registered her purchase with the company, and therefore never received the recall notice.

It was an accident, just like the other twelve fires caused that year across the country by the same coffeemaker. Of course, none of them had resulted in anything worse than charred linoleum.

This one had resulted in Karen Scuderi's death.

If you've got a thing for Tessa, buy her some flowers. Don't dig up her dead mother. It isn't romantic. He could hear Matt Tarpey's voice as clearly as if he were in the room. And damned if the man didn't speak some sense.

There was nothing in those pictures that hadn't been there before, and there was nothing he could do that would make Tessa see him as anything other than the brother of the guy she really wanted.

Joe pushed himself up from the table and put his bowl and spoon in the sink, washing them absently as he wondered what he was doing. The thing with Tessa had been short-lived, and a long time ago. He'd moved on, she'd moved on, and the two of them had been doomed from the start, anyway.

So if it wasn't for her, why was he doing this? Why was he so obsessed with the fire that preceded Karen Scuderi's death? He leaned over his counter and stared at his own coffeemaker, trying to remember if he'd registered it or not. It was amazing how many thoughtless decisions could lead to disaster. You buy an innocent appliance one day, the next day it kills you.

Coffee.

Something buzzed in his brain and he couldn't quite place it. He stood up and looked at the pictures from the slightly greater distance. Then he took some steps backward until he was leaning against the wall and the pictures were too far away to get any good detail.

Coffee. It was the coffee that bugged him. Something about the coffee.

Next to him, in the corner of the dining room, a squawk sounded. Joe looked down at the cage on the floor, housing the macaw. Its chest was a brilliant gold, its face a strange white-and-black zebra pattern, and the wings and back feathers were a bright shade of blue he'd seen only in crayon boxes. It was a pretty bird, but it looked kind of . . . well, pissed off. Could a bird look pissed off? Joe leaned down to get a better look and the thing squawked at him and flapped its wings violently.

Yep. Definitely pissed off. Maybe it was hungry. Or thirsty. He'd picked it up from Tarpey's place yesterday afternoon, then left it in the corner of the dining room with a handful of seed and a small cup of fresh water, but he didn't know what else he was supposed to do for it. He was an electrician. What the hell did he know about parrots?

Maybe he should find another foster family. Of course, the perfect one came to mind immediately, and he instantly decided against it. He was sure there were other people in town who could take in the bird. If he brought that bird over, it would just be an excuse to see her, and he wasn't desperate or stupid enough to keep trying with Tessa.

Buy her flowers. Dig up her dead mother. Give her a bird. It doesn't matter. Far as she's concerned, you're a eunuch.

Well, that was true enough. And he did need to find someone to foster that bird . . .

"What do you think?" he said to the bird. "You wanna go live with a couple of cute girls? Gotta be better company than me, right?"

The macaw answered this by turning its back on Joe and taking a huge dump on the newspaper that lined the bottom of the cage.

"Yeah," Joe said, turning his attention back to the kitchen table. "That's what I . . ."

He trailed off.

The coffee. Or the coffeemaker, rather. He leaned in, looked closer at the picture.

That wasn't Karen Scuderi's coffeemaker. At least, he didn't think it was. It was a long time ago, and he couldn't really remember for sure, but there was one person who might.

Joe stuffed the pictures into the manila envelope, lifted his coat off the back of the kitchen chair, and grabbed the birdcage to a resounding squawk of annoyance from the macaw.

"Cute girls," Joe said, tucking the envelope under his arm as he pulled the front door open. "Quit your bitchin'."

Finn woke up to the sounds of pans clattering in the kitchen. He rolled over on the sofa and tried to go back to sleep, but it was no use.

Something smelled good. Must be Tessa cooking.

Tessa. The woman was definitely going to be the death of him. They'd spent yesterday afternoon calling every hotel in Bimini, and with all the fire and death and mayhem hanging over them, all he could think about was taking her up to the bedroom and making her forget her own name.

But he didn't. Instead, he made call after call to hotel after hotel, and came up with one very interesting, though not really surprising, fact: Vickie Kemp wasn't registered at any hotel in Bimini. Finn's gut told him that Margie Fletcher was lying, which led to another interesting question—why?

But it wasn't a question either he or Tessa had the energy to try to answer last night, though. Instead, they'd talked around things for a while, had a quick dinner with Izzy and Babs, and then Tessa had gone to bed.

Finn spent the night on the sofa, tossing and turning and trying to think of any excuse good enough to get him upstairs and into her room. Twice that night he'd made it as far as the landing on the stairs before turning around and going back to Sofa City.

Aside from the fact that Tessa had her fight back—which turned him on even more, if that was possible—nothing else had changed since yesterday. If Tessa was really going to take that social worker on, the last thing she needed was to be associated with a bird thief, reformed or not. The best way Finn could help Tessa defeat Mary Ellen Neeley was to distance himself as much as possible.

Hell, it was the only way he could help her.

He sat up and ran his hands over his crumpled jeans and T-shirt. He'd never been a pajamas kind of guy, and sleeping on a sofa in a house full of women was no place to go *au naturel*. He got up and shuffled through the living room and through the kitchen door to find Babs standing at the stove, humming to herself. She was wearing a fluffy apron over her blouse and slacks, and appeared happy as a pig in shit, which with Babs usually meant trouble of some sort.

"Oh, Christ," he groaned. "You're cooking again? Tessa told me what happened yesterday."

Babs grinned. "Good morning to you, too, Mr. Grump."

She lifted the cast-iron skillet and slid its contents—two eggs, over easy—onto a plate that already sported a few perfectly cooked bacon strips.

Finn raised one eyebrow. "That actually looks good."

Babs nodded toward the kitchen table. "Tastes good, too. Sit down."

He did as ordered, and Babs put the plate down in front of him, twirling back toward the counter to retrieve a fork.

"You made this?" Finn said, looking down at the food.

"What happened to the family curse, Aunt Clarice and whatnot?"

"It's Aunt Corrine," Babs corrected, sitting down at the table across from Finn. "And your uncle is what happened." She nodded toward the plate. "Go on, you big coward. Give it a try."

Finn picked up the fork, separated a bit of egg and some bacon, and put the combo in his mouth.

"Wow," he said, amazed at how good it was. "So . . . what? Max taught you how to cook?"

Babs nodded, hopped up, and moved back to the stove. "It was slow last night, and he showed me a few things." She took two eggs out of the carton, cracked them simultaneously with one hand, and sent them sizzling onto the skillet. "He's an amazing man, your uncle."

Finn took another bite. "Yeah, he's gotta be if he can teach you to cook."

"I know," she said. "It's unbelievable, isn't it? It was like, he explained things to me and suddenly—" She snapped her fingers over her head. "I got it."

"That's . . . that's amazing," Finn said.

"Which reminds me, I hardly harangued you at all yesterday about your relationship with your uncle, which means I have loads to make up for today."

The doorbell rang and Finn hopped up. "Hold that thought. Or, actually, dump that thought and get a new one. I'm gonna answer the door."

"You can't avoid this forever," she called after him as he zipped through the swinging kitchen door. Finn ignored her, licking a bit of bacon off his thumb and crossing through the foyer to the front door.

And of all the things he might have expected to see on

the other side, his brother holding a birdcage with the macaw in it was not one of them.

"Hey, it's not my birthday," Finn said.

Joe looked at him, his eyes narrowing. "What are you doing here?"

"No room at the inn," Finn said. "What are you doing here?"

"I need someone to foster the macaw until we get a hold of Vickie Kemp," he said.

Finn smiled. "Well, come on in, then."

Joe eyed Finn warily for a moment, then stepped inside.

"I also have something I need to talk to Tessa about," he said.

Finn worked up a subtly smug expression. "She's still in bed. Maybe I can relay a message for you?"

Joe raised an eyebrow at Finn, and Finn raised one back. He knew Tessa would very likely kick his ass six ways from Sunday for insinuating to anyone in town, let alone Joe, that there was anything going on between them, but it had been ten years since he'd had any opportunity to aggravate Joe. He had a lot of lost time to make up for.

"No," Joe said finally. "I need to speak to her in person."

At that moment, footsteps thundered down the steps, and Tessa came flying down, pulling a flannel robe on over her sleep set of a concert T-shirt and a pair of lounge pants. Her eyes were half-open, and her hair was all lopsided, and he really wanted to take her back up to that bedroom and . . .

"Who's cooking?" she said as she landed at the bottom

of the steps. "And why? No one cooks. Those are the rules. My rules. No cooking."

Finn put one hand on her shoulder. "It's okay. Babs had some sort of religious experience last night, and now she can cook without burning anything down."

"Oh." Tessa blinked, looked at Joe, then glanced down at the cage. The macaw squawked. "You brought me a bird?"

"Uh, yeah," Joe said. "Actually, I kinda need to find someone to foster it and—"

"Well, Joe! Good morning!" Babs's voice cut him off as she came out from the kitchen, wiping her hands on her apron. She caught sight of the bird, squealed with delight, and clapped her hands.

Joe exchanged a look with Finn. Finn shrugged.

"She's a morning person," he said.

"What a beautiful bird!" She bent down and made some kind of weird smooching noises at the thing, to which it oddly seemed to respond. Babs straightened and grinned at Joe. "What's its name?"

Joe hesitated for a moment. "Um. I dunno. Bird."

"Oh!" Babs said. "That's no kind of name for a gorgeous little thing like this. How about Honey?"

"Honey?" Finn asked flatly.

Babs bent over and made some more clicking noises as she took the cage from Joe. "Isn't that right, Honey? You like that name, don't you?"

The bird squawked and seemed happy enough. Tessa turned to Joe. "Guess you've found your foster family."

"Yes, absolutely," Babs said. "And you couldn't have found a better one. Finn is a bird expert."

Joe shot a skeptical look at Finn. "You're an expert?"

Finn shrugged. "Define *expert*."

"Joe," Babs said cheerfully, "I am so glad you stopped by. Your uncle has been telling me all about you."

Joe's surprise registered on his face. "He has? Max? Has been talking?"

Babs shook her head at the brothers. "You two. For the boys he raised into men, one would think you'd know the man a little better. Would you like some bacon and eggs, Joe? Fresh off the griddle."

"Thanks. No. I've already had breakfast." He leaned toward Tessa and spoke in low tones, but Finn could still hear him. "Do you think we could talk about something? Privately?"

Finn felt an odd stab of territorialism. Sure, he was planning on taking off and leaving her forever, but not yet. What, Joe couldn't wait till the skidmarks were cold?

"Sure, Joe," Tessa said, rubbing her hands over her eyes. "Can I get some coffee first?"

"Absolutely!" Babs turned back toward the kitchen, squawking bird in tow. "Coffee for everyone!"

No one followed Babs, but she didn't seem to mind. Finn could hear her humming and clattering away in the kitchen like the madwoman she was, and he couldn't help but smile. The woman was six different kinds of crazy, but it was part of her charm.

"Actually," Joe said, watching the kitchen door with a slight expression of bewilderment, "I have to get to work, and it's just a quick question." He shot a distrustful look at Finn before turning his attention back to Tessa. "It's about your mom."

Tessa's eyes widened, and Finn could see that Joe's bomb was waking her up.

"What about her?" Tessa asked.

Joe shot another look at Finn. "Maybe we should talk in private."

"Maybe you shouldn't," Finn said.

"This doesn't concern you," Joe said.

"Does if it relates to my case."

"Your *case*?"

"I'm investigating the fires."

Joe cocked his head to the side. "Yeah? Who hired you?"

"Can't tell you."

"Why not?"

Finn leaned forward in mock discretion. "Client confidentiality."

"Oh, hell." Tessa rolled her eyes. "Joe, Izzy hired him."

Joe scoffed. "*Izzy* hired you? What's she paying you with, Girl Scout cookies?"

"Samoas, actually. Doesn't make it any less my case."

Joe rubbed his forehead, letting out a sigh of frustration. "Okay. Fine." He turned to Tessa. "Do you remember the coffeemaker your mom had at the shop?"

It was Finn's turn to scoff. "That's the big private question you had to ask her?"

Tessa shot him a *shut up* look. He shut up. She turned to Joe. "Yeah. I remember it. Why?"

Joe shook his head. "Look, this is gonna sound weird, but . . . didn't she break it?"

Tessa thought for a moment, then smiled. "Oh, my God. I'd totally forgotten about that."

Joe smiled back. "It was that Saturday I was helping out at the store . . ."

Tessa laughed. "Right! The day Mom burned her hand with the glue gun."

"Yeah, and she went to make some coffee and broke the top off the well, right?"

"Yeah." Tessa giggled. "And then she kept cursing the coffeemaker out and then Randy Williams came in with little Jana, who was like three at the time—"

Joe laughed harder. "And she kept repeating after your mom"—Joe's voice went high-pitched—"'Fucking coffeemaker! Fucking coffeemaker!'"

The two of them laughed comfortably together, like old friends. Which, of course, was exactly what they were. Joe had been here, all these years, and had developed a relationship with Tessa that was independent of Finn. Big deal. It was only natural. This knowledge, however, did nothing to lessen Finn's desire to throw his brother through the front window; in fact it was growing stronger by the moment.

Finally, Tessa's laughter subsided, and she looked at Joe, her eyes serious. "So, what's with the coffeemaker?"

Joe looked from Finn to Tessa and headed toward the dining room, motioning for them to follow. Tessa gave Finn a questioning look, which Finn ignored, still rankled by the buddy-buddy display he'd just witnessed.

"Oh, Christ," Tessa muttered. By the time they caught up to Joe, he had already pulled some pictures from a manila envelope and laid them out flat on the table. He pointed to one of them.

"That was only about a week before the fire. Did your mother get a new coffeemaker?" he asked.

Tessa leaned over the photo, examined it for a few seconds, then shook her head and looked at Finn.

"I don't think so." She pointed to a detail on the picture. "And this one doesn't have a clock display. She wouldn't have bought one without a clock display."

Finn leaned over the pictures, spreading them out on the table. "Where'd you get these?"

"Matt Tarpey made a call to County for me so I could get a look at the files," Joe said. "Something has bugged me about that fire since day one, but I could never put my finger on it."

Finn clapped his hand down on his brother's shoulder. "Congratulations, bro. It only took ten years, but I think that's exactly what you just did." He leaned over the photos. "They determined it was the coffeemaker that started the fire?"

Joe nodded. "Yeah, it had just been recalled. For shorting out and catching on fire."

"So someone planted it in Mom's shop," Tessa said.

"Could be the same someone who put that insane array of extension cords in Vickie Kemp's office," Finn said. "A fire inspector sees that, they wouldn't necessarily look any deeper. Right?"

Joe looked from Finn to Tessa, then back to Finn. "You think Vickie's fire is related to Karen's?"

"That's the prevailing theory, yeah," Tessa said.

Joe nodded. "I think so, too. I think Matt Tarpey has suspicions as well. The case went to the county Cause and Origin team, but I saw some pictures he'd taken himself in his office."

"Great," Tessa said. "What are we gonna do about it?"

"Gee," Finn said, his voice dripping with sarcasm. "I don't know. Maybe . . . and I'm just free-associating here . . . go to the police?"

Tessa closed her eyes and sighed.

"What?" Joe said, looking back and forth between Finn and Tessa. "Look, you know I'd be the last one to say this, but I think Finn's making sense."

"We can't go to the police," Tessa said. "We don't have enough evidence, and Izzy kinda bent a few laws getting us what we do have. I don't want her in trouble."

Joe let out an exasperated sigh and looked to Finn, who held up his hands.

"Preachin' to the choir, bro."

"All right," Joe said. "What are you thinking? You're gonna just go after this guy yourselves? That's just stupid."

"Hey, just a minute there—," Finn started, then looked to Tessa. "Oh, no. Wait. He's right. 'Magine that."

"I'm not saying go after the bad guy ourselves," Tessa said. "I'm saying get something more substantial than my memory of my mother's coffeemaker. If we give the police strong enough evidence, they can take it from there. But right now, if we give them what we've got, they're only going to ask questions about Izzy, and I can't risk the knowledge of her involvement getting out to whoever's doing this."

"So," Finn said, looking at Joe. "It's quite a quandary. If only we knew someone who had access to privileged information . . ."

He focused on Joe, and counted internally.

One . . . two . . . three . . .

Joe's eyes widened.

Bingo.

"What?" Joe said. "Me? What do you want me to do?"

"I don't know," Finn said. "For starters, maybe break into Matt Tarpey's office and get us those pictures of his?

Then, on your way home, you could pick up a pizza or something."

Joe laughed. "Break in?" His eyes connected with Finn's and he stopped laughing. "You're serious?"

"As a heart attack."

Joe looked at Tessa, then back at Finn. "I'm not going to break into his office. Why don't I just ask him?"

"Because we don't have time to fart around playing *Mother, May I?*" Finn said.

"No," Joe said firmly, looking at Finn. "I don't do stuff like that. That's your area. You do it."

"I'd love to," Finn said. "But I don't know that place near as well as you do. And if you get caught there, it's easier to create a cover story."

"You two could go together," Tessa said.

"No," Joe and Finn said in unison.

"Fine," Tessa said, gathering up the pictures on the table. "Then I'll do it."

"Yeah, right," Finn said, as Joe said, "No way."

Joe grabbed the pictures from Tessa and tucked them in the envelope, then turned to Finn, the displeasure on his face crystal clear. Not great at masking the emotions, that Joe.

"Tarpey usually leaves the office around six," he bit out after a few moments.

Finn grinned at his brother. "Wear something black."

Joe grumbled something rude under his breath and shook his head.

"If I go to jail," he said, shooting a harsh look at Finn, "I am so going to kick your ass."

Chapter Eighteen

Izzy put the last of the potted baby roses on the Valentine's display table in the middle of the gift shop, then wiped her hands on her apron. She glanced at the clock; it was 3:05. Quitting time was usually around three.

Not that there was any big rush to go home. It wasn't like she was going to be included in anything, anyway. She'd woken up that morning to Babs singing and cooking in the kitchen, Tessa and Finn looking tense but pretending nothing was going on, and some weird bird sitting in a cage in the living room. Izzy asked a couple of questions about what was happening, and received three variations on the simple but classic, "Eat your breakfast and get to school."

Part of her felt better that she'd told everyone what she knew. Sorta like a weight had been lifted. But now, she was just a kid again, on the outside. Nothing to offer, nothing to do but lie low and be protected.

Pffffft. Boring.

She pulled the strings on her apron loose and headed out toward the front. Margie was finishing up with a customer, so Izzy waited until she was done before leaning forward and tapping the counter with her fingertips to get Margie's attention.

"I'm gonna head on out," Izzy said. "If I don't get home on time, Tessa'll freak."

"Oh." Margie bit her lip. "Okay. I actually . . . I had something . . ." She leaned over the counter, looked around. Izzy looked, too. There was nobody there. February in Vermont on a weekday—not a huge crunch time for a nursery. Margie looked back at Izzy, her face crinkled in thought. Izzy stood up straight.

"What?"

Margie held up her index finger, sped around the counter, locked the front door, and flicked the OPEN/CLOSED sign to CLOSED.

"Margie—what?"

Margie held up her finger again, hurried back to Izzy, grabbed her by the hand, and led her through the back door of the greenhouse, locking that behind her as well.

"Margie," Izzy said as Margie led her up the short path that connected the greenhouse with Margie's house. "What's going on?"

"You'll see in just a minute," Margie said.

Two minutes later, they were headed down the stairs into Margie's basement, and Izzy was starting to get a little creeped out.

"Margie, I really think Tessa might start to—"

Izzy stopped talking as they hit the bottom step. The basement . . . It was . . . crazy. Bright orange floors. A weird avocado green minibar in the corner. A big futon. Beanbag chairs. And . . .

"Oh, my God, is that a *disco ball*?" Izzy said, pointing

to the sparkly sphere hanging from the middle of the ceiling.

"Yes," Margie said, "but that's not what I brought you here to show you. Vick!"

It was then that Izzy noticed a door slightly ajar at the back of the room, and the sound of running water.

"Just a minute," a voice came from behind the door. There was the sound of spitting, and then the water turned off.

"I was brushing my teeth. Jesus cannoli, can't a girl brush her—"

Vickie Kemp stopped midsentence as her eyes fell on Izzy. Izzy felt her mouth drop open in similar surprise.

"Hey, Vickie," Izzy said. "Have you been in Margie's basement all this time?"

Vickie smiled at her, then turned a significantly less pleased expression on Margie.

"So, this is your plan B?" Vickie said.

Margie nodded, put one arm around Izzy's shoulders. "If she's smart enough to get this whole ball rolling, well, then she's smart enough to help us stop it."

Izzy felt pride swell in her chest.

She was smart.

They needed her help.

She was plan B.

Vickie crossed her arms over her stomach, then finally smiled and nodded.

"All right, fine." She looked at Izzy. "You'd better call Tessa first, honey. You're gonna be here awhile."

Tessa sat on her sofa, watching two stupid Irish brothers bicker like a couple of old church ladies.

"I told you to be inconspicuous," Finn said, motioning at Joe's top-to-bottom black outfit—knit cap, coat, turtleneck, jeans, boots, all dark as pitch.

"You said wear *black*," Joe said. "So I wore black."

"It was a joke," Finn said. "I was being ironic. I didn't mean it literally."

"Then you shouldn't have *said* it literally," Joe said. "I'm not a criminal. I never got the criminal codebook where 'black' means 'inconspicuous.' "

"I'm not a criminal, either," Finn said. Joe raised an eyebrow and Finn added, "Anymore."

"Speaking of which," Joe said, "what the hell have you been doing all these years, anyway? And don't try to sell me that private detective crap, because I don't buy that for a minute."

Finn's eyes widened. "You want *me* to explain myself to *you*? You look like a fucking ninja on holiday."

Tessa glanced at the clock: 5:47. This had been going on for eight minutes, and there was no end in sight.

"And what the hell is this?" Finn said, pointing to the big white canvas laundry bag Joe had slung over his shoulder.

"If there's evidence, we're gonna need something to carry it in," Joe said.

Finn flicked a finger at the tremendous bag. "What kind of evidence are you planning on taking? You think we're gonna find a confession scribbled on some dry cleaning?"

Tessa patted the sofa a couple of times as an invite to Wallace, who accepted it without a moment's hesitation. She looked down at him and made a kissy face, and he slobbered all over her. She wiped her face on her sleeve and scratched his head as they watched Finn and Joe dig in for another round.

"I don't know what kind of evidence we're going to get," Joe said. "I'm an electrician. This isn't the kind of thing I do on a regular basis."

"What the hell does being an electrician have to do with not having common fucking sense?"

"Any more of this," Tessa said to Wallace in cutesy tones, "I'm going to have to go find a fork and stab myself with it."

Wallace licked her face again.

"Whatever, man," Finn said, dismissing his brother and turning to Tessa with a *Do you believe this guy?* expression.

Tessa sighed and pushed herself up from the sofa. "Do you girls think you could possibly put aside your catfight long enough to get this done? Because you're both starting to freak me out."

Finn huffed and gestured to indicate Joe's ninja-on-holiday outfit, as though that was all the defense he needed. Tessa put her hand to her forehead.

"Look, just . . ." She glanced at the clock. "Go now."

Finn checked his watch. "Might as well."

"But Tarpey's probably still there," Joe said.

Finn sighed heavily and spoke to Joe with a tone most people reserved for petulant toddlers. "That's why we wait outside, in the car. We watch him leave, we'll know he's gone, then we go inside."

"You can do this by yourself, you know," Joe said. "I don't have to help you, you freakin' leprechaun. What is up with the hair, anyway?"

Finn's eyes went wide and Tessa stepped in between them.

"You know what, guys?" Tessa said. "Just go. Izzy's gonna be home from dinner at Margie's soon and . . ." She looked at Joe. "I don't want her getting weirded out by you two."

"He said wear black!" Joe said.

"I *meant*—," Finn started, but Tessa grabbed his hand and squeezed it to silence him.

"Joe, would you go warm up the car, please?" She reached into her pocket and gave him her keys. "Take the Mazda. It's the darkest-colored car we've got."

Joe looked from Tessa to Finn, then took the keys, slung the laundry bag over his shoulder, and left. Tessa turned to Finn.

"Look—," she started.

Finn rolled his eyes. "Yeah, I know. *Be safe. Don't kill your brother. Wear clean underwear.*"

"I love you," she said, pushing the words so they got out before she lost her nerve.

Finn went quiet. That wasn't encouraging, but she'd already started. There was no point in stopping now.

"All right . . . ," she stammered. "Yeah, okay, that was sudden and awkward but . . ."

"No," he said. "It's just . . . you know. Got a little whiplash going from 'You're freaking me out,' to . . ." He paused and looked at her. "Well. You know."

She sighed and regrouped. "Remember the day you brought me the Tootsie Rolls?"

"Yeah." Finn laughed lightly. "You remember that?"

She nodded, feeling the tears threatening as the memories rushed through her. Man, cry once, and suddenly it's Niagara Falls. She bit the inside of her cheek, pushed back the weepy, and kept going.

"Since that day," she said, "I have loved you. I loved you when we were growing up, I loved you when you left, and I loved you while you were gone. I tried not to, lots of times I wished I didn't, but I did. And, God help me, I still do."

Finn opened his mouth, but didn't say anything. Great. The one man with an answer for everything, and she'd rendered him mute with her *looooooooooove*. She wanted to roll her eyes and make a joke, push all this back to the depths she'd kept it hidden in all these years, but she didn't.

She was a grown-up, damnit, and she was going to act like one.

"I just wanted it said," she added quickly. "I don't know when you're going to disappear again. I don't know if you're going to send Joe back with whatever you get and take off . . ."

Something flashed on Finn's face. She gasped and hit his shoulder.

"Oh, my God, you were gonna send Joe back and take off?"

Finn huffed. "All right. Yeah, I thought about it, okay? Tessa, every minute we're together, it's just . . ." He sighed and met her eyes. "It's only gonna make things harder."

Tessa wanted really badly to slug him one, but she didn't. She was a grown-up. Instead, she crossed her arms over her chest and narrowed her eyes at him.

"You know what? I take it back. I don't love you. You're stupid."

Finn nodded, his expression hard. Tessa sighed. *Grown-up. Be a grown-up.*

"Oh, crap," she whined. "I don't mean that. I mean, yeah, you're stupid, but I still . . ."

Finn reached up and put his hand on her face, his thumb caressing her cheek as he pressed his forehead to hers.

"Five tomatoes for a dollar," he said softly, his voice laced with an irony she could detect but didn't fully understand.

She pulled her head back.

"What the hell is that supposed to—?"

He kissed her softly, one hand cradling her face as the other wrapped around her waist, pulling her to him with gentle need. He stopped, took a breath, then kissed her again, this time with force and desire and nothing held back. Tessa stopped thinking, stopped worrying, just let herself fall into the kiss and the *zing,* because damnit, she needed some *zing.* She'd earned herself some *zing.*

A moment later, when they broke the kiss, she rested her hands on the back of his neck and breathed in deep.

"You come back to me tonight," she said, "or I swear I will hunt you down like the dog you are."

A horn blared from the street. Tessa laughed. Finn closed his eyes and cursed.

"I really hate that guy," he said.

"No, you don't," Tessa said.

He looked at her, his eyes crinkling at the edges as he smiled.

"I'll be back," he said.

"You'd better," she whispered.

Tessa watched him leave, and in that moment, she understood the *zing.* She understood that it was rare, and precious, and she finally understood why she'd never been able to re-create it with anyone else.

Because Finn was The One. He was her Soul Mate, he was her Destiny, he was all those things she'd never wanted to believe in because they were all dorky as hell. But she was tired of fighting off what she didn't want. The time had finally come for her to start fighting for what she wanted, and if that meant she had to fight Finn to keep the *zing* . . .

Well, then. So be it.

Sosie McGovern stood on Uncle Matt and Aunt Grace's porch, staring at the doorbell.

Just do it, she thought. *Just tell them and if Izzy gets mad, Izzy gets mad.*

She nibbled on her lip and sighed. Izzy wasn't going to be just mad. She was going to be furious. Telling this secret was a very serious breach of the best friend code, and Izzy would probably never speak to Sosie again. But last night, when Sosie had told her mother some of the basics without revealing any specifics, her mother had said that a real friend does what's right, even if it means losing a friend. And it wasn't right to let Izzy get into trouble over this when Sosie could get her some help. And who better to help Izzy than Uncle Matt?

No one. That's who.

Sosie had been worried about Izzy ever since that day in the bathroom, when they discovered that Izzy's mom had been killed by a nut job. What if that pyro/psycho found Izzy and hurt her? Sosie would never be able to forgive herself for keeping quiet.

So, okay, she thought as she raised her finger to hit the button. *Just do it.*

She pulled her hand down. She couldn't. It wasn't right. Maybe what she needed to do was talk to Izzy, convince Izzy to tell Uncle Matt. That made sense. And it wouldn't break the code, and she wouldn't lose her best friend . . .

The porch light switched on, and a moment later Aunt Grace pulled the door open.

"I thought I heard someone out here," Aunt Grace said, her smile fading as she looked at Sosie. "Sosie? Baby? What's wrong?"

Sosie sighed, felt her chin start to quiver. She didn't know what to do. She just didn't know what to do. She didn't want a psycho/pyro to kill her best friend, but she didn't want to lose her best friend, either.

"I don't know what to do," she squeaked at her aunt.

Aunt Grace reached out and put her arm around Sosie's shoulder. "You come on in and I'll get you some cookies, okay? And then you can tell me all about it."

Sosie smiled, and let her aunt guide her inside, comforted by the familiar scent of gardenias in her aunt Grace's perfume.

Chapter Nineteen

Finn leaned forward and glanced up to the nondescript two-story concrete box of an office building they were staking out. Tarpey's office was on the second floor, three in from the back. The light was still on. He glanced at the clock in the dash.

6:01. He'd been in the car with his brother less than ten minutes. And it felt like forever. He seriously couldn't believe glaciers hadn't formed and melted back into the ocean in just the time he'd been sitting in this car. And the longer he just sat, staring at the building, the more he thought of Tessa and how much he wanted to get back to her.

Which wasn't good. There was a world of hurt waiting there, and now that she'd lain her little confession at his feet, he knew he didn't have only his hurt to worry about. He took a deep breath and decided to focus on the task at hand.

"So, why isn't Tarpey's office at the fire station?" Finn asked.

Joe shrugged. "There's barely enough room there for

the truck and the guys on call. Town puts him up here, but there are grumblings that they're gonna build a new fire station sometime in the next few years. Which will be great, because the electrical setup in that place is old as hell. I wouldn't be surprised if it goes up—" Joe shrugged off Finn's look. "What? You don't want an answer, don't ask the question."

"You're right," Finn said, leaning back against the headrest and closing his eyes. "Wake me up when Tarpey comes out."

"No," Joe said. "Why do you get to sleep?"

Finn opened his eyes. "Fine. You wanna sleep, you sleep. I'll keep an eye out for Tarpey."

"Okay." Joe leaned his head back, closed his eyes for a second, then raised his head again. "I can't sleep. You sure you know what you're doing?"

Finn sighed. "Did I give you a plan?"

"Yeah," Joe bit out reluctantly.

"Then what's the plan?"

Joe paused for a moment, then said, "I tell the guard that I need to return this to Matt." He held up the manila envelope. "And that I'm just gonna shove it under the door."

"Check that out, folks. He can be taught."

"Yeah, that's fine for getting upstairs, but how are we gonna get into his office? I don't have a key."

Finn rubbed his thumb and index finger over his brow, trying to keep the brother-induced headache at bay. "We don't need a key."

"What are you gonna do, bust the door down?"

Finn stared at him for a moment, then declined to answer on the basis that that was the stupidest fucking question he'd ever been asked. Instead, he jerked his chin to indicate the building.

"You know the guard?"

Joe nodded. "Yeah. Gerard."

Finn gave a slow blink. "Gerard? The security guard's name is Gerard?"

"Yeah," Joe said. "And when we talk to him, speak up. He's a little hard of hearing."

Finn had to laugh at that one. "The security guard is *deaf*?"

Joe let out a rough sigh. "He's not deaf. He's hard of hearing."

Finn shook his head. "It's amazing this town hasn't been robbed blind."

"No, it's not. Because regular people live here. Regular people don't rob each other blind."

"It's fucking Mayberry, is what it is," Finn grumbled.

"Then leave," Joe said.

"Planning on it."

"When?"

Finn shot his brother a dark look. "When I'm ready."

Joe stared at the building and blinked. "Shit."

Finn glanced up. "What?"

Joe motioned up toward Tarpey's window. It was dark. "Did you see him leave the building?"

Finn took a deep breath and resisted the urge to knock his brother out. "No. Is his car here?"

Joe leaned forward and scanned the lot. "Don't see it."

"Oh, for Christ's sake." Finn yanked at his door handle and jumped out of the car. "You were supposed to be watching, idiot."

He heard the other door slam, followed by Joe's footsteps catching up to him.

"You think you can handle Gerald the deaf guard on your own, or do you need mc to hold your hand?" Finn asked.

"It's Gerard," Joe corrected.

Finn took a deep breath, pulled on a casual expression, and pushed into the lobby of the building, praying to God to give him the strength not to kill his brother before they got what they came for.

Afterward, though, all bets were off.

Tessa sat on her sofa, staring at the ceiling. Wallace sat by her side, his head resting on her knee, while she petted him absently.

I loved you when we were growing up, I loved you when you left, and I loved you while you were gone.

"Oh, God." She cringed, put her hand over her eyes. How was she ever going to face him again? What had she been thinking?

But most of all, why the hell didn't he say it back? And worse, when he did say something, it didn't make any sense. *Five tomatoes for a dollar?* What the hell was that supposed to mean?

She raised her head and looked at Wallace.

"What's up with men?" she asked. "He loves me. I know he does." She paused. "I think he does. He might." She nibbled her lip. "He does. He has to. If he doesn't, I'll kill him."

Quit worrying. He's crazy about you. He's just a big, dumb ass about it.

Tessa blinked. That was a male voice. In her head. She

didn't typically have male voices in her head. She looked at the dog, who just stared back at her, blinking his eyes and looking all puppy dog.

"Great," she said. "To top it all off, I'm losing my mind."

The front door burst open, and Wallace simply rolled on his side, exposing his belly for scratching.

"Some watchdog," she said as Izzy blew into the living room, followed by Margie and . . .

Holy shit.

Tessa hopped up off the sofa, sending Wallace flying with a small yap.

"Vickie!" She ran and threw herself into Vickie's arms. "When did you get back? We've been looking for you. I need to talk to you about some things."

"Vickie's been in Margie's basement all week," Izzy said, a bright smile on her face. "I'm plan B."

Tessa looked from her sister to Margie to Vickie, then back to Izzy.

"So you knew where she was the whole time?" she asked. "And what's plan B?"

"No, I just found out," Izzy said. "And I don't really know what plan B is."

"Plan B basically starts and ends with telling Izzy," Margie said, heading into the kitchen. "Where's your liquor? Still in the cabinet over the fridge?"

"What's left of it, anyway," Izzy said, just loud enough for Tessa to hear. Tessa shot her a look and they shared a smile.

"Come on in," Tessa said, motioning toward the sofa. Izzy sat next to Vickie, and Tessa took the rocking chair. Margie came back with two drinks, handing one to Vickie, and then paused as she was about to settle herself in the easy chair, completing the circle.

"I'm sorry, Tessa. Sometimes I forget you're of age. Would you like something?"

Tessa shook her head. "No, I just wanna know what's going on."

Izzy sighed and rolled her eyes. "This is where she's gonna try to send me upstairs."

Tessa looked at Izzy. "Why would I do that?"

"I'm too young. I'm too impressionable. My virgin ears. Etcetera."

"No way," Tessa said. "You started this whole thing, you're gonna stay and help me finish it."

Surprise washed over Izzy's face. "Really? You're not gonna try to protect me from all the harsh reality blah blah blah?"

Tessa reached over and squeezed Izzy's hand. "Baby doll, you are my harsh reality."

Izzy smiled, and her posture straightened. "Really?"

Tessa returned the smile and sat back. "Really."

"Cool."

"Besides, I'm assuming Lucy and Ethel here have already told you more than I know."

Vickie and Margie exchanged guilty glances.

"Yeah," Izzy said, the pride coming off her in waves. "They did."

"Well, then, we're all in," Tessa said, turning her focus on the older ladies. "Let's dish, girls."

Finn knelt down, his ear to the door as his trusty lock pick worked its magic. Two clicks down, working on the third . . .

"Aren't you done yet?" Joe said in a stage whisper.

Finn sighed, pulled the lock pick out, jiggled the door handle to reset the pins.

"There isn't any video surveillance, right?" Finn said in his regular voice.

"Right."

"We've established the floor is completely deserted, right?"

"Right."

"And Bernard is half deaf, right?"

"Gerard."

Finn shot Joe a harsh look.

Joe sighed. "Right."

"So relax and shut up so I can pick the fucking lock, okay?"

Joe grumbled something but went quiet. Finn put his ear to the door and started over.

Click.

Click.

He felt around, pushed the pick a bit to the left, then the right . . .

Click.

He stood up, turned the knob, and pushed into Matt Tarpey's office. It was dark and small and . . .

"Christ!" Finn yelled as he stumbled over something in the dark. "What the—"

"It's his office golf-putter thing," Joe whispered. "And be quiet!"

"Why?" Finn asked, kicking the putter thing back against the wall. "The guard is deaf."

"Hard of hearing," Joe said. "He's got an aid."

"Oh, well, in that case . . . ," Finn grumbled. Joe walked

over to Tarpey's desk and motioned to Finn. Finn pulled out his baby Maglite and tossed it to Joe, who caught it and flicked it on in one swift motion.

"The pictures aren't here," Joe said, sweeping the light over the clean desktop.

"Well, then, maybe he put them away. Where would he put them?"

"I don't know," Joe said. "I've never rummaged through the man's office before."

"Well, get cracking," Finn said, walking toward the filing cabinet in the corner. "You take the desk, I'll do this."

Finn pulled on the top drawer, and it opened easily. The fire chief didn't even lock his cabinet. Fucking Mayberry.

"Hand me the flashlight," Finn said.

"I'm using it," Joe said.

"Fine." Finn pulled up the shades, letting in some of the light from outside, and started riffling through the files.

"Here's what I don't understand," Joe said. "How is it that after everything you did and disappearing for ten years, she's still even talking to you, let alone letting you stay at her place?"

"It's my irresistible charm," Finn said. "And I told you I'm not talking about her with you."

Joe slammed one side drawer and opened another. "Fine, don't talk. Listen. Should be a shiny new experience for you."

Finn let out a curse under his breath and shut the top filing drawer.

"I'll give you a shiny new experience," Finn muttered.

"Go for it," Joe said.

Finn turned and looked at his brother. "Don't tempt me. I've been dying to knock that sanctimony off your face since the day I got back in town."

Joe straightened, shutting the second drawer with his knee.

"Go for it," Joe said.

Finn stared at his brother. "You gotta be kidding me. You wanna fight now? Here? No. Find the goddamn pictures. Then we can go out to the parking lot and I'll happily kick your ass all the way back to Tessa's."

Joe shook his head and moved to stand next to Finn. "That's fine. None of it matters anyway, because in a week, you'll be gone again. And I'll be here to pick up the pieces. Again."

Finn straightened up and took a step closer to his brother, his fist clenched at his side.

"Yeah? She hasn't wanted you for the last ten years, what makes you think she's gonna want you now?"

"Because, when you leave, she's gonna finally figure out that you were never anything but a waste of her time."

"And what the hell do you think you were?" Finn said. "Nothing but a distraction."

"Maybe," Joe said. "But don't worry. Soon as you're gone, I'll be happy to give her all the distraction she can handle."

That's when the first punch landed, although Finn wasn't sure who threw it. All he knew was that he didn't care about anything at that moment aside from smacking his brother down. He swung and caught Joe across the chin. Joe rallied pretty damn quick and got Finn in the stomach, sending him crashing back against the far window, the venetian blinds clattering loudly in response.

Finn pushed against the window and sailed into Joe, knocking him back into the wall, sending the flashlight rolling under the desk. He got one, two good punches in, and then Joe suddenly had him turned around, one arm pulled up behind his back. A second later, Finn's face was slamming down on the desk.

"Jesus," Finn said. "Where'd you learn to fight?"

"I spend two nights a month in the fire station with five burly guys," Joe said. "It's either spar or paint each other's toenails."

"Heh," Finn said. "That's funny. When'd you get a sense of humor?"

"About three months ago," Joe said. "I found a good deal on eBay. Are we done here?"

"Not even close," Finn said, rising up suddenly, catching Joe off guard and butting his brother's face with the back of his head. Joe cursed and released Finn, who spun around, grabbed him by the collar, and tossed him over the desk, sending the desk skidding a few feet as it took the brunt of Joe's momentum.

"We done *now*?" Finn said. Even in the dark, he could see Joe's lip bleeding. When they were kids, the first appearance of blood usually called the end of the fight.

But they weren't kids anymore.

Joe pushed himself up off the desk and started toward Finn.

"You think you're some big tough guy?" he said. "Think again."

Joe swung, Finn ducked, and Joe's fist connected with the wall, taking a chunk out of the plaster. Finn pushed against the wall and slammed his shoulder into Joe's gut, sending them both flying. They bounced off the desk and onto the floor, where Finn scrambled to the top and got in one more punch across the chin. Joe's face went to the left, and he started to recover when he suddenly froze and looked back to the left.

"Guess we're done now, huh?" Finn said.

"I think we are," Joe said. His voice was quiet. Finn looked to where the flashlight's beam illuminated a manila folder with tape on the sides, as if it had just been ripped from a hiding place.

Like, perhaps, under the desk.

Finn scrambled off Joe and grabbed the folder, pulling it open. Inside were about ten Polaroids of Vickie's charred office, along with a clipping from the *Lucy's Lake Weekly.* It was a page dated ten days ago, with one classified ad circled: *M. I know what you did. V.*

"Think we've found our smoking gun," Finn said, handing the pictures and the ad to Joe. Joe picked up the flashlight and scanned over the items.

"Jesus," he said. He looked up at Finn, all animosity gone from his face. "What do we do now?"

Finn glanced around the office.

"We put this place together as best we can, and get back to Tessa."

Joe nodded, stood up, then held his hand out to Finn. Finn took it and let his brother pull him up, feeling a sharp pain in his knee as he got to his feet.

"I think it's safe to say," Finn said, wincing as they pushed the desk back, "that we are officially too old for this shit."

Chapter Twenty

Tessa looked back and forth from Vickie to Margie, then finally to Izzy, who was gnawing on her lower lip.

"So, what are you saying?" Tessa said. "Matt Tarpey's been setting all these fires?"

Vickie nodded. "The signs point that way."

Tessa sat back in the rocking chair and let out a sigh. "But we still don't have any evidence solid enough to take to the police."

Vickie shot a look at Margie. "We would if someone hadn't fallen asleep."

Margie flipped Vickie off. "Bite me, lady. Next time you do the stakeout and we'll see how well you do."

Vickie stuck her tongue out at Margie. Margie chuckled and took a sip of her drink.

Tessa laughed. "So I guess this is what happens when best friends are best friends for too long, huh?"

Both Vickie and Margie looked at her blankly.

"What?" Margie asked.

"Nothing." Tessa stood up, put her hands on the small

of her back, and stretched from her shoulders, trying to clear her head.

Matt Tarpey. Jesus. All these years, she'd been giving her mother's killer free coffee and had no idea.

"So," Izzy said, "what do we do now?"

"We wait for Finn and Joe to get back," Tessa said. "See if they found anything in Tarpey's office."

She released a breath and glanced at the clock. It was almost seven o'clock. Where were they? What if Tarpey found them? What if . . . ?

At that moment, the front door opened. Tessa ran to the foyer as Finn and Joe walked in, looking like they'd been in a damn train wreck. Without thinking, Tessa threw herself into Finn's arms.

"Oh, my God." She pulled back and put her hands on his face, his shoulders, feeling for damage. "Are you okay? What happened? Did he catch you?"

Finn took her hands and squeezed them gently. "We're fine."

Tessa looked over at Joe. Whatever happened, he'd taken the worst of it; his chin was bruising up and his lip was bleeding.

"What the hell happened to you guys?"

"Don't worry about it," Finn said. "We found something. Maybe you should sit down."

"Yeah, it's Tarpey. We know." She touched Joe's bruising chin and he winced. "What happened to Joe?"

Finn touched her arm. "You know? About Tarpey? How do you know?"

Vickie and Margie stepped out of the living room into the foyer and Finn let out a big rush of air.

"Hey, Vickie," Finn said, not missing a beat. "How was Bimini?"

"Oh, my God." Tessa held up Joe's hand and inspected his bruised and bleeding knuckles. "What the hell happened to you?"

"Wall," Joe said.

"The wall? Tarpey threw you into the wall?" Tessa ducked down and grabbed the first-aid kit from under the half-moon table by the door. "Go sit on the sofa, and then you guys can tell me what happened."

"He's what happened," Joe said, jerking his thumb toward Finn.

Tessa straightened and turned glaring eyes on Finn. "What?"

Finn's eyes widened, and he pointed at Joe. "He started it."

Tessa blinked, able to believe what she was hearing but still a bit stunned by the sheer stupidity of it. "Wait a minute. Are you saying that I sent you guys to get evidence and you ended up in a *fight*?"

Joe and Finn exchanged guilty glances. Tessa tucked the first-aid box under her arm and grabbed them both by the elbows, leading them into the living room.

"Izzy, go show Vickie and Margie your room," she said.

Izzy huffed. "What? Now we're back to protecting my virgin eyes? I've seen blood before, you know."

"Not this much." She pointed to the sofa and the boys sat down, both grumbling, then she turned to Izzy.

"Izzy, please. I just need a few moments with the Hardy Boys here, okay?"

Izzy shrugged and looked at Vickie and Margie. "I have a PlayStation."

Margie's face brightened. "Do you have Super Monkeyball?"

Izzy laughed. "Yeah."

"Super Monkeyball it is, then." Vickie grabbed her drink off the coffee table. "Lead the way, Princess."

Tessa waited for them to clear out before settling herself on the coffee table and staring down both Finn and Joe. Finn was mostly just dirty. His jeans were scuffed with dust, and his shirt had a small tear in the shoulder.

Joe, on the other hand, looked like he'd been hit in the face with a frying pan. Tessa grumbled under her breath, ripped open an alcohol pad package with her teeth, and shot Finn a dirty look as she leaned over Joe.

"I can't believe you did this," she said.

"Me?" Finn said. "He was there, too. And why does he get the Florence Nightingale treatment?"

"He's bleeding!"

"Oh, so what? He gets all the sympathy because he bruises easy?"

Tessa ignored Finn and lightly dabbed the cuts on Joe's knuckles with the alcohol pad.

"What the hell happened?"

Joe and Finn exchanged glances, but both of them remained quiet. Tessa sighed, balled up the alcohol pad, and pulled out a Band-Aid.

"I don't need a Band-Aid, Tessa," Joe said. "I'm fine."

"Fine," she said angrily, tossing it back into the box. "Be a big man about it, then." She ran her hand through her hair and sighed. "What did you guys find?"

Joe told her about the pictures and the classified ad, and she filled them in on what Vickie and Margie had told her.

"Well," she said when she finished, "I guess we have enough to interest the police now. Where is it?"

"Taped back under his desk," Finn said. "The police have to go in with a search warrant in order for anything to be admissible in court."

Tessa met Finn's eyes. She knew what he wanted her to say, and she gave him a small smile.

"So I guess next we go to the police and tell them everything."

Finn smiled back at her. "Except the part about us breaking into Tarpey's office."

Tessa felt a rush of warmth fall over her, and it took a moment for her to pull her eyes away from his.

"Okay," she said, "with Vickie's and Margie's testimonies, that should give them enough to get a search warrant, right?"

"God willing and the creek don't rise," Finn said. There was a long moment of uncomfortable silence, and then Joe stood up.

"I'm gonna get going," he said, holding up his injured hand to Tessa. "Thanks for the ace medical care."

Tessa shot a look at Finn, who made no move to get up and talk to his brother. Big idiot. Tessa got up and hurried out to the foyer, stopping Joe at the door.

"Hey," she said. "You okay?"

Joe shrugged and offered a weak smile. "Yeah."

"I'm sorry," she said.

He looked confused. "For what?"

"For dragging you into this," she said. "I know Matt Tarpey is one of your good friends. I know you look up to him. I know you're not the breaking-and-entering type, but I asked you to do all this and you did it." She smiled up at him. "I just want you to know that I appreciate everything you've done. And I'm really sorry."

He met her eyes, and she knew they were both getting the subtext. Joe reached over, pulled her to him, and kissed her on the forehead.

"I will never understand your taste in men," he said quietly.

She put her arms around his neck and hugged him. "I'm obviously insane."

They released each other. Joe gave a small chuckle and let himself out. Tessa shut the door and leaned her head against it, gathering her strength for what she knew was waiting behind her.

Finn leaned against the columned open frame that separated the foyer from the living room, watching Tessa. He knew he had no right to be angry or jealous, but as fate would have it, he was both, and was also way too tired to fight off either emotion.

"So," he said after giving her a moment to gather herself, "what was that all about?"

Tessa leaned back against the door, looking seriously unamused.

"Knock it off, Finn," Tessa said. "There's only so much jealous brother crap I can take in one night."

"I'm not jealous," Finn said. "I just want to know what the hell's going on between you and Joe. It's just garden-variety, wanna-kill-my-brother-with-a-pitchfork curiosity."

"You know what?" Tessa said, her voice tight with anger. "That was a big deal for Joe to do for us tonight. He's not like you, Finn. He plays by the rules, and—"

"Oh, so I suppose slamming me into a desk is 'the rules' now, huh?"

Tessa put her hand to her forehead, and Finn could see how much he was frustrating her. Still, he couldn't help it. The idea of Tessa and Joe made him crazy, and his response was to pass the crazy on.

"Look," she said, "I've gotta think about what I'm going to do, what I'm going to tell the police, how I'm gonna keep all this from blowing up in my face, and I can't deal with your crap right now. Good night."

She started toward the stairs, and he tried to let her go. He knew it was best to drop it, let her go on up to bed angry and thinking he was an asshole, but at the last minute he reached out and caught her by the arm. She stopped, but didn't look up at him.

"Tessa, I know I'm not very good at this."

"At what?" she said tightly. "You're going to have to narrow the field for me a bit. There are so many things you're not good at."

He smiled and released her arm. "You know what I mean."

"Oh, what?" she asked, her voice full of mock innocence. "Are you talking about how, not two hours ago, we stood right in this spot and I told you I love you and you gave me some line about tomatoes? Is that what you're talking about?"

"Yep." He felt like a fucking idiot. "That'd be it."

There was a long moment of drawn-out silence, and Tessa made a move toward the stairs again.

"Tessa—," he started.

"What?" she snapped, stamping one foot. "What, what, *what*? Are you going to say something or are we going to dance around this all night? Because I'm too tired to dance anymore, Finn."

Why was it so hard for him to say the words? The verbal always came so easily to him, but when it really mattered . . .

"It doesn't matter," he said finally. He raised his eyes to hers. "I could tell you everything, but there's really no point."

"No point?" Her voice hit a weird, high pitch. That couldn't be good. "No *point*? Did you just actually stand there and tell me there's no *point*?"

Finn went quiet. Based on the look on her face, it was probably his safest choice. She advanced on him, stopping when they were only inches apart.

"Let me tell you something," she said. "Even if you run off like a coward in the night, and even if this thing between us never goes further than this moment right now, there's a point. The point is that I said it, and you didn't. Take it from me, as the one who gets left behind, there's a fucking point."

She turned her back on him and started toward the stairs again. Yep. She was pissed. Well, in for a penny . . .

"What if I do say it?" he said. "What good is that gonna do you?"

She stopped, but kept her back to him. Finn moved closer to her. He wanted to touch her, to pull her to him, but instead he tucked his hands in his pockets and spoke to the back of her head.

"When I leave, the only thing you should be thinking is 'good riddance,' and if I tell you what being with you does to me, how the thought of leaving you tears me up inside, how is that gonna help you when I'm gone?"

Tessa let out an angry laugh, then went silent. When she turned around, her face was filled with revelation.

"That's why you stole the Thing," she said, a touch of amazement in her tone, although Finn didn't know if it was at his wisdom or his stupidity. If he were a betting man, though, his money would go on stupid. "You took the Thing so I wouldn't miss you? So I'd think I was better off without you? Am I getting this right?"

Finn ran his fingers over his eyes but didn't say anything. She stepped forward, closer to him, until he allowed his eyes to connect with hers. The amazement was gone, and he could see she'd doubled back to fury.

"You arrogant son of a bitch."

He allowed a small smile. "Well, that's another topic entirely—"

"Don't joke!" she said, giving his shoulder a rough shove. "Don't you dare joke with me right now!"

Finn threw up his hands in frustration. "Don't joke? That's what I do, Tessa. I don't take things seriously, I don't think about anyone other than myself, and I don't have conversations like this." He swallowed hard. "Which is why, when you think about it, you'll realize you're better off without me."

He could see her eyes brimming with tears and it killed him not to reach out to her, but he stayed put.

"You're so stupid." She swiped angrily at her face. "You're so stupid, and I love you, so what does that say about me?"

There was a long moment of painful silence. Finn ran a hand over his face and laughed lightly.

"You know, there are very few moments in life when I'd be relieved if someone came at me with a bayonet . . ."

"I loved you." Tessa's voice was quiet, but sharp. Finn met her eyes, saw how much pain he was causing her, and felt his gut torque violently. "And here's a news flash, Finnegan. You protected me from *nothing*. I spent ten years missing you, wondering what the hell I did wrong to make you do that to me."

"That's crazy," Finn said. "How could you possibly think it was your fault?"

"I was an eighteen-year-old girl," Tessa said. "I thought global warming was my fault. And even when I got over that, I still knew what I'd lost, Finn."

Finn took a step forward, leaning his face down close to hers so she was forced to look at him, to understand what he was saying.

"What did you lose, Tess? Some stupid kid with no future who was gonna drag you down with him."

"You . . ." She blinked against the tears in her eyes. "You were the one who made me laugh when I had a crappy day. You were the one I vented to when I was mad, the one I shared all the good stuff with. You always knew when I was full of crap, and you always called me on it. You were smart, you were funny, you were good-looking. You were mine. And then, suddenly, you weren't."

He stared at her, not sure what to say. He thought he'd done her a favor. And he had.

He was sure he had.

Hadn't he?

"I knew every day exactly what I'd lost," she continued, her voice tight and quiet, "and I missed you every day and I believed in you every day, and my heart broke *every day*. That's the big favor that you did for me. Thanks so much."

Finn kept quiet, kept his focus on the door. Tessa took a

step closer to him, their bodies practically touching as she spoke in quiet tones.

"Here's the kicker," she said, a bitter laugh in her voice. "You weren't even protecting me. You were protecting yourself. If you'd given half a thought to me, you would have said good-bye."

He looked at her, could feel the emotion curling around his neck like a noose, and something inside him urged him to say something, to do *something*. Reach out to her. Hold her. Tell her everything. Instead, he stood there and did nothing.

"I have to get out of here," she said finally. He watched her as she snatched her coat and keys and fled, leaving the door open behind her.

Finn wasn't sure how long he stood there, frozen in the hallway. It was long enough that the chill finally snapped him out of it, and he walked over to the door and shut it. He ran his hands over his face, closed his eyes, heard her voice.

You weren't even protecting me. You were protecting yourself.

All he'd wanted to do was return the stupid car. How had he managed to fuck everything up so monumentally in the process? Every instinct he had was wrong, every word he said was an exercise in stupid. Yet, as he stood motionless in Tessa's hallway, his gut told him to go after her, to say more to her. To say everything.

"God," he said under his breath, running his hand over his face. "All I wanted to do was return the fucking car."

He plodded up the stairs and made a beeline for Izzy's room, knocking gently twice.

"Come in," Izzy said.

He opened the door to see Izzy, Margie, and Vickie sitting around the PlayStation, stricken expressions on their faces. He pulled on a tight smile.

"Guess you guys caught the show, huh?"

Izzy shook her head. "We heard, you know, voices." She paused for a moment. "She's really mad, huh?"

"You could say that," he said. "If you're into understatement. Look, I'm, uh . . . I'm gonna go after her, try to talk to her." He looked to Margie and Vickie. "Can you guys stay with Izzy until Babs gets home?"

Margie nodded, smiled lightly. "Sure. You bet."

Izzy huffed. "I don't need babysitters."

Finn walked over to her, knelt down in front of her.

"I know," he said. "I need them. I made a promise that I wouldn't let anything happen to you, and it's a promise I intend to keep. Think you can humor me on this one?"

Izzy smiled. "Yeah. Okay."

"Okay," he said. He straightened up, kissed her on the top of her head, and let his leaden feet carry him downstairs, out the door, and into the cold in search of Tessa.

Chapter Twenty-one

Finn sat down at the bar in Riker's and checked his watch. Tessa had been gone for over an hour, and every minute that went by without her made him edgier. She wasn't skating at the lake, she wasn't hiding in the shack. She wasn't on the swings in the park, and she wasn't wandering around town. He knew; he'd cruised every street in town twice looking for her. She probably had just taken the Thing for a long drive.

"Let me guess," Surly said, settling a bar napkin in front of Finn. "Pepsi?"

Finn shook his head. "Get me a Jameson's."

Surly raised one eyebrow but didn't say anything as he pulled the whiskey off the shelf. Finn knew he shouldn't drink. He got stupid when he drank. Then again, given the events of the night, it wasn't like he could get much stupider.

Surly set the Jameson's down in front of Finn. Finn tossed a ten on the bar and slammed the drink back. It was sharp and hot going down, and it reached out into every corner of Finn's being, pushing away the crazy that Tessa had put there.

Hmmm. Maybe there was something to drinking after all. He raised his glass to Surly. "Keep 'em coming."

A hand landed on the ten and pushed it back toward Finn.

"I'll cover that."

Finn glanced up. "Mr. Dale."

Mr. Dale smiled. The glass eye was actually a quality piece of work. As a matter of fact, if he hadn't known to look for it, Finn might not have even noticed.

Mr. Dale settled onto the bar stool next to Finn's. "I heard you were back in town."

"Funny thing about rumors," Finn said as Surly poured another round. "On occasion, they're true."

Mr. Dale chuckled lightly. "I'm glad I bumped into you. I never got the chance to thank you."

Thank me for what? Finn thought, but a split second later he put it together.

Tessa. The money. Helping people. Glass eye.

"So," Mr. Dale said, "thank you."

"It was nothing," Finn said, which was true, since Finn had nothing to do with helping Tony Dale.

That was all Tessa.

Tessa. Who loved him. Who, for whatever reasons beyond all logic and common sense, loved him. The only woman Finn had never been able to shake told him she loved him and he said . . . nothing.

Finn downed the second whiskey.

"It wasn't nothing." Mr. Dale took a sip of his beer, then settled it down on the napkin in front of him. "It meant a lot that you'd help me out, especially after I almost flunked you in geometry."

Finn chuckled. "Yeah, you almost did that, didn't you?" He clinked his glass with Mr. Dale's. "Can I ask you a question, Mr. Dale?"

"Sure. I guess."

Shut up, Finn thought to himself, but he kept going. "You know how there are women, and then there are *women*?"

Mr. Dale gave a brief smile, then waved to Surly. "I think we're gonna need another round here."

"So, here's the thing, Mr. Dale—"

"You can call me Tony, you know," Mr. Dale said.

Finn looked at him for a moment, tried to imagine his old geometry teacher as *Tony.*

"No, I really can't." He took another sip of his drink. "Mr. Dale, there are a lot of women in the world."

Mr. Dale nodded. "Yep. Sure are."

"And they're great. Pretty, funny, smart. Great. Right?"

"Yep."

"And then . . ." Finn shook his head. "Then there's the girl . . . the woman . . ." He clenched his fist, then released it. "The one that makes you crazy. The one that makes every breath so fucking hard, but even if you only got one moment with her a day, she'd still be worth it."

Mr. Dale sipped his beer, sighed knowingly. "Yep."

"You can't be with her, you can't *not* be with her . . ." Finn sighed, shook his head.

"I'm sorry," Mr. Dale said after a moment. "Was there a question in there somewhere?"

Surly set another Jameson's in front of Finn, and Mr.

Dale dropped some more cash on the bar. Both men lifted their glasses and drank.

"She told me she loved me," Finn said after a moment, "and I didn't say anything."

"Well," Mr. Dale said thoughtfully, "do you love her?"

"I'm sitting at a bar drinking Irish whiskey and pouring my heart out to a one-eyed geometry teacher," Finn said. "It's not looking good for Finnegan."

Mr. Dale laughed. "No, it's not." He took another sip of his beer. "Listen, Finn. I've been dating for a very long time, and in all these years, I've learned exactly one thing about women."

"Yeah?" Finn twirled his whiskey under his fingers. "Then you're one up on me. What is it?"

"It's not what you say, it's what you do."

Finn took a second to absorb this. "Yeah? You think?"

"Hell, yeah," Mr. Dale said, suddenly animated. "Look, we say stuff to women all the time. We say we'll call them, then we don't. We tell them they're beautiful, then we spend the evening looking at other women. We say we don't love them when we do, and we say we do when we don't. Christ, if I was a woman, I wouldn't listen to a god-damn thing any man ever said to me."

"You make a good point there, Mr. Dale," Finn said, "but it doesn't help me. See, the only way for me to show how much I love her is to get out of her life."

Mr. Dale went quiet for a bit, then shrugged. "Well, then, you're pretty much fucked."

"Yep."

They each stared off into space for a while.

"So, what happened to yours?"

"My what?" Mr. Dale said. "My woman?"

"Yeah."

Mr. Dale sighed. "She married an ophthalmologist."

Finn was horrified. "A what?"

Mr. Dale gave an ironic snort. "An eye doctor."

Finn stared at Mr. Dale, and clarity suddenly fell over him. In that moment, he knew with more certainty than he'd ever known anything in his life that he did not want Tessa to marry an ophthalmologist. His heart started beating erratically, and he couldn't sit still. He hopped off the bar stool and clapped Mr. Dale on the shoulder. "I gotta run. Thanks for the drinks, man."

Mr. Dale continued to stare out into the middle distance. "Yeah. No problem."

Finn walked out of the bar and into the cold air, breathing it in deep, hoping it would smack the effects of the alcohol down. He had to find Tessa. He didn't know what he'd say to her once he did, but he could cross that bridge when he came to it. He knew he couldn't be with her, couldn't stay, but damned if he was going to let her marry a fucking ophthalmologist.

He stopped where he was, at the edge of the Riker's parking lot, and realized he'd fully lost his mind. He couldn't talk to Tessa like this. If he did, he'd screw things up even worse. No, the thing to do was hike into town, hole up at the shack, something—anything—that would keep him away from Tessa until morning, when he'd gotten his sanity back.

Which would have been a good plan if the Thing hadn't pulled into the parking lot at just that second, whipping into a spot at the side of the building and trapping Finn in the glare of its headlights. He froze there, momentarily blinded as the lights shut off. By the time his eyes adjusted, she was standing in front of him, leaning against the grille of the car.

"Where the hell have you been?" Tessa said. "I came back, Izzy told me you'd run out. I've been looking for you all night."

Finn stuck his hands in his pockets and laughed a weird, nervous laugh. Christ, he was gonna mess this up bad.

"Well, you found me. I'm fine. Everything's fine." He glanced around. "I'm just gonna go for a walk, or something. See you tomorrow."

Her eyebrows twitched toward each other, and she pushed herself up off the grille of the car and walked toward him.

"Are you drunk?"

"Pffft," he scoffed, then shrugged. "Mr. Dale bought me a whiskey, yeah."

A smile spread over her face, and her eyes seemed lit from within. How had he never noticed that about her before?

"Tony Dale bought you drinks?" she asked.

Finn chuckled. "You can call him Tony? See, I couldn't do that."

Tessa shrugged. "I've known him as an adult a lot longer than you have."

Their eyes met and held for a moment. A slight smile curled on one side of her face. God, she took his breath away.

"You're so beautiful," he whispered, reaching up and touching her face with the backs of his fingers and it felt so good, she felt *so good*. He leaned forward until their foreheads were touching.

"Don't marry the ophthalmologist," he said.

"What?" She pulled back, looking at him like he was crazy, and the moment was broken. "Okay, Hoss. I'm taking you home. We'll come back for the other car tomorrow."

"I love you, Tessa." He breathed it more than said it, but he knew she heard it, because she took a step away from him and stared at him with an unreadable expression.

"Are you kidding me?" she said. Then, louder, "Are you *kidding* me?"

Suddenly, the expression was readable. She was pissed off.

"Tessa—"

"No," she said, waving her finger at him. "No. You do not get to go out, get drunk, and say that to me."

"That's not—," Finn started, then regrouped. "Well, okay, that is what happened, but I'm not just saying this because I'm drunk."

"Then why?" She put her hand to her forehead, closed her eyes, and sighed. "I can't deal with this right now. Look, Finn, if you have to come here and get stoked up on tequila—"

"Irish whiskey, actually."

"*Whatever*," she said through clenched teeth. "If you have to get drunk in order to tell me you love me, then you don't love me. So let's just drop it, okay?"

She turned to go back toward the car, but he caught her by the arm and spun her around to face him. There was no point in going back on it now. She was already pissed off, and honestly, now that he'd finally said the words, he couldn't stop himself.

"Tessa," he said quietly, "I love you."

She pulled her arm from his grip. "Let's go home. You

can sleep it off. And in the morning, if I don't kill you in your sleep, of which the odds are fifty-fifty, we'll talk about this then."

"No. I need to say this. In the morning, I might not say it all, and I need to tell you . . ." He paused, took a breath, and dived in. "You were right. Back then, when I took off, I was protecting myself. I didn't want ten years to go by with you regretting that you'd ever stayed with me. I thought you deserved better."

She rolled her eyes. "I have such a deep, deep desire to clock you one right now."

He put his hands on her shoulders and licked his lips. His mouth was dry, but he knew that if he didn't say it all now, he never would. "And maybe, yeah, maybe I was being a big idiot, but Tessa, you married the ophthalmologist and you've gotta get out of that."

She squinted slightly at him. "Exactly how many drinks did Tony Dale buy you?"

"You don't paint anymore," Finn said. "You don't laugh, you don't cause any trouble, you don't have any fun. You work hard, I know you do, and I have no idea what it's like to raise a kid alone when you're barely more than a kid yourself. I know I don't understand anything you've been through and I've been a big asshole, but Tessa—you just . . . you gave up."

She inhaled like she was going to say something, but then didn't. He took the opportunity to keep going, to get it all out before he sobered up and chickened out.

"I love you," he said. "And yeah, maybe it took a drink or two for me to be able to admit it. Maybe I'm not a guy who always knows what's going on in his own head, but I know that I love you. And I will cop to being an idiot and a jackass, but don't tell me I don't love you, because there is no other explanation for what you do to me."

Tessa's eyes brimmed with tears, glistening in the moonlight. She swiped at her cheek, then looked up at him again.

"Yeah?" She sniffled. "What do I do to you?"

"I'm not a noble guy," Finn said. "I'm in it for me and me alone, and you know what? I'm okay with that. But you . . . being around you . . ." He exhaled, tried to wrap his mind around the whirling mass of thoughts running wild in his head. "Mr. Dale just bought me drinks because he thought that I'd helped him. And you know what? It felt good. It felt good to know I'd helped someone else, done something unselfish for once in my life. I've never felt that before. That's not me, Tess. That's you."

Her fingers tightened slightly on his. He looked down at her hand in his. "There is nothing in the world I want more right now than to wake up in your bed every day with the chance, just the slightest chance, of being the man you believe me to be." He raised his head back and looked into her eyes. "If that isn't love then it's insanity and what's the fucking difference, right?"

She watched him, her mouth slightly open, just showing the tips of her bottom teeth and suddenly the reality of everything he'd said fell over him.

"Look," he said. "I'm an idiot. I don't know why I just dumped all that on you. I know that's not fair. I'm just gonna . . . Whew. I'm gonna walk back to the shack, you know, sober up a bit—"

She put her fingers to his lips.

"You're not going anywhere."

She slid her hand to the back of his neck, her fingers

twirling in the hair there, and a moment later pulled Finn into a kiss that made the rest of his world fade away.

Oh, my God, Tessa thought as the kiss took them over. It started out soft and gentle and moved to a house on fire in 3.5 seconds flat. She could feel his hands going under her coat, fisting her sweater at the base of her back and . . .

Oh. My. God.

Her hands were in his hair, his arms were gripping her tightly, and they twirled like they were the center of a cyclone until finally they bumped into the side of the Thing. Tessa pulled back a bit to regain her balance, but Finn reached under her sweater and his hands were cold on her skin and . . .

Oh. God.

"Let's sit in the car and talk," she said.

Finn sucked at the hollow of her neck. "Talk?"

"Or, you know, whatever," she said. She turned toward the Thing, trying to unlock the door as Finn stood behind her, his hands running over her abdomen, traveling lower . . .

Yeah. That works.

She pulled the door open and they both crashed inside, crawling over and pulling at each other until they were in the backseat, the very place where he'd first charmed her out of her underwear ten years before. He sat in the middle and she straddled him, hiking up her skirt until she could comfortably press against him. She put her hands on either side of his neck and kissed him, shifting slightly over him . . .

Oh. Yeah. That.

He groaned and she could feel him hardening under

her. She reached down and worked the button and zipper on his jeans, kissing his neck as she went. He tasted so good, felt so good, and it had been so long—

He grabbed her hand just as she freed him and placed his other hand on her face, gently moving her back until she looked at him.

"I love you," he said.

"Oh, yeah, I know," she said, leaning in for another kiss as she shimmied out of her underwear. He nipped his way down from her lips to her neck, his breath falling over her in warm, heavenly waves as he tucked one finger in the V-neck of her sweater and yanked it down so he could get to that spot between her breasts.

Oh. Man.

And then he pushed her back, just a bit, just enough to make her want to kill him.

"What?" she said.

He reached up and ran a hand through her hair. "I just want to look at you for a second."

She smiled down at him, turned her head to kiss the palm of his hand. Slowly, she started moving against him, and his hand tightened, gripping her hair.

"Enough looking," she whispered.

He smiled, reached his hand up under her sweater, and undid her front clasp of her bra in one swift movement.

That's what I want, she thought. *That's exactly . . .*

He freed her right breast as he moved his hand over it, his thumb and forefinger working together over her . . .

"Wow," she said. "You've gotten better at this."

He let his hand slide downward over her abdomen. "I was nineteen the last time we did this. If I haven't gotten better, for God's sake, don't tell me."

She arched backward as his fingers slid lower, curving around her and into her.

Oh, man. Has he ever gotten better at this . . .

Just as she was about to lose control, he grasped her by the hips and slid her up and onto him. The shock of having the whole of him inside her brought her back, and she locked her fingers behind his neck and looked into his eyes.

This is what I want . . . , she thought, and a rush ran through her. This was the first time in a long time that she had exactly what she wanted, and the realization felt like waking up. She opened her eyes, slowed, and looked at Finn.

"This is what I want," she said, her voice registering the surprise she felt. Finn looked at her, reached his hand up, ran his fingers through her hair.

"Good," he said. He pulled her down to him and kissed her, slow and deliberate, still inside her but not moving. As they kissed, motionless, she felt the need building up within her, pressure increasing. She rocked forward, sensations blazing through her with the movement.

This is what I want.

She rode up and then plunged down over him and he gasped. She worked it just to the edge, then slowed and switched rhythms, not wanting it to stop, not wanting to lose this moment to memory any sooner than absolutely necessary. It wasn't much longer, though, before it was absolutely necessary, and Tessa finally let herself release control, moving faster and faster until she heard him scream her name. A moment later she fell onto him, her breath shooting her hair out from her face in staccato gasps as she hugged herself against him.

"Oh, my God," she said after a moment. "We have gotten so much better at this."

He laughed, and she felt his arms come up and around her, holding her tight against him.

"You think?" he said.

"Well," she said, kissing him lightly on the tip of his nose as she pulled back to look at him, "practice makes perfect."

Chapter Twenty-two

When Finn woke up, he was alone in Tessa's bed. It took him a moment to remember what had happened the night before, everything that he and Tessa had done to each other, first in the car and then on that very bed. It had been wild, like coming home and exploring new territory all at once. She had been unrestrained and demanding, then she'd concentrate on him and send his world rocking. They shushed each other to keep from waking Izzy and Babs, then giggled together as they cuddled in exhaustion. Tessa's head had fit perfectly into the nook of his shoulder, and Finn couldn't remember a time when he'd felt so complete and at peace.

He was pretty sure it was never.

He pushed up on his elbows and looked at the open closet door.

"Tess? Babe? You in there?"

There was no answer. He glanced at the clock next to the bed—it was not even seven o'clock yet. On a Saturday morning. And they'd been up until . . . well, he had no idea, but it was late. He fought sleep as long as he could, keeping her awake with him, until neither one of them could fight sleep. After all, they both knew he was going to have to leave soon. No need to waste precious time sleeping.

He got up, threw on his jeans and T-shirt, and stepped out into the hallway. Both Izzy's and Babs's doors were shut, but the door to the attic was open. Finn ran his hand through his hair and climbed up the first few steps.

"Tessa?" he called quietly.

He heard a scuffle and then saw her head poke out into the open stairwell. She grinned and looked down at him, her hair hanging down, framing her flushed face. She looked alive and happy, and Finn smiled.

"Come back to bed," he said.

She shook her head, and crooked her finger at him to come up, then disappeared again. Finn laughed and started up the steps, knocking his head against the hanging bare lightbulb at the top.

Tessa sat yoga-style in the middle of the attic, surrounded by piles of open boxes. Random items were spilled out onto the floor. There was a pile of Christmas ornaments, a bunch of straw kitchen matron dolls, a few ceramic cats. Some of it was unfamiliar, and some of it he recognized as the kitschy stuff Karen had always had around the house. It was funny, because up until this moment, he hadn't realized that it was missing. He sat down behind Tessa, wrapping his legs around her, and picked up one of the kitchen matrons.

"Hey," he said, laughing. "I remember this lady. She was giving me the evil eye the first time I kissed you."

Tessa laughed and grabbed it from him.

"That wasn't our first kiss," she said, leaning back

against Finn's chest. He wrapped his arms around her and lowered his face into her hair, placing one gentle kiss on her neck. "Our first kiss was at Annie Lateri's birthday party."

Finn chuckled. "Who the hell is Annie Lateri?"

Tessa twisted in his arms, looked at him. "She had a lisp and you used to call her Annie Lisperi."

Finn blinked as the memory of a little girl in dark pigtails rushed over him. "Oh, yeah. I was a little bastard, wasn't I?"

"Yep." Tessa turned back to the boxes, reaching into one. "The best revenge is living well, though. She's married to the Vermont attorney general and has a house larger than this town."

Finn moved her hair out of the way and kissed her neck again, a familiar and not unwelcome pressure building up below.

"Anyway," Tessa said, her voice a little raspy, "we had our first kiss in her bathroom at her ninth birthday party. Remember?"

Finn pulled back. "Yeah, but that one doesn't count. No tongue, no play. And I was only ten years old. I didn't have any moves."

Tessa curled her leg in and twirled to face him, gracefully easing up to straddle him. "Well, you sure have moves now, sailor." She giggled, looking so happy and brilliant, like a light had turned on inside her.

She was amazing. He pulled her tighter to him, began kissing down her collarbone, pulling back the collar of her T-shirt to get at her bare skin.

"Whoa," she said, giving a quick gasp. "Anyway, I was

uh . . . oh . . ." Finn smiled and pulled back. She opened her eyes and smiled down at him. "I had a thought."

"Forget it," he said.

"No." She pushed back off him and the space between them, small as it was, physically hurt. They only had so much time, and he didn't want to waste a second of it not touching her.

"I was thinking of putting all this stuff back," she said, motioning toward her mother's things. "Well, some of it, anyway. And I was thinking I might paint some of the rooms. I think I'd like my bedroom to be yellow, you know? Bright. Cheerful." She smiled. "Hopeful." She tilted her head a bit to the side. "What do you think?"

Finn sighed, tried to imagine her bedroom in yellow, could only imagine Tessa naked on the bed, and that was fine by him. "I think that would be great."

"And I was thinking of maybe starting to paint again, for real. You know, like I used to. Just for fun, I mean, I wouldn't quit my job or anything, but . . ." She sighed, happiness radiating from her face. "It's just something I'd really like to do."

God, he loved her. Sitting here in this attic with her, talking about these little things . . . It was such a small moment, just watching her face light up as she talked. If he could do this for the rest of his life, he would.

If . . .

Her expression darkened, and she tilted her head at him. "What?"

Finn took her hand and kissed her fingers. "Nothing. Just thinking about how I'm going to miss this. You know, when I leave."

Her eyes went hard. "When you leave?"

"Well . . ." Oh, Christ. She knew. She had to know. Didn't she? "Yeah, Tessa. I can't stay. You know that."

She pushed up on her feet and took a step back. "No. I didn't know that."

Fuck. Finn stood up as well. "I don't know what to say. I thought we were on the same page here."

"Apparently not."

He could see her lower lip trembling and it made him feel sick and raw. How was it possible to go from feeling so good to feeling so shitty in just a few seconds? How did people survive this kind of thing on a regular basis?

"Tessa . . . ," he said, reaching out to her. She batted his hand away.

"No, you're right. I should have known. All that about 'I want to wake up next to you every morning and be the man you believe me to be,' blah blah blah. I mean who says that? Guys don't say that. Guys like you *definitely* don't say that. Jesus, I'm so stupid."

"You're not stupid," Finn said. "Now will you calm down so we can—"

"What? Talk? Why? So you can feed me more crap about how you love me, how you want to be with me?"

His chest felt like it was caught in a vise. "I do want to be with you. God, Tessa, you have no idea—"

"Right," Tessa said, bitterness cutting through her words. "You want to be with me, just not enough to be a real man and actually do it."

They stared each other down for a long moment, and then she turned toward the stairs. Finn caught her by the arm and pulled her back.

"So you tell me," he said quietly, "would a real man stay here with you, even if it meant you losing custody of your sister?" He released her arm. "Is that what a real man would do? 'Cause, you know, I'm kinda unfamiliar with their ways. Why don't you explain it to me?"

Tessa let out a heavy sigh, but didn't say anything. Finn took a deep breath and spoke calmly.

"What do you think that social worker is going to think if she finds out we're together? I haven't had a real job on paper in ten years, Tessa. How do you think that's gonna help your situation? You think that's gonna look good for you?"

"I don't care," she said, but he could tell the conviction in her voice was weakening. He put his hands on her shoulders. Touching her was both comforting and painful at the same time.

"You do care," he said. "And I care. And whether we like it or not, that's the way it is and nothing can change that."

Gently, he pulled her into his arms, leaning his face into her hair and breathing in deep. He felt a knot of emotion in his throat and swallowed against it as he kissed the top of her head.

"It's okay," he said. "We've still got a little time. We haven't got Tarpey yet. Maybe it'll take a while."

"That's what you're waiting for?" she asked. "Us getting Tarpey?"

Finn nodded. "I'm certainly not gonna leave while he's still out there—"

She pushed back from him. "Then get your stuff and go."

Her words hit him like a slap. "What?"

"Tarpey turned himself in last night," she said.

"Why?"

"I don't know. Maybe he saw what you guys did to his office and knew the jig was up." She swiped at her left cheek. "I don't know. I went looking for you to tell you, but then we got . . . distracted and I figured it could wait for morning."

Finn put his hand on his stomach, which was suddenly killing him. "Okay."

"So, mission accomplished. We're out of danger. And since you've turned over this new leaf of nobility, here's how you can be noble, for me. I'm going to go skating at the lake, clear my head a bit." Her eyes met his and even in the dim light, he could see the tears there. "When I get back, you can have your stuff cleared out, and you can be gone. The faster you leave, the faster I get over you."

She turned and walked out, ignoring him as he called her name.

Babs flipped over one last pancake on the griddle. She and Izzy had been happily making plans for Finn and Tessa all morning, since they'd noticed Finn's keys and wallet sitting on the table in the foyer, while the sofa was strangely unoccupied. However, a few minutes earlier, Tessa had stormed out, slamming the door behind her, and they'd quieted down, waiting for the second wave from Finn. Even Wallace had gone silent, curling up in the corner like a depressed puppy rather than begging for bacon.

Babs scooped her spatula under the pancake and held it up for Izzy. Izzy shook her head no, and Babs placed it on the stack. Footsteps sounded slowly down the stairs, and they heard Finn moving about in the living room. Babs exchanged a look with Izzy.

"We should probably wait for him to come in here," Izzy said.

"Oh, definitely, we *should*," Babs said, "but we're not going to."

With that, they both hopped to it, pushing through the kitchen door into the living room, where Finn was packing up his yellow backpack.

"Hey," he said, giving Babs a weak smile that was not at all up to Finn's usual standards. Something had gone horribly, horribly wrong. And so soon after it all seemed to be going so right.

Oh, Finn, she thought. *You abominable putz.*

Finn zipped up his pack and threw it over his shoulder.

"Hey, look," he said. "The rental car is at Riker's. I left it there last night. I'm gonna hike on out and get it, and then it's gonna be time to go."

"What?" Izzy said. "You're leaving? Why?"

Finn smiled at her. "Tarpey's confessed, kid. You're safe, I'm outta here. That was the deal."

"No," Izzy said. "I'm the boss here. I'm the one who hired you. I should get to say when you leave."

Finn let out a breath and honestly, Babs had never seen him look more miserable. He looked up at Izzy and tried to smile.

"Deal's done, Angel Face."

Izzy looked from Babs to Finn, then stomped her feet and tore up the stairs to her room. Finn watched her, his emotions raw on his face in a way she'd never seen before.

He turned to Babs. "You gonna be ready to go in about an hour?"

"No, actually."

Finn raised his eyebrows, looking surprised. "What?"

Babs pulled on a bright smile. "I'm staying. I spoke to Tessa about it last night before she went out looking for you. She's going to rent me her mother's room, and I'm going to work at the diner."

For a moment, Finn's expression of misery was replaced by one of total surprise.

"So, you're gonna live here?"

"Yes," Babs said. "The penthouse belongs to Bryson's partners, anyway, and the money from his insurance will certainly stretch farther here than in New York. I've been thinking about going for a while now; I just didn't know where I wanted to go, until I came here." She smiled. "And I think there are things I can do here."

Finn let out a halfhearted laugh. "Yeah, you fit right in here. But you manage to do that everywhere."

Wow. That was an oddly genuine thing for Finn to say. If there was any doubt in Babs's mind about what happened last night, it was gone.

"I'll miss you," she said quietly. "When I made the plans, I half thought you'd be staying, too."

"Well, you half thought wrong," he said. "I'm not a small-town guy. The pace here is a little slow for me."

"Now that's a crock of crap if ever I heard one. You've been happier in the last few days here than you ever were in New York."

"Yeah, well . . ." His expression tightened, and he looked back at Babs. "I'll return the car for you, and uh, you give a call when you're in the city next, okay?"

Babs was surprised at how potent her sadness was at

the thought of her redheaded thief going away. "You won't be coming back to say good-bye?"

Finn shook his head, let out a bitter laugh. "I think I've said it."

"All right, then," Babs said. She moved closer, put her hands on either side of his face, and pulled him down so she could kiss his forehead. She wanted to tell him he was a good man, that she believed in him, that she knew he would do well, but instead she just smiled and said, "I'll miss you."

Finn smiled, started toward the door. Behind Babs, the kitchen door swung open and Wallace came darting out. Finn looked down at him.

"What? You're coming with me?" He paused for a moment, then looked up at Babs. "Guess he's coming with me."

Babs watched, unsmiling, as Finn made his way to the door. He paused for a moment, cursed under his breath, then walked back and grabbed the macaw cage. Babs raised an eyebrow.

"I don't have a job at the moment," he said. "Tell Vickie that I'll pay her back. Tell Tessa . . ." He shook his head. "Tell Tessa I stole it."

"You are stealing it," Babs said.

Finn let out a harsh laugh and nodded. He met Babs's eyes for a moment, gave a wan smile, and left.

Babs stood there for a few moments, then marched up the stairs and pushed open the door to Izzy's room.

Izzy flipped over from where she was lying on her stomach and set her feet on the floor. She sniffled and rubbed at her eyes.

"Is he gone?" she asked.

Babs shut the door behind her. "Yeah."

Izzy nodded, her pain clear on her face. Babs walked over and sat down next to her on the bed.

"You know, New York isn't that far away," Babs said quietly. "We could go visit. See a Broadway play. Do some shopping."

Izzy's chin twitched.

"She was almost happy," she said, a tear tracking down her cheek. "I just wanted her to be happy so bad. She's given up everything for me and she was almost . . ."

Babs pulled Izzy into her arms and let the child cry on her shoulder for a minute. But just for a minute.

"You know, sweetheart," she said, pulling back a bit from Izzy, "it's one thing to express sad feelings. It's another thing to indulge them."

Izzy nodded, swiped at her face, and straightened her posture. "Okay."

Babs tucked her index finger under the girl's chin. "I've got an errand to run right now, and I'd really love it if you'd come with me."

Izzy gave a soft smile and sniffed. "Sure. Where are we going?"

Babs stood up and held out her hand. "To the post office. I'm expecting a fax from a friend, and with any luck, it'll stir things up a bit."

Chapter Twenty-three

Finn sat in Babs's parked rental car, staring through the windshield straight ahead as he white-knuckled the steering wheel. His view wasn't great; mostly the ivy that clung to the brick walls of Village Pizza, which jutted up against the parking lot at Max's. He looked to his left, through the length of the parking lot to Max's Diner.

Just go, you idiot, Wallace said from the seat next to him.

Finn shot the dog a look. "You know, there are a thousand ways to get rid of a dog in New York City, and a lot of 'em are painful."

Go, Wallace said, turning around twice in the front seat before lying down, snout on his paws.

Finn sighed, undid his seat belt, and got out of the car. Every step toward the diner, he had to resist the urge to go back, but eventually, he was there, his hand on the doorknob.

He just couldn't turn it. He'd sworn he'd die before setting foot in that diner and . . .

Oh, fuck it. It wasn't like he was a man of his word, anyway.

He pushed the door open and stepped inside. The gregarious morning chitchat came to a sudden halt, and all that was left was "All My Exes Live in Texas," playing on the crackly old radio. Pammy, one of the waitresses who had been a fixture at Max's Diner forever, froze with the last plate for a table of four in her hand. The woman who ordered the eggs had to grab the plate and place it on the table herself.

"Hey," Finn said, giving a short wave to the crowd.

A few people said hello, one or two men nodded, and then Abigail Husteff got up and threw herself into Finn's arms, sobbing.

"Thank you so much," she said. "I never would have been able to afford Mr. Peabody's leukemia treatments if it wasn't for you."

Finn reached one arm up and gave her a few awkward pats on the back, then looked to her girlfriend, Cindy Simes, who mouthed the word "cat."

Finn cursed under his breath. He wanted to tell them all he was no hero, that it was Tessa; it had all been Tessa.

But he couldn't. Instead, he patted Abigail on the shoulder again. "Yeah. Hey. No problem."

A moment later, Cindy huffed, got up, and peeled Abigail off Finn, giving him a grateful smile as she guided Abigail back to their table. Finn glanced around the room, and they were all looking at him with that mixture of happiness at seeing him, and genuine gratitude. He smiled back at them.

"Yeah, um," he said. "Is Max here?"

Pammy, who had regained herself sometime during the

scene with Abigail, pointed toward the kitchen. Finn nodded, gave one last wave to the crowd, and curled around the counter to get to the kitchen door.

And there was Max. His hair was a little whiter, his build a little stockier, and when he turned around the cranky-old-fucker lines had etched even deeper between his eyebrows, but it was Max.

And it felt good to see him. Somehow, Finn had never imagined this moment without physical threats and kitchen utensils being used as weapons. But both he and Max stood there, perfectly quiet. The old clock on the wall ticked loudly as they stared at each other, and then finally Max spoke.

"You're okay, then?"

Finn felt a huge lump in his throat, and tried to swallow it down. "Yeah. I'm okay. You?"

Max gave a curt nod. Finn took a deep breath.

"Look, I'm on my way out of town . . . ," he began.

There was a slight change in Max's expression, but Finn couldn't quite read it.

"Back to Las Vegas, then?"

"No, actually," Finn said, smiling lightly. "I thought I'd try New York."

Max's brows rose a touch. "Oh, yeah? Pretty close by, then?"

"Yeah."

Max cleared his throat. "You taking your crazy assistant with you?"

Finn was confused for a moment, then let out a small chuckle when he realized who Max was talking about. "No. She's decided she wants to stay here, and what Babs wants, Babs gets."

Max huffed. "The woman's been making me insane. Did you know she wanted to organize a karaoke night?"

Finn laughed. "No, but it doesn't surprise me."

There was another long moment of silence.

Now or never, idiot, Finn thought.

"Look, Max, I'm sorry about—"

"Aw!" Max gave a violent wave of his hand. "Get on out of here. I've got cooking to do."

With that, he turned around and tossed some pancake batter on the griddle. Finn stood there for a second, not sure if he'd accomplished what he came to do, but hell. Coming meant something. And Max knew it. That had to be enough for now.

He crossed the kitchen and was about to slip out the back door when Max called his name. He stopped and turned to face his uncle, who looked at him with his typically gruff expression.

"You'll call this time, though, right? Babs will worry about you and make me crazy if you don't."

Finn smiled. "Yeah, Uncle Max. I'll call."

Max flashed a short smile at him. "Well, go on. Get out of here, then."

Finn nodded and ducked out the back, grateful for the cold air in his lungs as he did.

One down, one to go. Then he could leave Lucy's Lake behind for good.

Somehow, though, that didn't sound as good to him as he thought it should.

"What's it say?" Izzy asked, poking her head over Babs's shoulder to get a look at the fax. Babs folded it in half and tucked it in her purse, leading Izzy outside as she did. She realized that Adele had done her a favor by letting her receive her fax there, but still. Adele had been very nosy when she saw that the cover page was from a detective agency in Brattleboro, and it was a good thing she'd told Derek Brown, P.I., to just fax her the evidence directly. Adele wasn't sharp enough to understand what the bank statement meant.

But Babs sure did.

"What is it?" Izzy said when they got outside. "Why are you smiling?"

"Oh, darling," Babs said, putting her arm around Izzy's shoulders. "I'm smiling because sometimes, every now and again, Fate will hand you exactly what you want at the exact moment you want it, and those moments are just too delicious not to enjoy."

Izzy nodded, but her knotted brow gave away her confusion. "So, what did you get?"

"I'll tell you while we walk," Babs said, stepping out to the street and looking from left to right, then glancing back at Izzy. "You don't happen to know which B and B Mary Ellen Neeley is staying at, do you?"

Tessa threw another log in the old woodstove at the shack. She'd been skating for hours but she hadn't been able to push it all away. Now, instead of the calm she usually felt, she was just empty inside. She wanted more than anything to run out and find Finn, track him down, try to convince him that he could stay and they could find a way to keep Izzy and . . .

But that was stupid. Finn was right. Mary Ellen Neeley would investigate him, and at the very least she'd see his spotty work record and take that into court as evidence of Tessa's unfit parenting.

Look at the man she loves, Mary Ellen would say. *Look at the man she lets live in the house with this poor, impressionable child . . .*

Tessa struck a match in a violent motion and stuck it in the paper and kindling at the bottom.

It was so stupid. Finn was a good man. Whether he wanted to admit it or not, whether his work record showed it, he was a thousand times better than all the men out there with good, steady jobs who lied and cheated and stole. At least Finn was upfront about it. He was a thousand times better than Matt Tarpey, who burned down buildings and then killed her mother when she figured it out.

And yet, prior to his confession, Matt Tarpey would have been exactly the kind of man Mary Ellen Neeley wouldn't object to.

Tessa felt a constriction in her chest.

The kind of man Mary Ellen Neeley wouldn't object to?

This was insane. What was she doing? She was letting Finn and Mary Ellen Neeley tell her what was best for her and damnit, the *zing* was best. Finn was best. And if it meant she'd have to fight harder and longer and messier with Mary Ellen Neeley and the State of Vermont to keep her sister, then damnit, she'd do it.

But whatever she had to do, she wasn't going to let Finn go. Not without a fight. Not this time.

She opened the door to the woodstove and poked around with a log, spreading out the fire so it would die down. But, damn, that would take too long. She grabbed the bucket on the floor. She could fill it with snow from outside, melt it on the woodstove, douse the woodstove—fifteen minutes, tops.

Then she could go find Finn, even if it meant driving out to New York to get him.

It was a plan. She grabbed the bucket and raced for the door, screaming in surprise as she opened it to find Vickie and Margie standing there.

"Oh, shit!" Tessa said, putting her hand over her chest. "You scared the hell out of me."

"We found her; she's at the shack," Vickie said, then flipped the phone shut and smiled at Tessa. "Izzy's on her way."

"Why?" Tessa said. "What's going on?"

"I'm so glad we found you," Margie said, stepping inside. "Luckily, you're always in one of three places—your house, Max's, or the lake."

Tessa felt slightly offended by that. "I go other places," she said weakly.

Both Margie and Vickie grinned at her. Tessa looked back and forth between them.

"What?" she said, her voice suspicious. When those two got together, things tended to get out of hand. Besides, she needed to go out and talk to Finn. "Look, ladies, I've got something I have to do—"

"Not right now, you don't," Vickie said, grabbing her by the arm and leading her back into the shack. "We're waiting right here until Izzy gets here."

"Don't worry," Margie said, hugging Tessa's shoulders. "This is gonna be worth it."

Chapter Twenty-four

Finn sat in the combination interrogation/visiting room at the Lucy's Lake sheriff's office. It was a small box of a room, with cement-block walls painted a sickly shade of green. It hadn't changed in the decade since he'd last sat there, but back then, he'd never sat there as a visitor.

The door opened and Marshall Evans escorted a hand-cuffed Matt Tarpey into the room. Finn stood up, looked at Marshall.

"Thanks, man," he said.

Marshall smiled. "No problem." He glanced at Tarpey. "You have ten minutes. That's all."

Finn looked at Tarpey, who was settling into the chair on the opposite side of the long table.

"I'll have him back to you in five."

Marshall nodded and shut the door.

"I don't know what you want with me, Finn," Tarpey said, his voice sounding rough and tired. "This has nothing to do with you."

"You killed Tessa's mother," Finn said. "That has something to do with me."

Tarpey met his eye. "Karen Scuderi died in a car accident."

"Running from a fire, which you set," Finn said.

Tarpey shrugged. "What do you want? You want me to say I'm sorry? I've confessed. It's done."

Finn watched him for a moment. It was just the one question. He needed the one question in his mind answered, and then he could leave, let the police deal with this asshole.

"Isabella Scuderi hired me to look into this case," Finn said. "I just need you to fill in the blanks for me."

Tarpey let out a breath and sat forward, his eyes on the table as he spoke in a monotone voice. "I set a number of fires over the course of seven years. I used defective or re-called electrical items, things that wouldn't raise suspicion. Karen Scuderi suspected I was setting the fires, and she confronted me on it. I went into her shop one night to burn it down. I intended to scare her into keeping quiet. I didn't know she was there. She must have been working in the back. As is typical in these cases, she suffered from a certain amount of smoke inhalation, which can cause dizziness and disorientation. Getting behind the wheel of a car in that state is just as bad as driving drunk. She drove into a tree, and that was it."

Tarpey finally raised his eyes to meet Finn's. Finn leaned forward.

"So you went ten years without setting a fire?"

"Yes," Tarpey said. "Then I saw a classified ad in the paper. I concluded it was Vickie Kemp, causing trouble, so I set her place on fire as well, to shut her up."

Finn nodded. "Okay. Couple things. Why would Karen be in the shop at two in the morning?"

Tarpey shrugged. "I think Karen's the only person who can answer that question."

Finn locked his eyes on to Tarpey's. "I have to give it to you. It was a stroke of genius, keeping that locket all these years. That never would have occurred to me, to use something like that."

And in that moment, Finn got what he'd come for—that flash of surprise in Tarpey's eyes. It was just a flash, and if he hadn't been watching carefully, Finn might have missed it.

But he didn't. Now, for the final test.

"I wouldn't have stuck it under the doormat, though," he said casually. "Too easy to find."

Tarpey, the confidence back in his eyes, shrugged and sat back. "Well, hindsight is twenty-twenty, right?"

"You stupid son of a bitch," Finn said. He pushed up from the table. "What did you think, no one would figure it out?"

A slight look of alarm crossed over Tarpey's face. "This has nothing to do with you, Finnegan."

"If Tessa or Izzy gets hurt because you were in here playing protector for your crazy wife," Finn said, "then you can bet your ass it'll have everything to do with me."

Finn pushed up from the table and knocked on the door.

"Wait a minute," Tarpey said, sitting forward. "Grace didn't . . . it wasn't . . ."

Finn shook his head. "We're done."

Marshall opened the door, and Finn stepped out.

"How long before he goes up to County?" Finn asked.

Marshall shrugged. "Couple hours."

"Don't let them take him," Finn said. "He's not your man."

Marshall laughed. "He's not? He confessed. Why would he confess?"

"Why does any man do something stupid?" Finn glanced at the door behind him, then looked back at Marshall. "You need to get Grace Tarpey in here. She's your arsonist. I have to go find some people, make sure they're okay." He handed Marshall a card with his cell number on it. "Call me when you've got Grace in custody, okay?"

Finn headed toward the door.

"Wait a minute," Marshall called after him. "He just told you all that?"

"No," Finn said. "But he'll tell you."

Tessa glanced at her watch. It had been fifteen minutes. At this rate she really was going to have to go all the way to New York to talk to Finn. She sighed.

"Can't you just tell me what it is?" Tessa asked. They were all three sitting on the cot with Tessa in the middle, and every time she tried to get up, they pulled her back down. "I really have to—"

There was a light knock, and both Vickie and Margie squealed, this time pushing Tessa up from the cot. Tessa shot an exasperated look back at them as she headed to the door. She had it open before she turned her head and looked, at which point she froze in her tracks.

The evil bitch-troll social worker from hell.

Tessa shot another look back at Margie and Vickie. This is what you held me here for?"

Mary Ellen stepped inside, followed by Izzy—who was grinning like mad—and Babs, who held some papers in her hands. Mary Ellen kept her eyes on the floor, and didn't look up until Babs cleared her throat.

"What—?" Tessa said, but then Mary Ellen started talking, as if it was a speech she'd memorized.

"I did a bad thing," Mary Ellen said. "And I am very, very sorry."

Mary Ellen looked at Babs, who raised her eyebrows, prodding. Mary Ellen turned back to face Tessa.

"Ten years ago, someone offered me money to keep you and your sister distracted. Every month, I've received five hundred dollars in cash to make things difficult for you and I'm very, very, very sorry."

Mary Ellen didn't look sorry. She looked pissed off. And her tone was extremely tight.

"So, wait," Tessa said. "What? Someone has been paying you to mess with us?"

"Oh, wait just a minute, sweetheart," Babs said, her voice dripping with glee. "It's just about to get really good." She gave Mary Ellen a sharp nudge on the shoulder. "Go ahead."

Mary Ellen rolled her eyes. "There are two ways we can handle this. One, you can go to the police, report me have me put in jail, and ruin my entire life"—Babs cleared her throat, and Mary Ellen cursed under her breath before continuing—"which I richly deserve."

Tessa felt a smile start to spread over her face. She couldn't help it. This was by far the most enjoyable interaction she'd ever had with Mary Ellen Neeley.

"Or," Mary Ellen went on, "we could keep this between ourselves, and I can make absolutely sure that you retain full and unquestioned custody of Isabella until her eighteenth birthday."

"And?" Babs prodded. Izzy giggled and whispered, "I love this part."

"And," Mary Ellen said, "if you choose option number two, I will personally show up at your house every Saturday until Isabella turns eighteen and"—she took a deep breath, closed her eyes, and bit out the last part—"clean your entire house."

"Including toilets," Izzy jumped in.

Mary Ellen opened her eyes and pulled on a tight smile. "Including toilets," she said through clenched teeth.

Tessa looked at Babs. "So, when you asked me how to spell Mary Ellen's name, that wasn't for numerology, then?"

Babs shook her head and held up the fax papers in her hand. "Derek Brown, P.I. We should send him a nice fruit basket. He went above and beyond for us, really."

Tessa couldn't help it; she laughed. "I don't believe this. I don't believe this!" Her heart suddenly lightened as she realized what this meant. She looked at Mary Ellen. "So, what this means is, I can do whatever I want and you'll protect us? You'll make sure I keep Izzy?"

Mary Ellen's nose lifted. "Well, there's only so much I can—"

Babs cleared her throat again. Mary Ellen clamped her mouth shut, then slowly nodded yes.

Finn, Tessa thought. *Finn. I have to tell Finn.*

Tessa laughed and ran to grab her purse from where it sat on the cot. Finally, *finally,* she was going to have exactly what she wanted. Finally—

"Wait a minute," she said. "Who paid you to do this? Who would—"

"Don't tell them, Mary Ellen," a sharp voice came from

behind them. Tessa turned around to see a tall woman with shellacked platinum blonde curls and a long white coat step into the shack. Her lips were bloodred, her eyes dark and angry, and she smelled vaguely of gardenias.

Grace Tarpey kicked the door closed; it was then that Tessa saw the gun in Grace's hand.

Grace's cold, beady eyes surveyed the entire group, falling finally on Tessa, her lips curling up into a tight smile.

"I so like to be the one to deliver the surprises," she said.

Chapter Twenty-five

When Finn pulled up down the street from Tessa's house, all he could see past the crowd and the fire trucks and the ambulance was smoke billowing out of the first floor. His heart cranked into overdrive and he pushed his way through the crowd, stopping only when a firefighter grabbed him.

"They're not in there," the guy said. Finn pushed himself away and looked up.

Joe.

"Tessa," Finn said.

Joe shook his head. "She's not in there. We've been through the whole place. It's empty."

Finn ran his hands through his hair. His heart was still pounding in his ears and he couldn't get his thoughts straight.

Except one.

"Where's Tessa?"

"I don't know," Joe said. "But she's not in the house. And even if she was, she'd probably be fine. The fire started in the basement, and we got to it quickly."

Finn stared at the black smoke rising into the sky. "It's Grace."

"What?" Joe asked.

"It's Grace. Grace Tarpey. Matt confessed to protect her. It's Grace and she's after Tessa and Izzy." Finn reached into his back pocket and pulled out his cell phone, dialing Tessa's number.

"I just tried to call her a few minutes ago," Joe said.

The phone rang for the fifth time, then went to voice mail. Finn cursed and flipped his phone shut.

"I'm gonna go look for them," he said, darting back toward the car.

"Finn!"

He turned around and saw Joe walking toward him.

"Need any help?"

Finn breathed a sigh of relief. "You'll cut my time in half if you can look at Max's. I'll go to the shack."

"You got it, bro," Joe said. "I'll call you if I find them. You do the same."

"Thanks," Finn said.

Joe nodded, then they both went their separate ways.

"You are a popular girl," Grace said as the last ring sounded on Tessa's cell phone, which sat useless in her purse. "Must be nice."

Tessa said nothing, just shifted on the cot, which was tight on the real estate since Grace made everyone, including Mary Ellen, sit on it. Meanwhile, Grace stood next to the woodstove, where the fire was still blazing pretty well.

A crazy arsonist next to a raging fire. It wasn't good.

"The thing about fire," Grace said, reaching into her

coat pocket with one hand while keeping the gun leveled at them with the other, "is that it's so hard to control. This woodstove, in a tinderbox like this? I don't know what Dick Lowery was thinking."

Tessa tried to see what Grace had pulled from her pocket, but it just looked like a vial of perfume.

"I don't understand what you're doing," Izzy said. "You can't just burn us all up here and think no one's going to have questions."

Grace rolled her eyes. "Yeah, let's talk about questions, darling Isabella. You and your incessant questions. I knew you'd have them someday, which is why I hired this nitwit"—she indicated Mary Ellen with her chin—"to keep you girls busy. But you, with your poking around and your questions. This is really all your fault, you know?"

Tessa saw Izzy's eyes widen, and she reached for her sister's hand.

"Don't listen to her," Tessa said. "This is not your fault."

"Oh, sure it is," Grace said. "All I did was play a little bit, burn down a few places that no one really missed anyway. No one got hurt. Hell, when I took out that barn on the edge of town, Melvin Cheeters made a damn fortune in the insurance. But then Karen had to start in with all the questions. What business was it of hers, anyway?" She looked at Vickie and Margie. "Or yours. Or Sosie's, or Christ's sake."

"Sosie told you?" Izzy said, her voice wavering.

"Did you think she wouldn't?" Grace said, her voice ripping with contempt. "Although, granted, she didn't until just yesterday. All sniveling on my porch." Grace's voice went up to an annoyingly high pitch. "'I'm worried about Izzy, Aunt Grace. Izzy's gonna get hurt. She's my best friend. Blah blah blah.'" Grace's voice went back to normal. "Honestly, kid needs to strap on a pair, know what I mean?"

Grace opened the vial in her hand and started to pour it in a long line on the floor. The cloying smell of gardenias filled the shack.

"You know," Grace said thoughtfully as she poured the liquid onto the dry wooden floor. "Perfume makes an excellent accelerant. You wouldn't even believe how flammable this shit is. And virtually untraceable." She held up the empty vial. "I didn't even figure that out until I took out Karen's craft shop, can you believe that? Man, she was pissed off. Clawing at me and yelling. But what did she expect I was asking her to meet me for at two in the morning? Not the brightest bulb in the box, your mother."

Tessa felt her sister start, and tightened her grip on Izzy's hand. As long as Grace still had the gun on them, they had to keep their cool.

"You're not going to get away with this," Izzy said, her voice tight with fear and anger.

Grace laughed.

"I don't plan on getting away with it, you stupid little bitch," she spat. "My life is over. Once they start investigating those fires, they're gonna know Matt didn't do it, that he was protecting me. But the thing is, if I'm going down, I'm damn well gonna take you with me."

Deftly keeping the gun pointed at her hostages, she gripped a rolled piece of newspaper and dipped one edge into the woodstove. It caught, and she dropped it on the line of perfume on the floor.

Which lit up like a line of black powder. Of course, the old warped wood of the shack didn't help matters. Grace might have been crazy, but she was right about one thing—that place was a tinderbox.

Grace stepped back toward the door, then stopped, keeping the gun trained on them. Tessa stood up as the fire started to edge toward her. Grace said nothing, just laughed. Tessa looked behind her to the window. She could block it while Izzy crawled out. The idea of taking a bullet to get Izzy to safety didn't bother her in the least.

"Izzy," she said, nodding toward the cast-iron skillet that hung on the wall, "grab that. Break the window."

"I don't think so," Grace said. She cocked the gun, aimed it at Izzy. "Anyone moves, the kid gets it."

Tessa exchanged glances with Vickie, Margie, and Babs. Mary Ellen whimpered and took a step forward. Grace glared at her.

"What did I just say? Anyone moves, the kid gets it. That includes you."

"But," Mary Ellen whimpered, "I was on your side."

"You were on my payroll, and if you'd done your job, we wouldn't be here."

"But—"

Mary Ellen didn't get a chance to finish the thought, because at that moment, all hell broke loose.

Finn pulled up next to the cars at the side of the lake. There was Tessa's Thing, the Mazda, Vickie's little Ford, and a Subaru he didn't recognize. When he hopped out and saw the Lucy's Lake Fire Association sticker on the bumper, he cursed under his breath and scanned the lake. There was no sign of Tessa. He looked up toward the shack and saw black smoke coming from the woodstove pipe. It took him a moment longer to realize that the smoke wasn't just coming from the pipe; it was also leaking through the walls, and he could see flames licking through the side window. He took off around the lake, skidding and sliding through the snow. The freezing air cut at his lungs as he ran, his only thoughts of Tessa. If he was too late . . .

If he was too late . . .

He shut off that train of thought and pushed harder, falling in the snow and pushing back up until he finally reached the shack, where he skidded to a stop, his breath raw in his chest.

Tessa, Izzy, Babs, Vickie, and Margie stood in a circle around two other women. As Finn gasped for breath, he could see that Grace Tarpey was one of them, lying unconscious on the snow next to a cast-iron skillet. The other woman was a skinny blonde who matched the description of the evil troll social worker.

Tessa looked up, saw him, and smiled. Finn rushed over to her and pulled her into his arms, kissing the top of her head.

"Shit, Tess, you just took ten years off my life." He pulled back and put his hands on either side of her face, looking into her eyes. "Are you okay? You're okay?"

Tessa smiled. "All things considered, I'm pretty great, yeah."

He wrapped her in his arms again and looked at Izzy, who grinned at him.

"I hit her with a frying pan," Izzy said, pointing to the unconscious pile that was Grace Tarpey. Finn had to laugh.

"You what?"

"Well," Izzy said, slight concession in her voice, "first Babs charged her and got the gun away."

Finn raised an eyebrow at Babs. "Gun?"

Babs gave a dismissive wave of the hand. "It's not as brave as it sounds. I used Mary Ellen as a human shield to do it."

Finn looked down at the blonde slumped on the ground next to Grace Tarpey.

"You're Mary Ellen?" he asked. "The social worker?"

"I could have been killed!" she sobbed.

Babs sighed. "Yeah, she could have. But luckily, Grace was too surprised to actually shoot. Mary Ellen and I took her down, didn't we, Mary Ellen?"

Mary Ellen didn't answer, just whimpered to herself.

Finn pulled back and looked at Tessa. "You're serious? She had a gun on you and you all took her down?"

Tessa smiled. "How did you find me?"

Finn shrugged. "I checked your house, Joe checked Max's. That pretty much left the lake."

Tessa huffed. "I really need to get out more."

Finn looked down at her, let out an awkward-sounding laugh, and felt his heart catch in his chest as he fully realized that he'd almost lost her. Almost really lost her. Forever.

"Oh, hell," he said, drawing her close in his arms so she couldn't see his face. He took a deep breath and blinked hard to ward off the . . .

"Finn?"

He swiped at his eyes quickly, then let her pull back to look at him.

"Sorry," he said. "Smoke was getting to me."

One corner of her mouth twisted up into a smile.

"Yeah," she said, "that can be a bitch."

He looked at her, taking in everything about her. The dark hair falling around her shoulders, the flush in her lightly freckled cheeks, the hint of laughter in her eyes, even when she'd just been through hell.

She was his girl.

He put one hand on her face.

"I love you," he said.

She smiled up at him. "Yeah, I know. The question is, what are you gonna do about it?"

Good question, he thought. Just then he heard footsteps behind him, and turned to see Joe running toward them, breathless.

"Fire," he gasped, gesturing toward the shack. He looked at Tessa. "Everyone okay?"

Tessa laughed. "We've had heroes running to our rescue twice in one day. We're doing great."

Joe straightened up, still gasping for breath, then pulled out his cell phone.

"Calling in the troops?" Finn asked.

Joe nodded.

Finn looked at the flames shooting up into the sky from the shack.

"Ask 'em if they got marshmallows."

Chapter Twenty-six

Tessa stood back and surveyed her canvas, tilting her head a bit to the left. She looked at the bowl of fruit that sat on the three-legged table, then back at the oil painting in front of her, and decided she needed better lighting in the attic. Which meant another trip to the store. Between fixing up the basement, buying products to get the smoky smell out of the first floor, and all the paint she'd been snapping up, she was pretty sure she'd managed to jump-start the town economy in the course of the last week.

Well, she thought, *there are worse things to do with money.*

She put her brush down on the ridge of her easel and pulled off her smock, then gasped as she saw the figure standing behind her.

"Sorry," Finn said, a smile creeping up one side of his face. "I didn't mean to scare you."

He leaned casually against the banister at the top of the attic steps, his eyes trailing around the space before landing on her again.

"I like what you've done with the place," he said.

"Yeah," Tessa said, "putting Mom's stuff back around the house really cleared the attic out. It's my art studio now."

"Sounds perfect."

She wanted to throw herself into his arms, but instead she quirked one eyebrow at him and tried to maintain a slightly pissed-off expression.

It'd be no fun if she made it easy for him.

"So, where ya been, Finnegan? A whole week. You don't write, you don't call. You attempt to save a girl from a burning building and then just disappear. What's up with that?"

"Had to see a man about a horse," he said, then shook his head and grinned. "I still don't know what that means."

"But you know what's weird?" she said. "Everywhere I went, everyone I talked to, they all kinda looked like they knew something I didn't. Little whispers. Little smiles. Very strange. You happen to know anything about that?"

"Feeling out of the loop?" Finn took another step closer, put one hand on her waist, and pulled her to him.

"Yep." She pushed his hand away playfully.

"Little cranky about it?"

"Little bit," she said, trying to hide her smile. Although, hell, if he could hear her heart bumping around in her chest like a mental patient, the jig would be up anyway.

He leaned his head down and grazed his lips against her neck.

Oh. God.

No, wait.

She pushed against his chest, moving him back, and he groaned, "Now you're just being mean."

"You don't get to leave me hanging for a week, breeze back into town, and kiss my neck like that. Where were you?"

He sighed. "No kissing until I tell you?"

She shook her head.

"Okay, then," he said with a smile. "I went to New York. Tied up a few loose ends. Sublet my apartment. Got a job."

She felt a stab of disappointment. "A job? A real job? In New York?"

"A job. A real job." He shook his head, his eyes playful. "Not in New York. I'm, uh . . ." He chuckled. "I'm gonna be a cop."

Tessa laughed outright, then clapped her hand over her mouth at Finn's mock-indignant expression.

"I'm sorry," she said. "But . . . how?"

"Marshall Evans was impressed by how I cracked the Tarpey case," Finn said. "He gave me a call. I've been in New York, uh . . . securing my background check."

"You're kidding? You committed fraud so you could be a cop?"

Finn nodded. "For the low, low price of one macaw."

Tessa gasped. "You really sold it?"

"To a good home for a great price," he said. "And Vickie's letting me pay it off in installments."

"Will wonders never cease?" she said.

His eyes softened as he looked at her. "Apparently not."

She couldn't help herself, and allowed a full smile. "You're lucky Babs broke down. I'd have been really pissed off at you if I didn't know you were coming back."

"Well," he said, tilting his head to one side as his arms snaked around her waist. "How could I stay away?"

He leaned down and kissed her lightly on the lips, then pulled back.

"No," Tessa whined, leaning into him, "that was good. I was liking that."

"Come on," he said, taking her hand and leading her down the stairs. At the bottom, he cut to the right, toward her bedroom.

"I like the way you think," she said. Then he opened the door and let her in.

"Finn," she whispered as she looked around the room. She clasped her hand over her mouth and her eyes filled with tears as she felt his arms wrap around her waist from behind.

Daisies. Pink, orange, yellow, blue. Everywhere. On her dresser. Sprinkled over her bed. Sitting in a vase on her nightstand.

"I wanted a thousand of them," he said, "but Margie could only get a hundred and fifty on such short notice."

She twirled in his arms to face him, biting her lip to stop from crying.

"I love them," she said.

He kissed her on the cheek and then held up one index finger. "But wait, there's more."

He ducked around her to the corner of the room, whisked some daisies off a drape cloth that he pulled back to reveal seven cans of wall paint.

"I got a lighter shade of yellow," he said, "but if you want something brighter, we can go back."

She swiped at her eyes and blinked hard. "It's perfect," she said, without looking at the paint.

Finn let out a sigh of relief. "Whew! If I had to fish that ring out of the paint—"

"What?" She raced past him to the paint cans. "You put the ring in the paint?"

She heard him laughing behind her and looked up to see him holding a small black velvet box.

"No," he said. "I'm stupid, but I'm not that stupid."

He held out his hand to her, and she took it, letting him pull her up. She was glad for the help because her legs suddenly felt very wobbly. She'd known it was coming. Babs had told her. But still, Dermot Finnegan was standing in front of her, promising forever. It took some getting used to.

She reached for the box and pulled it open and . . .

"Oh my God," she breathed. It was gorgeous. Platinum, with a beautiful round diamond sparkling in the center. Finn plucked it out of the box. He looked at her, and for once, his expression was completely sincere.

She liked that.

"I don't know how to ask you this," he said.

She smiled and felt her eyes tearing up. *This is it,* she thought. *This is what I want, what I've always wanted. I'm finally going to have it.*

"I know I don't have a great track record," he said finally. "And I know I've been a total idiot. But if you give me this one chance, I'll spend the rest of my life making sure you don't regret it."

"I won't regret it," she said, feeling a tear plop down her face. He raised a finger to her cheek and whisked it away.

"Tessa Scuderi, will you—?"

"Oh, yeah," she said, sniffing as she cut him off. "You bet I will."

He smiled and slid the ring onto her finger. Gently, he leaned down and kissed her, and things were just beginning to get interesting when they were interrupted by a barking at the door. They broke the kiss and turned to see Wallace running toward them. The dog jumped up on Tessa's legs, and she bent down and scratched his ears.

"Guess I should have warned you," Finn said. "Wallace and I seem to be a package deal these days."

"I can live with that," she said, standing up. Finn wrapped his arms around her waist and pulled her in to him, lowering her down into her bed of daisies.

Yep, she thought as his lips grazed her collarbone, *I can definitely live with this.*

About the Author

Hello, Readers! I've been asked to provide a bio and . . . well . . . I'm not really good at bios. Despite the fact no one is more qualified to write about me than me, I'm terrible at it. "Lani was born in Poughkeepsie, New York. She likes piña coladas and getting caught in the rain . . . zzzzzzz." So, I'm going to shake things up a bit by providing some True Confessions. Prepare to be shocked.

Aside from Adam and Eve, I am related to absolutely no one famous, although I did meet Bill Cosby once. Oh, and I know a guy who was an extra in *The Princess Diaries II*.

I met my husband while hurling salmon in a cannery in Alaska. However, I do not recommend that single women go to Alaska to find husbands. I happened to get lucky, but what they say about Alaskan men is generally true—the odds are good but the goods are odd. And frequently running from either the law or the IRS. Sometimes both. I'm just saying.

I have been known to feed my children Cheerios for dinner when on deadline. And sometimes when not on deadline. I'm a bad cook. Trust me, they're better off.

I once stole ten tables and forty chairs from the student center at Syracuse University. Two hours later, I returned them. No one said a word.

If you're interested in finding out more about me and my books, please visit me at *www.lanidianerich.com*. Thanks so much for reading!

More
Lani Diane Rich!

Please see below
for a preview of

Hard to Get

AVAILABLE FALL 2007

Chapter One

"Here lies Esther Goodhouse." Emma Bartlett leaned forward in her foldout nylon camping chair and poured the freshly made vodka tonic from the red plastic party cup onto the soft mound of grave dirt. "She had sex, and it killed her."

Across the grave, sitting in a matching camping chair, Mercy giggled into her own red cup. In any other forty-eight-year-old woman, the giggle would seem affected and a little silly. Coming from Mercy, though, it was pure charm. Emma lifted her drink, enjoying the sound of the rattling ice as she did. Esther had always loved the sound of rattling ice.

"To Esther," she said.

Mercy raised her cup. "To Esther."

They drank. Emma glanced around for a sign of Herman, the cemetery caretaker. When he'd told them there was no alcohol allowed at Forever Acres, she'd slipped him twenty bucks and an impromptu coupon scribbled on her business card, good for a free night's stay at the Goodhouse Arms——worth significantly more than twenty bucks. She'd hoped that would buy them enough time to finish off the bottle of Stoli, but who knew? People were sensitive about public drinking these days, even if most of the public in this particular situation were dead.

Damn teenagers. Ruined it for everyone.

Emma splashed some more vodka and tonic into Esther's cup, this time digging a little indentation into the dirt and settling the cup there. It seemed much more festive.

"Saint Esther," Mercy said softly.

Emma smiled at the thought of Esther Goodhouse as a saint. They'd have to bend some rules of sainthood to allow it, but she liked the idea. "Think you can get a bulk rate on those medals?"

"Probably," Mercy said. "I'll make some calls in the morning."

Emma nodded and went quiet. She was beginning to feel softened by the vodka, which was good. In the past three days, since she'd gotten the news of Esther's passing, she'd felt stiff and tired and way older than she was. Now, with all the planning and public mourning behind her, she kicked her heels off and pulled her feet up onto the camping chair, crossing her legs yoga-style in front of her, finally comfortable. She was still in the black dress she'd worn to the funeral, and if there'd been anyone aside from Mercy and a thousand dead people around, she'd have placed her comfort below the fact that someone might be able to get a slight visual on her underwear. As it was . . .

Go for it, dead guys, she thought. *Least I can do for you.*

They drank. An automated streetlight flickered on over

the meandering road that cut through the cemetery, and Emma realized it was starting to get dark.

"So." Mercy nibbled her lip a bit the way she did whenever she was about to broach unpleasantness. "How are you doing?"

"Me?" Emma shrugged. "I'm okay."

Mercy nodded. "You sure?"

"Yeah," Emma said. "I'm drinking vodka tonics in the middle of a cemetery. Why wouldn't I be great?"

"Point taken," Mercy said. "What do you think is gonna happen to the Arms?"

Emma let out a heavy sigh. For the last three days, she'd made a point of not thinking about the fate of the Goodhouse Arms.

"I don't know. I'm sure your job is safe, though. Don't worry."

Mercy's laugh was, like everything about Mercy, hearty. "Oh, I'm not worried about my job. I'm the best chef in New York State. Possibly, in the country." She took a sip of her drink. "Maybe even in the world."

Emma couldn't help but smile. "You know, some people find a total lack of humility unattractive."

"Yeah, but I don't like those people." Mercy's smile faded. "What are you gonna do?"

Emma shook her head. "I don't know. I guess it depends on who Esther left the inn to. For such a prestigious family, they've sure got a lot of assholes."

"Like Evan."

"Evan wasn't that bad," Emma said. This wasn't exactly true, but it didn't seem right to talk smack about Esther's great-nephew in her presence. Even if Esther didn't like him much herself.

And even if Esther was dead. Emma sighed.

"You could go back to school," Mercy said.

"Oh, right," Emma said. "You don't go back to school at thirty-two."

Mercy snorted into her cup. "Not if you're stupid enough to say something like that, you don't."

"It would feel weird to be anyplace else," Emma said, trying to imagine living somewhere aside from the old servant's cottage at the back of the Goodhouse property. She couldn't do it. She wondered what that said about her. Probably nothing good.

"How old was that plumber again?" Mercy said. It took a moment for Emma to realize she was talking about Esther's latest—and last—conquest.

"Sixty-four."

"A younger man," Mercy laughed, then lifted her glass and her voice to the heavens. "To Esther!"

"To Esther!"

They both drank, and then a moment of silence fell. Emma stared at the drink in the center of the mound of dirt that covered Esther Goodhouse's earthly remains.

"It doesn't seem right," Emma said. "That an entire life just settles down to be a mound of dirt and a gravestone, you know?"

"Unless you believe in God, and heaven, and life after death, and . . ."

Emma groaned. "Oh, hell, Mercy."

"Okay. Sure. We can talk about hell."

"I don't want to have this argument again. At least not now, okay?"

Mercy eyed Emma for a moment, then nodded. "I don't need to argue. I know I'm right."

Emma sighed, concentrated on the mound of dirt in front

of her. "She was so much more than this grave. A mother figure, a boss, a friend, a mentor . . ."

"An eccentric crackpot," Mercy added.

Emma laughed lightly, then sniffled. "She was the last family I had left, and she wasn't even family."

"She was family." Mercy paused for a moment, then added, "So, not to beat a dead horse, but what are you gonna do?"

Emma swiped at her face. "What do you mean?"

Mercy leaned over the cooler, grabbed the vodka with one hand and the tonic with the other, and splashed both into Emma's cup. "She would have wanted you to go back to school."

"Don't start, Merce." The last thing Emma wanted to hear right now was a lecture on how she was living her life—or not living her life, as the case may be. Emma looked up at the stars that were just starting to become visible in the twilit sky, wishing she believed in an afterlife, because the idea of Esther watching over her right now would be a real comfort.

"Look, you did your duty. You came home when your dad got sick, and you took over managing the Arms after he died. Esther's gone now, and she probably left the place to one of her asshole relatives. It's a sign that it's time for you to do what you want to do."

Emma said nothing, just took a big swig of her drink. Mostly because she didn't have an answer. Aside from three semesters at college, where she mostly studied How to Drink Your Ass Off and Still Make It to Class 101, she'd never lived anywhere else, never done anything else. The Goodhouse Arms was her life. She knew where George Washington had actually slept, which tree in the courtyard was the one Eleanor Roosevelt had planted.

She didn't know anything else.

Good God, that was depressing. She took a breath and drank again.

Then her hip started buzzing. She put her drink in the little cup holder that was built into the arm of her nylon camping chair and looked at the caller ID on her cell phone.

Esther Goodhouse. Her heart gave a small, painful jerk at the sight of Esther's name on her phone, then accepted the reality of it; someone was calling from Esther's office. She flipped open the phone.

"This is Emma."

"Emma." It was a man's voice, one she couldn't quite place, but that sounded vaguely familiar. "It's Brendan Blair. I'm with Valentine and Linehan, the firm that's handling Esther's estate. I introduced myself at the funeral."

Ah, yes, along with about a thousand other people. "Of course, Mr. Blair. Do you need my help with something?"

"Well, I'm sorry to bother you, but I'm heading back into the city tonight, and there's something we really need to discuss."

Whatever it was, it was going to have to wait. The bottle of Stoli was only about half gone, and the clock was ticking. "Yeah. I'm not really available right now. Can I call you tomorrow?"

Brendan Blair cleared his throat. "Actually, it's kind of pressing. See, Esther has left you the Goodhouse Arms, and . . ."

Brendan Blair from Valentine and Linehan kept talking, but Emma's brain stuck on *Esther has left you the Goodhouse Arms,* circling it from all angles, trying to get a full understanding of what it meant, and failing.

"Esther what?" she said finally, interrupting something about signing papers.

"She left you the inn," Brendan Blair said. "Congratula-

tions. Your net worth just went up about two-point-five million dollars."

Mercy's hand landed on Emma's forearm, and Emma glanced up to see Mercy mouth the words "Are you okay?"

But her brain was circling around *Your net worth just went up about two-point-five million dollars,* and she couldn't quite answer the question.

She made some plans with Brendan Blair of Valentine and Linehan to visit the city later in the week and sign the paperwork. Then she flipped the phone shut and downed what was left of her drink. A slow smile spread over Mercy's face, and Emma knew she'd heard enough of the conversation to put the pieces together.

"Holy shit," Mercy said.

"Holy shit," Emma responded, and her brain started circling that as well.

Holy shit.

Holy shit.

Holy shit.

"Ladies." A flashlight bounced over them. Herman the caretaker stepped up toward them, glancing around, as though the dead might be watching.

"You can't stay here," he grumbled through clenched teeth. "I could lose my job."

Emma blinked up at him. "I just inherited the Goodhouse Arms."

The caretaker snorted, then, when neither of the women joined him, his eyes widened. "No way."

Mercy giggled. "Way."

"My life has just changed dramatically, Herman," she said. "Can we have ten more minutes?"

"Um . . . ," Herman said.

"I'll throw in a free meal for two. Cooked by our own Mercy here."

Mercy grinned up at him. "Best chef on the planet."

Herman looked from one to the other, then smiled at Emma. "You don't need a handyman or anything there, do you?"

Emma paused for a minute. Did she need a handyman? Eh. Not really.

But she certainly could afford one.

She held her hand out to Herman. "Sure."

Herman took her hand, shook it, and settled down on the grass between them. "Then let's toast."

Emma lifted the bottle of vodka out of the cooler. She felt oddly disconnected from everything, buffered from her feelings by shock, grief, and uncertainty. She didn't feel like she'd just inherited one of the most prestigious and famous inns in America.

She mostly just felt thirsty.

Emma filled both their cups, and one for Herman, and they all stood, raising their cups to the air.

"Here lies Esther Goodhouse," Emma said. "May we all live to be just as old and half as crazy."

All three lifted their cups in unison, and drank in silence. It wasn't much of a toast, but Emma knew Esther would have loved it.

In Stephanie Rowe's *Date Me, Baby, One More Time* (on sale now), Justine Bennett is cursing her life. She's the Guardian of the Goblet of Eternal Youth, she hasn't left the house in ages, and it's been over two hundred years since she's had sex. But she's a survivor and here are a few tips from her Guardian handbook:

Survival Tip #1:
Get your priorities in order. See cute guy. See cute guy reach for the Goblet (yes, the one that has recently shape-shifted into an espresso machine). Kill cute guy immediately. Yeah, it's a thankless job, but that Guardian Oath you took pretty much limits your options. Not that the Goblet ever appreciates the sacrifice. Espresso machines can be so ungrateful.

Survival Tip #2:
Abandon all plans of having a personal life. You're married to the Goblet, end of story. (I know, I know, what's the point of staying young forever if you're locked in your New York City condo with no one but a cranky, oversexed dragon to keep you company?)

Survival Tip #3:
Whatever you do, don't trust the gorgeous pretzel mogul standing outside your door. Why? Because he's the one ready to behead you and steal your legacy, all in the name of saving the men of his family from a deadly Curse that's going to kill him in less than a week.

Survival Tip #4:
Never, ever, ever, ever, ever have sex with the gorgeous pretzel mogul working his way into your soul. If you do, not only will you wind up being tortured in the Chamber of Unspeakable Horrors for all eternity, but you also may lose your heart, and he just might lose his head.

Stephanie

www.stephanierowe.com

Authors Dish

Dear Reader,

Do you think it's weird to have such an overpowering crush on a character that I have to give him his own book? Should I be seeking counseling? Eh, maybe. But I don't care. I love Finn and I don't care who knows it.

Every now and again, if a writer is really good and eats all her veggies, a character will walk into a scene fully formed, requiring almost no work; that's what Finn did for me. I was writing *Maybe Baby,* and had no idea where I was going with it (that's how I write, hence the need to dye my grays) and BOOM! There he was. All redheaded and bird-thieving and wisecracking; I just loved him. So when I had the opportunity to write a second book, I knew it had to be Finn's.

What made *The Comeback Kiss* so much fun to write was that I had this carefree, live-by-the-seat-of-your-pants guy in Finn, and I just had to send him back home again. There was so much fun stuff waiting for him in Lucy's Lake—his cantankerous uncle and goody-goody brother, and his regret personified in Tessa, the one woman he couldn't forget—that I couldn't resist slamming this slick guy into the one situation he couldn't scam his way out of. Plus, I love reunion stories. They make me all warm and fuzzy inside. Hope it does the same for you!

Happy reading!

Lani Diane Rich

www.lanidianerich.com